THE

SYRIAN

TERRORIST

An Intelligence Thriller

By David Mackenzie

ISBN 978-0-473-42686-6

First published in January 2018. Chatham Rise Publishing.

The Syrian Terrorist

THE SYRIAN TERRORIST

Prologue

Paris, Wednesday 7 January 2015

Dressed in black and with their faces partially masked, the two gunmen moved quickly along the quiet avenue in the 11th arrondissement towards the building in which they knew the people they were targeting would be found. Each of the gunmen was carrying a Kalashnikov assault rifle, a brutally efficient automatic weapon with a fearsome reputation.

It was late morning, but the winter chill had kept most people indoors and the avenue was deserted. Puddles from overnight rain blackened parts of the roadway and trees stood bare and gaunt in some form of acknowledgment of the bleak winter locals were describing as one of the coldest they could remember.

If anyone had seen the gunmen approaching the building they may have noted there was an air of professionalism in the way the darkly dressed figures moved and in the way they held their weapons.

But no-one was watching, and the gunmen entered the building unobserved. In an outer reception area they encountered an employee. They forced him to give them access to the building's secure internal offices.

After passing through the opened security door the gunmen saw a meeting was underway in an adjacent room. They silently approached the room and then, following a quick hand-signal from the leading figure, threw open the door and invaded the room.

Those meeting in the room were stunned by the sudden noise and the presence of two masked and armed gunmen. They were unable to immediately comprehend what was happening.

One of the masked figures called out a name.

'Yes, that's me,' said a bespectacled middle-aged man sitting at the head of the long table around which those at the meeting sat. He had replied automatically to his name without pausing to think why the gunman might be asking. Without a word the gunman raised his weapon and calmly shot the man in the face, killing him instantly.

After a moment of stunned shock, a dreadful realisation dawned on those seated around the table which carried their papers, laptops, and other meeting paraphernalia. Slowly, much too slowly because they were in shock, people in the meeting began to respond as they started to make some sense of what they were facing.

Then the gunmen started shooting at all those they had found in the room. Some, who moments ago had been earnestly engaging in editorial discussions concerning their next scheduled publication, died where they sat. Others sought refuge under tables, behind shelving, anywhere to try to escape the deadly fusillade.

Not many of those who took cover escaped the shooting. The gunmen simply walked around the room and calmly fired their weapons into people as they stood over them. After just a few minutes the slaughter stopped, and the gunmen walked from the building they had invaded. Most of those who had been meeting in the room attacked were left dead or dying.

As the gunmen got into the small black car they had left in the avenue to make their escape a lone policeman appeared in his vehicle, driving towards them. He was responding to reports of multiple gun shots.

The gunmen leapt from their vehicle and fired at the police-car which stopped, and reversed hard, but the gunmen were capable shooters as the grouping of bullet holes through the police-car's front windscreen immediately in front of the driver's position would later attest. Seriously wounded, the lone police officer staggered from his vehicle and collapsed on the pavement. He was unable to do anything more because of his wounds. One of the gunmen ran to where the officer lay, helpless, and coldly fired his weapon into the officer's head at close range.

Back in their car, and speeding away from the scene the two gunmen rejoiced in their achievements. They had killed the infidels who had insulted Islam.

'Allahu Akbar,' they recited as they drove. "God is Greatest".

Within hours the world would know about the murderous shootings of journalists and editors in a meeting at the offices of a small Paris-based satirical magazine, Charlie Hebdo.

Video of the cold-blooded execution of the wounded police officer in the avenue outside Charlie Hebdo offices, taken on mobile phones by people cautiously peering down from nearby buildings, would appear on the internet and be viewed some millions of times.

The two gunmen, brothers Saïd and Chérif Kouachi, would themselves be shot dead within forty eight hours during a firefight with French police.

Items found in the Kouachi brothers' lodgings would show they had been inspired by the writings of Anwar al-Awlaki. Al-Awlaki had been the al-Qaeda regional commander considered responsible for a number of terrorist atrocities against the West. He had been killed in a drone strike carried out by the United States military in northern Yemen in 2011 as part of its War against Terror.

People in France, and around the world, would react with horror and disbelief at the attack on Charlie Hebdo's offices, and the killing of innocent journalists and editors, to say nothing of the very public murder of a helpless police officer.

But, what no one would know for several months, was that this was just the beginning.

Chapter One

It was Friday, the end of another working week, so while most of her colleagues had left the office promptly at 5pm Anne Davis had decided to work on into the evening. She had been unable to find any time during her day to review reports she had received the previous afternoon. Anne was particularly conscious of the fact some of the reports were marked "For Early Attention", indicating a requirement they be reviewed within at least forty eight hours of receipt. If she could get a few uninterrupted hours reading this evening she would be able to clear the backlog and get away for her weekend free from the overhang of work pressure.

It was just after 8pm, as she was beginning the last of the priority reports, when she received a call on her mobile phone from Helen Frost, the Assistant Director's personal assistant. Anne's relationship with the crisp and efficient Ms Frost had always been amicable and polite, but some in the organisation had little time for Helen Frost, finding her a very difficult personality. Frosty by name, frosty by nature, some of the office wits would say. And then be quite pleased with themselves, particularly if they went on to say something about how they were not able to warm to her, or similar.

Anne understood the banter, but she had little time for anyone who took it a step further than was acceptable. During an end of week drinks session some months previously, a colleague, believing he was being very funny and insightful after consuming more rounds than had been wise, had proceeded to pronounce that Ms Frost, with a name like that, must of course be frigid. He had then gone on to crudely deliver his view on what it was she really needed to resolve that characteristic. Anne hadn't hesitated.

She didn't get angry or raise her voice, but in a calm and measured way provided the group present with a hilarious allegory that spoke to their drunken colleague's failed insight into women, likely lack of ability to cope in any normal relationship, and various other character flaws, some recognised as she spoke, others just invented by Anne but receiving the approval of the group anyway as they laughed at the expense of the offender. The colleague glowered at Anne, but he understood he was in a poor position to retaliate, so said nothing. He never made comments about Ms Frost in that vein again.

Personally, Anne acknowledged Helen Frost could be difficult. She was unnecessarily demanding on occasions, and sometimes a bit short, but Anne had long ago accepted that in life some people are different and Ms Frost was one of those people. It was just a personality quirk, and in Anne's view it was not productive to fail to get over it quite quickly if Helen Frost was being annoying.

Anne liked efficiency so she would never dwell on such incidents. In any event, she had observed over time that everyone felt and reacted to the pressures of the office differently, and she took the view someone like Helen Frost was far from the extreme end of the office behavioural spectrum. There were others in the organisation whom Anne had thought super odd on occasions, and worryingly they were further up the pay scale and had greater responsibilities than Ms Frost.

Helen Frost was pleased to have found Anne in the building, particularly given it was a Friday night. She knew Anne would often enjoy the end of week by having some drinks with others from the office at a local bar. Usually it was Jerry's, a hostelry popular with professionals in the thirty to forty, or thereabouts, age group, so finding Anne in the office was a bonus.

'Anne, could you be in the Green Room in thirty minutes for a meeting with the Assistant Director?' Helen Frost asked.

The fact the request was posed as a question was not meant to indicate to Anne she had any choice in the matter.

'Sure,' said Anne, wondering what it was that could require her to meet at such short notice on a Friday evening with the Assistant Director. Whatever it was it must be serious she was thinking as Helen Frost, true to form, simply said "Right then" and disconnected the call without further comment.

Anne finished reading the report she had been reviewing and then signed out of her screen. After securing her office she made her way to the western side of the building where the Green Room was situated, again wondering what to expect.

Dr Anne Davis had been with the Central Intelligence Agency of the United States of America, a security agency of the federal government universally known simply as the CIA, for nearly eleven years. She had been based at CIA headquarters in Langley, Virginia, all of that time, although she had made some "field trips" outside the United States. She had participated in those trips only as an observer and had been kept well back from the sharp end of any CIA operational activity. She was an analyst not an operative she had been told when she had asked about what she could do while on her first field trip. Just observe and learn had been the message.

An expert in Middle Eastern affairs, particularly Islamic fundamentalism, Anne had been recruited by the CIA just after she had finished her doctoral thesis at Columbia University, a prestigious academic institution in Upper Manhattan, New York City. She had been 28 at the time and wondering what scope she had to gainfully use her new qualifications and well developed knowledge of Islam.

Academia was of no interest, but possibly a public service role she had thought, maybe the diplomatic corps.

As someone with expertise in Middle Eastern affairs and Islamic fundamentalism, Anne was the perfect person to help fill the expanded needs identified by the CIA following 9/11, as the 2001 World Trade Centre attacks in New York City had become known throughout the world. Additional specialist expertise in matters of Islam was highly sought after to help the CIA and Homeland Security identify and analyse potential threats to the United States of America.

Anne had accepted the CIA role after some persuasion from senior CIA officers, who had finally convinced her of the value she could offer in the War against Terror the United States was conducting. In her wildest imaginings as a student she had never thought she would become involved in counter-terrorism, but here she was, a key player in the CIA, dealing with Islamic terrorism threats. And she was good at what she did.

Anne was known within the CIA as a very competent operator, a person who spoke her mind and who was clinical in her analysis of information. She had a reputation as an intelligent, incisive woman, and, when she had to be, as a person who would be quite direct. There was never any risk of Anne's view being side-lined without a fulsome discussion and, if she thought it necessary, a challenging debate. Anne's capabilities were well-respected by her colleagues.

Many of the events noted in the field reports continually flowing in to the CIA's Counter-terrorism Centre where Anne worked appeared disconnected, but often there were hidden linkages buried in the data received. Finding a linkage enabled the development of opinions about activity that might be indicated by the data. There had been occasions where it was Anne who had seen linkages which other analysts had missed. It was recognised within the Agency that Anne's insightful analysis and clear presentation had facilitated, on more than one occasion, the development of an appropriate response to meet concerns about risk to the security interests of the United States.

Privately, as the Agency was always careful not to over-stimulate egos, although there was no risk of that with Anne who was a well-balanced and considerate individual, Dr Anne Davis was acknowledged by the CIA leadership to be a star with a great future in intelligence.

The previous year her acuity had been amply demonstrated. Not by any high level cerebral analysis, although she was perfectly capable of that when required, but by something more practical. As part of an analytical review triggered by some information received Anne had seen a pattern in observed sightings of persons of interest which others hadn't picked up on. Actually, non-sightings as it turned out.

An Imam, based in Turkey, and known for his radical views, had been under general surveillance. That meant the surveillance did not extend to electronic eavesdropping or mail intercepts, nor was he actively followed. He was simply part of the regular reporting undertaken by various watchers paid to inform a field agent about the comings and goings of persons of interest they had seen during various reporting periods.

Anne noted the Imam's regular activities so often observed and included in the reports, had not been referenced in the field agent's reports for a period of nearly two weeks. No-one else seemed to have noticed the absence of any comment about the Imam's activities, or if they had, they had given it no weight. Just an Imam who hadn't been seen during the reporting period. Anyway, now he was back, as noted in the latest report which referred to the Imam being seen in a spice market with a group of three other men. The other men were unknown to the watchers but appeared to be foreigners the report had said.

That report of the Imam meeting the three men had caused an initial flurry of interest among some of the analysts, but because no-one identified any further information they could link, the sighting itself was treated as inconclusive. While Anne agreed the spice market sighting didn't mean anything on its own, she thought the circumstances warranted further enquiry about the Imam's activities. What took Anne's interest in this case was the fact that prior to the meeting observed in the spice market the Imam had dropped out of sight for a short period.

Anne went looking further because she wanted to know if there was anything in the fact he had disappeared from reports for two weeks. She found something which immediately aroused her suspicions. Another radical Imam, based in London, had also disappeared from general surveillance reports during the same two week period. He too, it turned out on enquiry, had not been noted in reports simply because he had not been seen during that time. Anne thought this was a linkage that was important.

Two radical Imams from different parts of the world both taking a holiday during the same two week period? Too much of a co-incidence Anne had argued, noting it was also an important time in the Islamic calendar and it would be unusual for an Imam not to be regularly engaging with the members of his mosque during that period.

She had kept pressing and eventually others agreed Anne may have something that should be followed up. As a consequence of the additional information Anne had identified and assessed, surveillance of both Imams and their cohorts was stepped up from "general" to "full". Within weeks the watching, listening, and reporting, human and electronic, provided some evidence a bomb plot was indicated for London.

Subsequent simultaneous raids by security forces in different parts of London prevented another co-ordinated suicide bomb attack on the British underground rail transport network. The London based Imam was arrested and held for trial. The Imam in Turkey escaped, just before Turkish security forces completed a raid on his home. Some of the cynics at Langley wondered whether his fortuitous avoidance of arrest was more than luck.

When Anne had noted the absence of both Imams during the same period it was too much of a coincidence in her view, and also it didn't sit well with her that any Imam would be away from his mosque at that time. As a consequence she had pushed for, and obtained, more surveillance.

The two Imams were watched closely to see if the fact they had both dropped out of sight for two weeks could mean something, notwithstanding initial resistance from some who saw no value in pursuing Anne's "hunch". But Anne had based her view on more than a hunch, and she had persevered and argued her point and eventually she had succeeded in securing the surveillance which ultimately led to the discovery of yet another major terrorist plan to attack the West. She was a quality intelligence officer.

In her personal life, which she tried to keep quite separate from her professional activities, Anne's friends would describe her as having genuine empathy and high levels of both intellectual and emotional intelligence. Anne enjoyed her friends, but she also enjoyed her independence. Sometimes she would head off for a weekend on her own at an uncle's holiday cabin in woodlands only two hours' drive from Langley. A good book was all she needed for a weekend like that.

Anne's commitment to her work and her enjoyment of her social independence were the principal reasons she hadn't formed any long term intimate relationship. Anne didn't take a nun-like attitude to men, but she had never wanted to take any close personal relationship beyond genuine friendship, with some very pleasant love-making when it suited her. She took the view any permanent relationship would be just too complicated at this stage of her career, besides, did she really want to be saddled with

13

having to adjust to all the habits of a live-in lover? She thought not.

As she entered the Green Room Anne could see that indeed, something serious was in play. The Assistant Director of the Counter-terrorism Centre was already there, as were his closest advisors Bob Newhill and Dave Luscombe.

Bob and Dave were both thoughtful, insightful men, and importantly would often act as the Assistant Director's conscience if he got a little too excitable and needed to be persuaded to back off an idea. Everyone knew that, including the Assistant Director himself, who was nearing retirement and was secretly grateful for any second-guessing that would help him finish his career with a clean record. Things could go wrong fairly easily when you worked in intelligence, where big calls were required on occasions. Get it wrong and the politicians, with their 20/20 hindsight, took you apart, especially if there were political points to be scored, and there usually were.

'Anne, come on in,' said the Assistant Director, 'thanks for making yourself available at short notice.'

'No problem,' she replied, thinking it fortuitous she had decided to work late at the office that evening. She nodded hello to Bob and Dave, both of whom muttered welcomes and continued to scan the material spread out in front of them.

'I will get straight to it Anne,' said the Assistant Director, 'earlier today, just after twenty one hundred hours Paris time, terrorists launched simultaneous attacks on different parts of Paris. They tried to bomb the Stade de France. They attacked a theatre hall known as the Bataclan where a concert was underway. People in the street and at restaurants and bars nearby were shot. First reports indicate at least one hundred dead. French security forces think they now have it under control but there's a lot of confusion, it only unfolded a few hours ago.'

Anne didn't react other than to nod her head in acknowledgement. Nothing surprised her these days after a string of terrorist attacks throughout the world, all made with callous disregard for human life.

'Anne, after Charlie Hebdo, and now this attack, the French government is in a state of shock. Hollande is angry, and demanding action and accountability from his security services,' the Assistant Director continued.

'And we think the attackers were trained professionals, carrying out a carefully planned operation, not just some random angry boys from the local Muslim quarter,' Dave Luscombe chimed in.

'Why do you think that Dave?' asked Anne.

'A number of reasons. The fact there were multiple co-ordinated attacks, reminiscent of the Mumbai attacks in two thousand and eight. All the required planning and preparation have been below the radar. I spoke to a contact in French intelligence earlier and he says they had heard nothing in the lead-up period, so the attackers knew how to operate quiet coms. The attackers also had some training apparently, as they used their automatic weapons effectively. They fired in regulated bursts and didn't simply spray automatic fire. And, they were equipped with an assortment of weapons, AK forty sevens and hand-grenades, as well as improvised explosive devices my contact tells me.'

'I think we all agree it looks like they had some professional training,' the Assistant Director cut in, 'and unlike Charlie Hebdo this wasn't al-Qaeda. We think it may be Daesh,' he said, using the acronym from the Arabic translation of *Islamic State of Iraq and the Levant*, also known as the *Islamic State of Iraq and Syria,* and avoiding the more common "ISIL" or "ISIS" used by the media.

Anne knew Daesh, a terrorist organisation now established in Syria and Iraq. If Daesh was responsible for this evening's attacks in Paris a new paradigm was emerging she thought. Daesh had not previously shown itself to have an extended reach, although it was being suggested the Russian airliner crash in the Sinai a few weeks previously might have been caused by a Daesh bomb.

'If it's Daesh then this is something new,' said Anne. 'That group has not been shown to actively operate beyond its own geographic frontiers in Syria and Iraq, other than trying to radicalise loners in the West via social media. If it's them that's a major escalation in focus and capability.'

'Agreed, and that's the preliminary view of the French as well,' Dave responded.

The Assistant Director nodded. 'That's correct and that's the concern. What's front of mind for me Anne is whether this shows a developing plan by Daesh to change focus and commit terror acts well outside their usual area of operation. These attacks reflect a new level of sophistication with what, at this early stage anyway, appear to be worryingly efficient operational control and command arrangements. I think this may actually confirm Daesh has invested some time and money in developing its operational skills and has decided to extend its operational reach.'

Anne looked concerned as she thought of one of the reports she had been looking at earlier that evening. The report had sounded ominous warnings about Daesh ratcheting up its campaign against the West.

"*Better organised…. better trained….committed to acting outside its areas, and inside Western cities….looking at the full gambit of attack methods….trying to recruit scientists in Syria and Iraq.*"

Anne had been appalled by what she had read. She knew it probably meant unpredictable and deadly attacks by Daesh in Western cities were being planned. There were no limits for such a rogue organisation. Until seeing the piece on efforts to recruit scientists Anne had not considered chemical or biological attacks a realistic terrorist threat. Now she accepted there was a real possibility of such an attack. Why else would Daesh be trying to recruit scientists? Anyone, anywhere, at any time, could now be a Daesh target she had thought. And here was Daesh reaching into Paris, demonstrating its increased commitment to bring terror home to the West.

'You are correct, Daesh is thought to be wanting to expand its area and mode of operation,' Anne said, 'and it may also be looking to hire scientists. I can only think of one reason they would want to do that.'

'Jeeezuss H Christ,' exclaimed the Assistant Director, 'tell me that Daesh developing biological or chemical capabilities is just a possibility-based assumption Anne, and not based on anything definitive.'

'Sorry,' Anne grimaced, 'we have field reports indicating a real world position involving Daesh looking to up its game by recruiting scientists. Not sure how successful the scientists would be though. Weaponising some of the material that could be used is not easy, but an old favourite like deposits in municipal water supplies is not too hard if reservoir security can be breached. The view has always been that chemical or biological attacks are just too difficult for an organisation such as Daesh. The materials are not easy to obtain and deliver. But nothing is certain in the world we are dealing with, so we need to think about all their options.'

'Fucking great Anne,' said the Assistant Director, getting fully into his invective stride now as he tended to do when under pressure, 'so it will come as no surprise to you the White House has advised that the President wants us to give analysis of the French attacks top priority, and to develop a strategy to assist French security beyond our current levels of intelligence cooperation.'

'The President plans to speak to his French counterpart tomorrow, expressing his concern and the willingness of the United States to help. He will then formally offer intelligence assistance, and I am to confirm to his office by eight tomorrow morning what form that assistance could take. My current thinking, and the reason for this short notice meeting, is that beyond stepping up information sharing we should offer the French a senior intelligence officer on secondment for up to six months.' Pausing momentarily, the Assistant Director quickly looked at each of them in an effort to gauge reaction so far, and seeing nothing indicating disagreement he continued.

'Anne, I want you to go to France in that role if the French accept.'

As the Assistant Director had been talking Anne had been thinking about what had just happened in Paris. The attacks had been cruel and deadly. Mass indiscriminate deaths in multiple locations. This was terrorism as bad as it gets she thought. She knew the French Government and its security services would be stunned. So would most of the Western world, although Anne also knew some in the Western world would have quiet satisfaction in seeing a NATO country attacked from within, but that satisfaction would never be seen or acknowledged. Anne also understood there would be wildly enthusiastic celebrations in other parts of the world. She knew enough about Arab culture and Islam to understand why many would dance with uncontained delight.

Just real bad luck for some they had been at the concert, or at dinner, or in a bar that night. Jesus, she thought, this was a serious escalation by the terrorists. Yes, I will give the French what I can, but she knew the task was not easy and her contribution on its own could not provide any resolution. This terrorist attack reflected a new security paradigm for the West, and she knew wide-ranging and unimpeded co-operation between Western governments and their various agencies would be essential if the developing threat was to be properly met.

'I would be happy to do that,' replied Anne. Then, more formally, 'this is a significant escalation in mode and reach of operation and of course we should do whatever is needed to help.' Her formality reflecting her view this was serious, and acknowledging the West was likely now to face more deadly terror attacks.

'Thanks Anne,' said the Assistant Director, 'the French will have to confirm formal acceptance of the President's offer and as you may appreciate it will have to go through various channels within the French government. Because of what has just occurred in Paris they will unlikely be ready to respond in any formal way for a week or so, at least. There is confusion there at present. Some French politicians are already baying for the blood of their security services, and the media will no doubt join them over coming days. Two successful terrorist attacks in ten months is considered unacceptable, and it is. The head of France's security service is on the receiving end of all this, so setting up this secondment, if the French want it, means you probably won't start until after Christmas. By then things should have settled down a bit internally within French security.'

'Dave and Bob will brief you on scope and authority once the secondment is confirmed. You will report to Dave throughout. Thanks Anne,' and with that the Assistant Director left the room.

Some weeks later, in early December, Dave Luscombe, Bob Newhill, and Anne, met to discuss proposed arrangements for her secondment to French intelligence.

'As expected, formal confirmation has now been received from the French,' said Dave. 'They propose you work with their counter-terrorism unit at the Central Domestic Intelligence Directorate, the DCRI, the *Direction Centrale du Renseignement Intérieur,*' he added, in a tortured French accent. 'They are keen for you to start soonest, but I have told them they should expect you in Paris no earlier than the second week of January. I know you have Christmas and New Year planned with your father Anne, so no point in going until after that, which is why I told them second week of January. I also reconfirmed with them the secondment term is a maximum of six months, as discussed earlier. That all okay with you?'

Anne was okay with all that, and appreciated Dave's thoughtfulness. He was a Very Nice Man so far as she was concerned, that accolade being her usual for any older man whom Anne had found to be especially kind. She was grateful Dave had recognised her commitment to spend the festive season with her widower dad, particularly as she was going to be away, in France, for six months.

Anne also understood why she would be working with domestic intelligence services in Paris, rather than external security services. The prevention of any further terrorist attacks within France would be getting absolute priority, and as part of that there would be very close liaison between external and domestic French intelligence services. Given what had been experienced in Paris over the last year those services would work together to ensure no gaps, but the prime domestic counter–terrorism responsibility was with DCRI. When DCRI had been formed it had assumed the functions of the former Central Directorate for General Intelligence. As counter-terrorism was one of the principal functions of the Central Directorate the role DCRI was now assuming in response to the attacks all made perfect sense to Anne.

What a mess in France she thought. Any further attack after Charlie Hebdo and now this attack at the Bataclan theatre and surrounds will have French intelligence pilloried by the media and the politicians. She didn't think that entirely fair, but nevertheless she knew the security services would be blamed in the event of another terrorist outrage. Someone always had to be held to account in such situations, and it would never be the politicians, notwithstanding they had responsibility to adequately fund and empower the security services. If the law did not allow the security services to undertake some action they saw as necessary, or, if the services had insufficient funding and resources to manage their watch lists and someone on the list became a headline with a terror attack, then it would be considered negligence by the services. It could never be a governance failure by the politicians.

'We are there to help as much as we can, but we are not passing our raw data to the French unless it's something we know they have already. We will analyse the data and give our view on what activity we consider is possible, or unlikely, as a consequence, but our sources are to be protected by keeping prime material within our knowledge. That's particularly so for material ex HUMINT,' said Bob, using his favoured description for human intelligence.

Anne understood names and source areas had to be kept as closely held as possible to protect assets. She would share the results and be able to give the French helpful information, but without divulging source. In the absence of knowledge of source the French would just have to trust her information credibility assessment.

'Your primary contact at DCRI will be René Sharen, their head of counter-terrorism, and just to forewarn you, while he is highly regarded in his professional role by both the French and us, he can be bit of a prick personally, so, just so you know…..' Bob trailed off.

'He's a good operator, but he's French and you are on his patch, so you will need all your diplomatic skills,' Dave added.

But Anne wasn't concerned. She had dealt with her share of difficult personalities over the years and she doubted the working relationships she would form within French security would be a problem. Too much for everyone to lose in the circumstances. In fact she was looking forward to meeting René Sharen, head of DCRI counter-terrorism, and getting on with the work that needed to be done. She understood the French were famously prissy about outsiders giving them advice, but she hoped that in the circumstances there would be recognition of the value her secondment could add to French counter-terrorism efforts.

21

Dave Luscombe continued. 'Briefing papers, with all we have on the attacks, as well as the information sharing protocols we want applied and an overview of DCRI including René Sharen's CV, are available for you to access on the ops system,' a reference to the in-house network used to distribute confidential operational material. 'And once the secondment is underway you should report to me, following SOPs of course, or Bob in my absence,' Dave added, referring to the Agency's Standard Operating Procedures which provided the framework for most activity when operating in the field, which is how Anne's secondment was to be classified. And on this occasion she was authorised to act operationally with French security if it became necessary. Observer status limitations when in the field were no longer applicable to this experienced CIA officer, particularly as she had now completed an analyst's Quick Course at "The Farm" as the CIA field training operation at Camp Peary near Williamsburg was known.

Dave concluded, 'Once you have briefed yourself come back to me with any questions Anne. Otherwise, if you have nothing further after briefing enjoy the festive season with family and friends and then get yourself to Paris and set yourself up there for the first six months of two thousand and sixteen. Paris station has arranged accommodation for you so you can get that detail when you arrive, from the embassy.'

'I'm pleased you are on this Anne,' said Bob Newhill, smiling, as the meeting finished up. The secondment offer of one of the Agency's best assets had been a big issue for Bob. While France had been the target recently it could so easily be the United States another day. Bob knew that right now international co-operative action was required to combat terrorism.

His view, happily shared by many, including influential politicians, was that there could be no free-riders. All western countries had to commit and cooperate, which is what the United States had always done and was reinforcing now, as far as he was concerned. Bob would not have been happy if the French had said they needed no help.

The threat was global, so must be the response, and a French refusal would likely have given rise to a less than optimal response to the renewed vigour being seen in the current levels of terrorist activity. If there ever was a reason and time for international co-operation, it was now, dealing with Daesh and its developing aspirations.

Chapter Two

Akash Prasad looked out over his castor oil plantation and smiled. For three generations his family had been growing castor oil plants on their plantation in a small sheltered valley about one hundred kilometres south west of the city of Chennai, previously known as Madras, not far from the town of Vandavasi in south eastern India. The valley had the reputation of being moderately fertile, and importantly it had the well-draining soil essential for castor oil plants to flourish.

Producing castor oil for a good living is not an easy task in south eastern India. Many of the growers in the area, one of the world's most concentrated regions for growing castor oil plants, have very small land holdings and struggle because of their inability to achieve any economies of scale. And there were other reasons as well which contributed to the lack of profitability in the industry.

When selling their castor oil, produced by crushing the beans contained in the plants, many of the growers found the buyers of their oil, while claiming independence from each other, had clearly talked about pricing between themselves. As a consequence growers rarely achieved the returns they needed as a result of what was effectively buyer pricing collusion.

Anti-trust regulatory controls in India were not sophisticated in any event, but those that existed did not permeate down to the grower level, so there was little legal protection for them. While the authorities exercised some control in the retail markets by ensuring no dominant participant used its position to influence price, they seemed to have overlooked the procurement market, which left growers exposed when they sought to market their castor oil to the various buyers operating in that market. Perhaps it was a reflection of the growers' lack of influence, being in the main solo operations on small holdings.

Added to these unfortunate market realities was the unpredictability of south eastern India's weather, particularly as the castor oil plants approached maturity. Harvesting required dry conditions. The difficulties growers faced were numerous and many of them struggled to turn a satisfactory profit.

The Prasad family had a large plantation and while they had experienced financial troubles in the past their castor oil business had been relatively successful in recent years compared to some in the business. The size of their operation had helped as it gave them economies of scale and more influence with the buyers seeking the oil processed from the annual crop.

Akash was the current administrator of the plantation on behalf of the wider Prasad family, having taken over from his uncle at the end of the previous season. Akash was anxious the plantation should perform well under his stewardship, and he wanted to improve profitability. He knew the family would be watching to see how "young Akash" handled his new responsibility as the plantation administrator. Akash knew they would judge him quite simply, on the year's profit. Issues of sustainability and reinvestment in the plantation were not for them. They wanted the cash, now.

Akash recognised that a good annual dividend was what would keep the extended Prasad family happy. He didn't like it, but there was little he could do about it at present. Once he had a couple of successful seasons behind him it would be different. Then, when the family had seen what he could do, he would have more influence and they would not quickly dismiss his suggestions for the business. He planned to propose more reinvestment of profits in the business at that time. The family, particularly a couple of big-spending aunts, would just have to take a longer term view and cope with some reduced dividend payments for a few years in that case.

When this season's castor oil plants had been harvested, Akash would extract the oil with the new crushing and extraction plant he had recently purchased and had installed at the plantation. That had been the family's one concession to further investment in the plantation, principally allowed because Akash had been able to demonstrate it would mean increased profitability in Year One. No extended pay-back period. The aunts, in particular, had liked that.

Akash was looking forward to using his own processing plant. Having his own plant would mean he could better control the timing of his oil production, and also it would enable him to avoid the expensive contractors near Delhi the Prasad plantation had always used in past seasons for processing their castor oil plants.

In recent times the prices for castor oil had been improving. Various buying agents had been to see him already this season, all trying to persuade Akash he should sign with them for his oil. Each one of them had told him their particular price for the castor oil he would produce was the best price in the market, and he should take the price offered while it was available.

Akash had noted all the prices offered were very similar, and it confirmed to him the castor oil procurement market was not really a competitive market. As a consequence, while Akash was keen to finalise a sale of his oil he had delayed committing to any buyer as long as he could. He thought the market prices would have to improve. The longer he left it the better the price was likely to be. And it didn't hurt to appear not to be too keen to finalise a sale. He didn't want buyers knowing cost overruns on his new crushing and extraction plant had put him under financial pressure. His need for some significant cash-flow as soon as possible, to meet the cost of the increased borrowing necessary to cover the processing plant cost over-run and other general plantation overheads falling due, was his private concern.

The longer he held off accepting an offer, the better the offers would be in the rising world market for castor oil in Akash's view. He could wait some weeks yet and then the buying agents might even begin to feel their own pressure as their principals started to question them as to whether they had successfully secured the castor oil quantities the principal sought for the season.

Setting up a crushing and extraction plant at the plantation, instead of contracting the processing of their castor beans to the plant outside Delhi, had been Akash's first significant commercial decision since taking over from his uncle. In Akash's view the family which owned the Delhi plant had used its position as the controller of scarce processing capacity to lift its processing charges significantly at peak harvest times, just when that capacity was most needed. Supply and demand in action he knew, but it was unsatisfactory. So far as the Delhi processor was concerned you either paid a premium to get your product processed when you needed it to be processed, or you took your chance on the timing of access to the processing facility and the availability of your oil, which had some price risk in the wholesale buyer market.

Now, with his own crushing and extraction plant, Akash controlled that situation. He could process his castor oil bean crop when he chose. He had also created a supplementary revenue stream by arranging to process some of his neighbours' crops after he had met the crushing requirements of his own plantation. His decision to price processing at a reasonable level, because he certainly didn't want to be guilty of squeezing his neighbours on price in the way the Delhi processors had in the past, had been recognised by his neighbours, most of whom had signed up for their processing to be undertaken by the Prasad operation. Akash was happy that what he may have lost in margin with his pricing was more than covered by the significant volumes his neighbours had committed.

As it was to turn out, Akash's plant harvesting and oil sale plans did not go as he had hoped. Continual heavy rain delayed his harvest. It was late November before the ground was sufficiently dry to allow harvesting to begin. The castor oil buyers, sensing, or perhaps hearing some of the industry gossip about non-payment of Akash's creditors, played a waiting game while offering Akash lower prices than previously offered.

Once his harvest was finally in, castor oil beans removed from the plant material surrounding them, and his new processing plant had started crushing the beans and extracting their oil, Akash was not the happy man he had originally thought he would have been at that point. He had received no acceptable offers for his castor oil from buyers and his sale margin were going to be substantially down on the level he had calculated if he sold at anything like the currently offered prices. So when he was approached with an unexpected business proposition early in the New Year, he listened.

The tall, olive skinned man in the well-tailored white jacket standing in front of Akash in the office of the building housing his new crushing and extraction plant smiled at him, and repeated, in his refined English accent, what he had just said; 'Yes, I want to buy some of your oil cake, one tonne, and the price I will pay is fifteen thousand US dollars, in cash, on delivery.'

He was repeating his offer because Akash had been so incredulous he was being offered so much for the cake. After all, it was just the dross left after crushing the castor oil beans and extracting their oil. It was usually simply disposed of to an approved dumping facility.

'Let me explain,' the man in the white jacket continued, sensing Akash's continuing disbelief.

'I represent a Swiss pharmaceutical company which is working to produce a drug that will help sufferers of arthritis if successful. There is material to be extracted from the oil cake which may assist. I know the disposal of oil cake is closely controlled in many countries and while my client could go through various formalities to get what it needs, it could pay you to provide what it wants to avoid the delay my client would experience in dealing with the bureaucracy to obtain the oil cake. Win-win for both of us really,' he smiled.

Akash looked closely at the man making him the offer, trying to decide if his visitor was genuine and if he was, whether this was a deal he should agree to undertake. Akash knew that while Indian regulators did not closely control what was done with the cake of castor oil beans after processing they wanted to know how it had been disposed of. The oil cake contained some residual toxins so secure disposal was expected. But the system in India was a very light-handed regulatory control compared to some countries. All every Indian castor oil processor had to do was file a return showing the amount of oil they had produced from processing and confirm amount, mode, and place of disposal of the cake. There was no check on the actual disposal of the oil cake referred to in the return.

Akash had not filed such returns before as the processors in Delhi, the people actually producing the oil and the resulting cake, had always handled the disposal and reporting formalities. But now as the administrator of a plantation undertaking its own processing it would be Akash's responsibility to report oil cake disposal for this season's processing. A fairly simple reporting requirement he thought, with no checks, so I can deal with it how I like.

Akash had already decided if he did go through with this the fifteen thousand dollars from the sale of oil cake would not show in any tax return. No sense in paying tax on this one-off windfall he thought. If revenue inspectors came looking any tax audit would only identify his castor oil sale income and any processing income earned from neighbours, all of which he would fully declare. No-one, including the dividend-expectant family members, would be looking for revenue from his oil cake as it wasn't normally sold. No tax on the fifteen thousand dollars and no need to share the undisclosed windfall with the family. This could be a very good outcome for me Akash thought.

Yes, he decided, I will sell oil cake to White Jacket. Good money I can keep for myself and tax free from a virtually undetectable cash transaction. And, he rationalised, the oil cake is going to be used by a reputable company in Switzerland for medical research so why should I decline to help just because it involves some short cuts through the officialdom surrounding oil cake disposal returns?

'We have a deal,' said Akash, reaching out to seal the arrangement with a hand-shake. As they shook hands Akash was already planning how he would spend this unexpected tax free bonus.

'Thank you,' smiled White Jacket, 'we will need to maintain absolute discretion about this transaction.'

'Agreed,' said Akash, thinking about his plan to keep it for himself, tax free. No one would know anything of this so far as he was concerned.

'When all your processing has been completed separate one tonne of oil cake and let me know it is ready by email to this address,' said White Jacket handing him a slip of paper with an email address written on it. I will arrange for a container to be delivered to your property once I receive your email confirming your processing is complete, and the cake can be loaded into that container and held until needed. The oil cake is booked for shipping in early March. Can you hold it for me until then?'

'Certainly. And my cousin manages a tea plantation,' said Akash helpfully, 'for convenience he could provide some empty tea chests. He always has some surplus to his requirements. I could have the oil cake loaded into those chests and placed in the container for your March delivery. I will need about forty chests for the amount you seek.'

'Excellent,' said White Jacket. 'I will arrange for someone to contact you about collecting the container at the beginning of March. When my contractor arrives to uplift the container he will pay you fifteen thousand in cash at that time. Is that acceptable?'

'A cash deposit now to show good faith would be most satisfactory,' said Akash. He noticed a brief shadow of annoyance cross White Jacket's otherwise smiling face, but he considered it necessary that he ask for a deposit. He thought it good business practice. He had to hold the cake until March and for all Akash knew the man may not proceed with his purchase.

'I will arrange for five thousand dollars to be given to you within the next week,' White Jacket replied, somewhat coldly Akash thought, but never mind, he would get his deposit.

'Thank you,' said Akash to White Jacket, delighted with his day.

Akash didn't know it, but the well-spoken, tall, olive-skinned young man in the white jacket with whom he had made the arrangements to sell some of the cake left behind from his castor bean processing was Aashiq Ahad, a Syrian who was an agent of Daesh. Acquiring the oil cake was a necessary preliminary step in a terror attack Daesh was planning to carry out in France.

Aashiq was considered the best person to help bring such a plan together for Daesh because he had been educated in the West, he was familiar with most aspects of western culture and habits, and most importantly, he was a secret asset of Daesh. Western intelligence had no idea Aashiq Ahad was a Daesh operative. He had always operated under deep cover keeping his connection with Daesh unknown to all but senior Daesh leadership. As a consequence he could operate under the noses of the infidels in the West and more easily travel about to make necessary arrangements.

Aashiq Ahad was the son of a wealthy Syrian trader who specialised in exporting raw cotton. A lot of money had been made by some in Syria from the cotton trade in the early days, but it had not been as lucrative in recent times. There had been water shortages caused by drought and the antiquated Syrian irrigation systems struggled to cope. They were both old and inefficient. Then there was the war. Times had changed, and while Aashiq spent some time in the business after finishing his schooling, it was always unlikely Aashiq would want to succeed his father in the family business.

Aashiq's childhood had been privileged. Growing up in a large home in one of the better areas of the Syrian port city of Latakia, he had attending Al Sham Oasis private school. On completion of his schooling, Aashiq spent some months working in the family cotton business, but then, with some assistance from his father who had decided it was an appropriate time to make an endowment at a London University, he had gained entry to the London School of Economics where Aashiq studied sociology and social policy. The LSE, as it is known, was a university with well-established connections to the Arab world. As a favoured UK institution for tertiary study by the children of the Arab elite Aashiq's enrolment there was unsurprising.

Aashiq had thoroughly enjoyed his student days in London, spending his first academic year as a resident in a student hostel, Carr-Saunders Hall, before moving into a private apartment nearby. The apartment was expensive, but his parents wanted him to have all he needed and he had told them living in an apartment rather than in the student hostel would improve his ability to study.

When he had graduated and returned to Syria he was a different person from the eager, somewhat naïve, young man who had left four years previously to attend university in London. He was now urbane, confident, and he had adopted a rather affected English accent. Many of the people he had met in London had found Aashiq an attractive personality, but some in Syria did not like the new-look Aashiq. He now appeared too western for a number of his associates.

But while Aashiq dressed like a westerner, sounded like a westerner, and had adopted some of their social behaviours, he remained faithful to the obligations imposed on him by the Qur'an. He didn't drink alcohol, often to the disappointment of some of the hard-partying students he had associated with during his university days. Some of the women studying at LSE, taken with the look and style of the tall olive-skinned Arab, had dated him, but while he was friendly and fun he would never take the relationship to a sexual level, despite not so subtle encouragement from some he went out with.

Aashiq had been quick to adopt modern western dress and some of its behaviours, but despite his apparent westernisation while at LSE he held deeply embedded Muslim beliefs about alcohol and sex. In particular he respected Zina, the Islamic law forbidding sex between unmarried parties, which was usually described pejoratively by Muslims as fornication. Fornication was something Aashiq would never commit.

While devoted to Islam, Aashiq did sometimes find himself wondering about the concept of martyrs being rewarded with large numbers of virgins, a favourite Daesh encouragement when seeking to persuade young men to die for the cause. It seemed a direct conflict with the teachings as he understood them, and Zina in particular, but then political expediency came in all forms. Aashiq understood that.

What his friends at LSE hadn't known about Aashiq was that he had developed a view Islamic teachings and law should be dominant in the beliefs and laws controlling people and culture throughout the world. To that end, on his return to Syria after completing his university studies he had sought out members of Daesh. He had told members of Daesh whom he had met he wanted to make a contribution to the cause.

Suspicious at first, they came to trust Aashiq over a period of some months as they heard him talk about issues of importance to Islam and the way the West, where most people still drank and fornicated every day, was trying to impose its will and ways on Muslims. For Aashiq, Daesh was the modern day saviour of a world that needed Islam and he was determined to help ensure Islamic dominance.

Soon, after Aashiq had been introduced to and spent time meeting with some of the leaders of Daesh in Syria, which was not without its risks given the armed clashes constantly occurring in the region, he had become established as a valuable resource for Daesh. He had good contacts in the West, was western educated, and understood the way westerners thought and acted. Also, and importantly, he had the knowledge and ability to introduce some in the Daesh leadership to the advantages of participating in social media. With its ability to facilitate communication and spread influence this became a particularly useful tool for the cause.

Aashiq knew suitably minded individuals could be reached via the internet and relationships established via social media sites. There was no need for them to be in our country or even in a mosque in their own country to facilitate radicalisation he had said to the Daesh leaders. He had been right. A number of lone wolf attacks in western countries had been encouraged in this way, undertaken by would-be jihadists living within the country concerned who without any warning had turned on their fellow citizens.

Aashiq was determined to keep his name and involvement with Daesh low key, limiting his connection to just a few leaders, all of whom completely understood the need for discretion. Aashiq knew he would be of much more value to Daesh if he did not become known to the western intelligence services. He fitted in well in the West, and as a person with an unknown connection to Daesh he could move relatively freely throughout the West.

Six weeks after his meeting with White Jacket, Akash had completed all his castor oil plant processing. He had sold his oil at a price above the previous year's price. He had also increased his margin as a consequence of reducing his processing costs by using his own crushing and extraction plant. The Prasad family was happy, with an increased dividend to be paid this year. Young Akash had performed well the family thought.

Akash was also very happy. He had been able to demonstrate to the family the wisdom of setting up their own crushing plant and he had skilfully negotiated good prices at sale of the castor oil to the buyers who in the end had been forced to lift their offers to get their required supply of oil. Production levels, once the wet start to the harvesting season was behind them, had been above average after a warm summer with moisture at optimum levels during the early part of the growing season. No torrential downpour to damage the crop's progress to maturity. And, coincidently, Akash had earned himself fifteen thousand US dollars, tax free. Just from disposing of part of his otherwise worthless oil cake by-product. A very good year.

When the container promised by White Jacket arrived in response to Akash's email confirming his processing was complete, Akash had arranged for it to be parked on a discreet site behind the crushing and processing plant building and loaded with forty tea chests containing the dried oil cake. Early in March Akash was contacted by a trucking firm about picking up the container he was holding in storage. Arrangements were made and the container was gone within twenty four hours. Akash had been paid the balance of his fifteen thousand dollars, contained in a sealed envelope given to him by the truck driver collecting the container, who had said nothing other than he had been instructed to give Akash the envelope.

Akash didn't know where the castor bean oil cake had been taken once the truck carrying the container had left his property, but by the end of March the container carrying the oil cake, carefully packed into tea chests inside the container, was being unloaded from a ship in the south of France.

Castor oil plants may seem innocuous, but their seeds contain a deadly toxin, ricin, which remains in the oil cake residue left after castor oil beans have been crushed and their oil extracted. When extracted from the oil cake pure ricin has the capability to kill an adult human. A small dose of purified ricin, no more than the equivalent of a few grains of sand, is all it takes. That is what Daesh had sought and what Aashiq Ahad had been sent to India to acquire. It was key to the attack being planned, aimed once again at ramping up terror levels in France.

Chapter Three

Daesh originated from the Iraqi division of al-Qaeda. It expanded rapidly in Syria from 2011, although Putin and Assad put it under real pressure there following Russia's intervention in the Syrian civil war. That intervention began in September 2015 after Putin accepted a request from Assad for assistance. A request by Assad considered to be a political master-stroke as Russian intervention, even at the cost of the conditions the Russians had required, acted to preserve his then tottering regime. The presence of the Russians also curtailed some plans by the United State that were, until that point at least, being prepared for activation.

As well as Iraqis and Syrians, many foreign fighters joined Daesh. They travelled to Iraq or Syria from around the world to join, notwithstanding the efforts of many western countries to stop their citizens from doing so. Some countries had made it a criminal offence for a citizen to leave their country to travel to join Daesh, and were arresting people at airports as they were about to fly out. Some were even being arrested prior to that point, if found to be planning to leave at some future date. Such was the concern about Daesh in the West.

Many of the foreign fighters joining Daesh were more compelled by a sense of adventure and excitement and a lust to fight than by their religious beliefs and attraction to participation in the Caliphate which Daesh was proposing. But the fighters would never openly admit that was what drove them. Better to be seen as avenging Islam and building a new Islamic state than simply embarking on activities involving cruel and psychotic behaviour, something for which Daesh had quickly become known.

Daesh was a prime concern for western intelligence services, who saw first-hand the results of some of the Daesh atrocities. A drone offensive by the United States military, targeting the Daesh leadership, had been extremely successful with a series of drone attacks decimating Daesh senior ranks.

As a consequence of the drone offensive Daesh leaders were now being much more careful and were maintaining a low profile in all their activities. They avoided attendance at large meetings of the group wherever they could. Sometimes they had no real choice but to meet for some particular reason, and in such cases much care was taken over keeping those meetings secret.

Messages were delivered in ways that avoided a meeting wherever practicable. The preferred communication method was for messages to be delivered by individuals of little importance in Daesh, simple couriers, or by the electronic equivalent of a dead letter drop, using an established email site. Daesh leaders knew that to be seen attending a meeting, or to use a mobile or satellite phone, was likely to trigger alerts that would start the process of a drone being tasked with a strike against them.

Abu al Khayr was pleased and honoured to have taken over recently as a senior operative of Daesh. As a senior commander responsible for attack strategy and planning he was proud of the way Daesh had grown and developed. He appreciated the order that now existed, with improved allocation of responsibilities to the right people, quality planning and preparation, and careful execution of plans. Daesh was no longer a rag tag group of tribal fighters. It had transformed into a properly organised and capable entity in al Khayr's view. He truly believed it would achieve the Caliphate talked of by both Daesh leaders and the frightened politicians of the West.

Al Khayr had plans to avenge Allah in the cities of the fat and bloated disbelievers in the West, and he wanted to do it in a way that the infidels would never forget. They could not escape just because they stayed at home. It was enough they were part of the society trying to impose its will on Islam, and assuredly they would experience retribution as a result he thought.

In his formal role in Daesh as a military strategist and planner al Khayr was charged with planning attacks in the West that would keep Daesh in the headlines, and remind infidels they must respect the concerns of Islam. He thought the West had become complacent and he wanted to shake that complacency by bringing Islam to their homeland. Members of Daesh were committed to the true faith and that would ensure eventual victory, he knew.

Al Khayr had experienced some recent success with the attacks centred on the Bataclan in Paris. Now he had another plan, also for an attack in France, which his clever young westernised lieutenant, Aashiq Ahad, had devised. He would meet with Aashiq soon to discuss these arrangements.

Abu al Khayr was very cautious whenever he proposed to meet his lieutenants or travel from his usual safe house situated in the countryside not far from the Syrian city of Raqqa. His home was a small mud brick cottage, with a large number of olive trees growing around it. Importantly it was a place where al Khayr could stay and be discreet, because the road which passed the property was at least eighty metres away through the natural screen provided by the olive trees growing around the cottage. No-one walking past could look in and see who was there, unlike many of the houses in the city itself where there was little privacy from the searching eyes of passers-by. Most of those passers-by were just being inquisitive, not purposefully seeking out anyone, but nevertheless al Khayr didn't want to be seen by anyone passing if he could avoid it. You never knew who may be looking.

Hakim, al Khayr's predecessor, had died a month previously when a missile from a drone had struck his car, instantly incinerated him in a huge fireball as he returned from visiting a seriously ill sister.

It was stupid of Hakim, al Khayr had thought at the time, as if the Americans would not have known of her illness and anticipated the possibility of a visit from one of the most wanted on the list of terrorists maintained by that great Satan, the United States of America. All they had to do was watch his sister and wait. And they did, and now Hakim was dead. Al Khayr knew he wouldn't be so foolish.

Abu al Khayr recognised that his lieutenant, Aashiq Ahad, as well as being indispensable in planning and preparing attacks, had been instrumental in persuading Daesh to modernise its public relations and how it communicated with potential martyrs and fighters living in countries outside Iraq and Syria.

Daesh now actively used the internet and social media to target susceptible young men and women living in the West, with some success. Potential recruits were encouraged by Daesh to rise up in the defence of Muslim women and children who, Daesh claimed, were being raped and killed by forces from the West, the United States in particular.

As well as being encouraged to use a rifle against any infidel, these potential terrorists were being urged to use everyday kitchen items to make explosive devices, such as a pressure cooker bomb, or to use their vehicle to drive into crowds of pedestrians. Good Muslims should conduct individual *jihad* the Supreme Leader had said, calling for individuals to undertake random attacks in the communities in which they lived if they were unable to undertake the *Hijrah,* the migration, to the land of the Caliphate, the *Khilafah* as he called it.

The Supreme Leader of Daesh was very supportive of the new approach developed as a result of Aashiq's urgings, particularly as the results had become more evident. Increased numbers of fighters were arriving to join Daesh's brigades. There had also been an increasing number of attacks conducted by individuals living within

Western communities on their fellow citizens. What the western media often referred to as "lone wolf" attacks.

In addition, some western media were also now writing stories which referred to the things Daesh was said to be doing in education and health, and food supply for the benefit of those living under its protection in its *Khilafah*. Al Khayr knew the truth was somewhat short of that, but he had faith Daesh would deliver many benefits to those it enveloped in its protection at some point in the future, once established, and he was happy to see the reporting by the western media of some of the good territorial governance being undertaken by Daesh.

The individual acts of terror carried out by occasional lone *jihadists* in the West were not enough for al Khayr. Charlie Hebdo had been a satisfying attack on western ideas and belief, getting world attention, even if undertaken by al-Qaeda in the Arabian Peninsula, effectively a rival organisation.

Daesh's own Paris attacks, centred on the Bataclan, had been beautiful, but al Khayr wanted more. As a consequence he had spent a lot of time thinking about how the West might again be attacked, and he had readily agreed to the suggested attack Aashiq had developed and raised with him. Now this next attack, again on France, was almost ready. Al Khayr had named the operation "*Haboob*", and now he needed to meet his principal lieutenant, Aashiq Ahad, to get an update on progress with key elements of the plans for *Haboob*.

Abu al Khayr kept his personal contacts with his fellow Daesh members to a minimum because it was too dangerous for members to gather together often. Eyes were everywhere, including the sky, and the Western powers were continually watching and waiting for an opportunity to identify such a meeting and destroy all its attendees.

Hand-delivered notes, and messages hidden in email sites that could be accessed and read from anywhere with an internet connection without the message having to be sent over the internet and risk interception, were the methods used to prepare for the Paris attacks. The French had not expected the Daesh teams at the Stade de France, the Batacalan, and in the nearby streets, restaurants, and bars attacked by the martyrs. The low profile adopted in planning those attacks and the techniques for communicating had worked well.

Al Khayr was breaking one of his self-imposed rules by meeting Aashiq, but he thought it necessary and he would be cautious. There was too much to discuss at this point in the planning. He was impatient with the time taken by some of the usual forms of communication. While they were safer, they were too slow, with messages, responses and counter-responses taking days. Face to face meetings allowed instant reporting and response, and facilitated decision making. He would be careful, but he had to meet with Aashiq to finalise arrangements for the next attack on France. Accordingly, al Khayr had decided to travel through the Syrian countryside to meet Aashiq in his home.

Al Khayr smiled to himself as he thought about Aashiq Ahad, a very intense young man who was totally committed to the cause. Aashiq was well-educated, with a university degree from London, courtesy of his wealthy parents, and he had developed a penchant for dressing in modern western style. No robes for Aashiq.

Abu al Khayr recognised that while a lot of the changes to the way Daesh now operated were down to Aashiq, some in the organisation did not like Aashiq's style. So far as al Khayr was concerned Aashiq was completely trustworthy and a very good organiser and thinker. He relied on Aashiq more than he would ever admit publicly, especially to those on the Governing Council who did not like Aashiq because of his "westernisation".

Aashiq Ahad had decided long ago to operate covertly, avoiding any public connection with Daesh. As a second layer of protection, in case he should become suspected of being a Daesh operative, he had decided he would live well away from areas where Daesh was active, and hide in plain view as one of many in the port city of Latakia where he had grown up. The city had experienced the ravages of the civil war in Syria during a siege in August 2011, but the fighting had since moved on to other areas. Now it was a government controlled area and Aashiq considered he was well undercover. He was confident his links with Daesh would remain unknown, and he took additional comfort from his belief Syrian forces would not expect a senior Daesh operative to be based in Latakia.

Aashiq's home in Latakia was close to Tishreen University. His home was typical in design of many houses in that part of the city. Its living quarters were arranged around a small courtyard, which in this house contained a spring-fed fountain, a rare luxury. The courtyard was decorated with citrus trees and a few grape vines.

When al Khayr arrived at Aashiq's home in Latakia, he and Aashiq embraced. Al Khayr was clearly impressed with the standard of living Aashiq had achieved in a country battered by what was referred to internationally as the Syrian civil war, although he and all his friends knew that in reality it had become a sectarian war. The high principles of the Arab Spring uprisings had long since been supplanted by a brutal sectarian reality. Now it was Alawite and Shia groups versus Sunni, with some foreign intervention added to really confuse things. It was this countrywide chaos which had helped some Daesh operatives stay unobserved and out of harm from the western intelligence agencies and their associated forces who were actively seeking members of the Daesh command.

Sitting in a room off the court-yard of Aashiq's home, they swallowed the coffee which had been bubbling on a small stove. It was strong and hot. The *kahwa murrah*, as the coffee they were drinking was known, had been brewing all morning on the stove, leaving the air in the room heavy with a warm sweet smell. Aashiq had served the coffee from a traditional Arabic brass pot into a small ceramic cup that took little more than a mouthful. Rather like using a shot glass al Khayr swallowed his coffee in one quick action, the Arab way. So did Aashiq. This coffee is never taken slowly and savoured. It is always taken quickly as part of a greeting acknowledgment when a guest enters the host's home.

'What progress can you tell me of Aashiq Ahad?' al Khayr asked.

Aashiq began to tell him about the progress made on the plan for the attack. He reported he had been to India and obtained the necessary castor oil cake, and it was expected to arrive in France at the end of the month. It had cost fifteen thousand US dollars.

He had also arranged the lease of a property in Montfavet, a small commune just outside the city of Avignon, in the south of France. Aashiq confirmed an agent had met with the owner of an empty warehouse situated in the light industrial area of Montfavet, near the airport, and negotiated a lease of the building for two years from the beginning of March as had been discussed when he had made his original recommendation to al Khayr. The warehouse was only needed for the period from March to July, but a short term lease would be unusual for such a building and it had been agreed early in the planning that it should be rented for a longer term to ensure the arrangement did not raise any queries from the landlord.

'The warehouse is near the Caumont airport in Montfavet. We have agreed to pay rental six months in advance through the term of lease. That avoided any question of a bank guarantee being sought which would have raised difficulties because of the questions banks always ask in relation to matters of ownership, identity, and financial worth when arranging guarantees. The warehouse has secure access and will fit our requirements well once the processing equipment is installed, which will be soon,' Aashiq added.

Aashiq went on to say contact had been made with a person who was known to be willing to take a bribe to assist the illicit importation of goods. That person worked in computer services in the inspector's office at the principal port serving the south of France, Marseille-Fos. Aashiq had arranged for a payment to this person in return for him agreeing to facilitate the release of a certain container to be shipped from Chennai, India. The person concerned had not been worried about what may be in the container and had not asked, but comments purposefully made but intended to seem as if inadvertent would have left the impression the container carried contraband cigarettes Aashiq said. The fact that Aashiq had arranged for the shipment of forty tea chests filled with castor oil cake from Chennai to France remained a matter known only to those in Daesh who needed to know.

Aashiq's plan for the container was based on the fact that Customs and Excise at Marseille-Fos could not check every container transiting through the port, there were just too many. He knew a system of alerts operated, based on identity of the shipper, point of origin, end destination, and declared contents. Aashiq hoped his container would not be selected as its shipper would be shown as a well-established and reputable international trader in agricultural machinery parts, based in Marseille.

If the container was selected for inspection the arrangements in place would ensure the container passed through the port without actually being opened. The port worker taking the bribe had agreed if the container was selected for inspection, and he could not deselect it within the system he operated without raising suspicion, he would ensure an official inspection sticker was placed on the container confirming that it had in fact been inspected and its release authorised. He was confident he could also place an equivalent note on the port's computerised records for the particular container confirming that indeed the container had been inspected and approved for release should anyone want to check that the inspection sticker attached to the container was correct.

Aashiq also confirmed arrangements had been made to have the container collected and to ensure no trail was left as to where it might have gone.

'The scientist who has agreed to help us with our plan will stay in a *pension* in Avignon. I don't want him in Montfavet,' Aashiq continued, 'it's too small, and he may be the object of enquiry as to who he is, where from, and what he is doing in Montfavet whenever he socialises at the few cafes and bars there. Better he lives in the anonymity of a larger place, and its only twenty minutes on a local bus to Montfavet.'

'I have also arranged for the commercial drones to be acquired,' Aashiq said, 'three of them, each capable of carrying a payload of up to five kilogrammes. They are relatively expensive, but for our purposes they are ideal. Stable in winds up to twenty five knots, good height-hold capability, and programmable to fly a precise flight path from take-off to landing. GPS units in each drone will ensure flight path accuracy,' he said, referring to the Global Positioning System carried in each of the drones. 'The drones have an area where we can fit the necessary hoppers underneath the main body. The hoppers will be made from light aluminium to keep weight to a minimum.'

'Thank you Aashiq Ahad, you are a worthy and capable person,' said al Khayr, pleased with what Aashiq had told him. After another hour of discussion about various elements of the plan, including advice regarding the hiring of a driver and provision of a van to move the drones to their launch position somewhere near the main square in the old city section of Avignon, and how Aashiq planned to get out of France after the attack, al Khayr was satisfied all necessary arrangements were in place and potential threats to success identified. So, excellent, thought al Khayr as he stood and completed a little dance to show his pleasure at progress, and his excitement.

The Avignon festival is an annual arts event held each year in July in the city of Avignon, in Southern France. Much of the festival takes place in and around the beautiful Palais des Papes, with its famous courtyard Cour d'Honneur being a favoured place for live theatre. Over the period of the festival upwards of one hundred and sixty thousand people can attend the various events, and it is a favourite of both locals and those from further afield in France.

The shopkeepers and restaurateurs of old Avignon, the area within the Old City walls built by the popes when Avignon was a papal territory in the fourteenth century, are always very busy during the festival as a result of so many visitors descending on Avignon to participate. It is a busy, merry, scene. Street performers can be seen entertaining with agile displays of gymnastic dance, while other performers may undertake comedic interaction with passers-by, to the delight of the gathered crowds, and musicians of all genre can be seen performing, often with some notable pieces of musical novelty.

In July each year, Avignon's main town square, Place de l'Horloge, is largely taken over by the throngs of people visiting for the festival who eat and drink their way through each day in the many outdoor bars and restaurants set-up in the square for the festival. The shops, particularly those selling Avignon memorabilia, do a roaring trade with the out of town visitors. The local traders all do very well during the early weeks of every July. It is a popular event for artists, traders, and the public.

It was *Le Festival d'Avignon* al Khayr planned to attack. Aashiq was well advanced with necessary arrangements to enable the attack to be executed on the 2016 Festival's opening day, Wednesday 6 July.

Aashiq had told al Khayr very early on in the attack planning sequence about the small commercial drones he would arrange to be acquired to deliver the highly toxic ricin dust they would place in the drones. The drones would be used to fly down the length of Place de l'Horloge, forty or fifty feet above the partying crowds, releasing the poisonous ricin dust as they flew overhead.

The use of drones would make the attack special Aashiq had said, and that was the important feature of this attack. It was about the media coverage, the fear, and the respect it would generate for Daesh. Not just the deaths the attack would cause. A large bomb could just as easily do that. No, this was about causing fear.

Al Khayr had liked the plan to use drones. It would be a spectacular attack, but he had been unfamiliar with the use of drones and the poisonous dust, ricin. After initially questioning why easily obtained explosives could not just be attached to the drones instead of the more complex poison dust attack, or indeed, why not use static explosive devices hidden in a parked car or in rubbish bins, he had become enthusiastic about Aashiq's plan. He agreed its terror level would be higher than a normal form of attack once it became known, and for that reason supported it.

Aashiq had persuaded al Khayr to allow the use of drone delivered ricin dust not only because it would be seen as a horrific attack, but because he wanted Daesh to be seen as a participant in biological and chemical warfare. Ricin was relatively easy to obtain and delivery by drone was efficient, and, more importantly, virtually unstoppable once the drones were launched. All that was required was some castor oil cake and someone who knew how to extract the toxin, ricin, from that cake, then you have a deadly weapon to put into the drones for delivery he had said. He knew that would get the West's attention.

Electronic jamming of the drones by security services was not an issue. Aashiq's advice was they could by-pass that defence by using the GPS installed in each of the drones to ensure the drones flew the track intended. The self-contained nature of that guidance meant once programmed and launched each drone would fly its planned track and any attempted jamming would be ineffectual. There would be no ground-based drone operator transmitted signals which could be jammed.

Even the release of ricin dust was free of any requirement there be a ground-based signal to activate release. A small solenoid attached to the hoppers carrying the ricin dust on the drones would have a timer which would cause the hoppers to open after the elapse of a certain time. There were to be two holes in each of the small hoppers containing the ricin dust. The hoppers would be attached to the underside of each of the drones. One hole was at the top of the hopper, at the front, facing the direction of the drone's travel. The other, larger hole, would be opened on the bottom of the hopper. Gravity, assisted by air rushing into the hole at the front of the hopper creating a positive pressure, would help cause the dust to flow through the opening at the bottom.

Al Khayr had understood that while there would be some deaths, it was unlikely there would be a large number because the dust would principally affect the elderly and, he was told, children. More important to al Khayr was that it would be seen as the ultimate terror attack. Poison laid by drones flying over a crowd at a public event would be a new horror for the West to face. Only some would die, others would be ill and suffer, but everyone would once again understand persecuting Islam brought consequences.

Al Khayr had been happy to give Aashiq the go-ahead, and now all was nearly ready. The name al Khayr had given the operation was fitting he thought. "Haboob" is Arabic for "dust-storm".

Al Khayr left after thanking Aashiq for his hospitality. He would now report to the Governing Council on progress with his next attack plan. As his vehicle picked its way along roads long ago damaged in the conflict, but remaining largely unrepaired, al Khayr felt a surge of enthusiasm for the attack. He hated the West, and all it stood for. Al Khayr knew graphic scenes of destruction in Syria and its human cost were being broadcast by Western media night after night for viewers sitting safe and comfortable in their homes. The ratings driven broadcasters often began a so-called news item with a viewer discretion advisory that "some images may be distressing", but they kept showing it and made little effort to provide any considered analysis of what was happening, and why, in his opinion.

Al Khayr would give the Western media something to broadcast, and a lot closer to home for their viewers than Syria. His plan to attack the French infidels, *Haboob*, was coming together and would soon be executed. Drones sowing poisonous dust over crowds of people on the ground below. Yes, it would be a spectacular attack that would shake Western governments, and France in particular.

He smiled broadly. *Allahu Akbar.* God is Greatest.

Chapter Four

René Sharen, head of DCRI counter-terrorism, loved Paris. He was fifty, and had lived all his life in the City of Light.

Educated at the Sorbonne, on completion of his degree he had joined what is now France's Ministry of Foreign Affairs and International Development, as a trade analyst.

Unfortunately, his personality was not an easy fit in the relatively restrained atmosphere of the Ministry, where delicate conversations were the norm. René was a very direct person. He saw that as being pragmatic and effective. While working in the Ministry as a trade analyst he often felt frustrated he was unable to call things as he saw them, particularly when political sensitivities were involved, which was frequently.

René had soon left the Ministry and joined the French national police as an international trade investigator, responsible for ensuring trade legality and monitoring international funding flows. He spent a lot of his time looking for evidence of money laundering and tax avoidance on international transactions. Specialist financial intelligence gathering and analysis to help prevent serious crime and funding of terrorism also fell within René's purview in his role with the national police.

After some years he had moved from that role to an intelligence role at France's former Central Directorate for General Intelligence, and eventually to DCRI after the Central Directorate was merged with that organisation.

In his personal life René was similarly impatient with the niceties of life. He was socially competent when he chose to play the required game, but he did struggle with close personal relationships. In his intimate relationships a number of the women he had dated had felt uncomfortable, although if you asked any of them why none would be likely to be able to say exactly what caused them to feel that way, other than perhaps that he had tried too hard to please.

Something René was passionate about, and did truly enjoy in his spare time, was his skeet shooting. Maybe it was just the release of energy after a long day at the office dealing with some very difficult issues, but whatever it was, it helped René relax to go to the range and fire some shots at targets as they flew through the air.

René was lead on a team of skeet shooters which competed regularly, made up of members of police and security agencies. There was something René found very satisfying in shooting down a target hurled into the air by a special machine on his call of "*tirez*", that call of "pull" being the signal to the operator to launch the target. Tracking the target with his shotgun as it flew through the air and blasting it out of the sky was one of René's skills and pleasures. The team, their shooting competitions, and the camaraderie, were all important to René in his personal life.

In his professional role with DCRI René's operational judgment had been impeccable to date, but he knew in the current circumstances he would need all his professional experience and judgment to help protect France from the terrorist threats that were growing by the month. His commitment, pragmatic approach, and innate insight into how terrorists thought, demonstrated by some spectacular successes in the field, had eventually led to René being appointed head of counter-terrorism at DCRI, a position he had now held for some four years. But, in truth, René was feeling the burden of that responsibility, and he was not comfortable.

The issue for René with Charlie Hebdo had been that it was such a success for the bad guys, as he called them, because every newspaper, TV channel, and radio station had covered it in detail, and the internet had been full of it, including some graphic video. It was a propaganda victory for the terrorists, and that's what they want he had thought.

His main concern following Charlie Hebdo had been the risk that it might set off local extremists intent on doing something themselves. Lone shooters, taking on easy, soft targets, like a school or a supermarket, to avenge some perceived slight against the institutions of Islam. Or maybe something as simple as using a car as a weapon by driving into pedestrians.

But as it had turned out it wasn't just a lone shooter or driver acting randomly that had followed, but a co-ordinated attack by multiple terrorists at multiple sites. The attacks at the Bataclan and on surrounding streets, restaurants, and bars, had involved mass killings by a well organised group of attackers.

He knew the Bataclan attacks had to have been carefully planned to be carried out as they were. This was totally removed from the local lone wolf situation he had been worried Charlie Hebdo might trigger. This was something else.

The more people involved in the planning of an attack the more likely the plan will be uncovered before it occurs. People who have to communicate with one another to plan and coordinate their operations have a better chance of being noticed than a solo operator. But René knew there had been no indicators before the Bataclan. No intelligence, no chatter. The attacks had come as a complete surprise to French intelligence. '*Merde,*' he muttered to himself as he thought about what had happened.

DCRI had been advised just before Christmas, by the Minister responsible for security, that the French Government had formally accepted the United States' offer of intelligence assistance. The Director General of DCRI had since confirmed to René the "Americans" were seconding one Dr Anne Davis, a CIA counter-terrorism specialist, for six months, and she would be arriving in early January to take up her role.

Normally René would probably have described himself as somewhat pissed at the idea of taking a CIA officer on temporary secondment, but now he would take all the help he could get. The security issues facing France and its citizens were extremely serious and René knew attacks of the nature France had suffered in the last year were likely to be repeated. It would be his task to make the terrorist attacks much more difficult to achieve, by identifying and neutralising the planners and suppliers. Yes, he would take all the help he could get.

René didn't know much about Dr Anne Davis of the CIA. He understood she was in her late thirties, and competent in her specialist field. Hope I can work with her he thought. René understood he had to make a real effort to keep it on the rails with Dr Davis, the stakes were too high to do otherwise. He knew the attacks on the Bataclan and other targets had marked a turning point in terrorist capability and will.

At the beginning of the second week of January 2016, just over eight weeks since the terrible attacks on the Bataclan, René was preparing the briefing he would give his seconded agent, Anne Davis of the CIA. She was due to start her secondment at DCRI the next morning.

When Anne arrived and was greeted by René in the counter-terrorism annex, a discrete area of the grey stoned building in which DCRI was situated, she was struck by how drawn and tired he looked. His cheeks had a dull grey pallor, the skin under his eyes was shadowed dark and had formed into small swollen bags of flesh, and he had an unhealthy sweaty sheen on his forehead. Beginning with Charlie Hebdo in January last year, through to the attacks at the Bataclan a few months ago, it had been a tough time for René Sharen she thought, and it was showing.

'Welcome Anne, I trust you had a comfortable trip,' said René, as he ushered her into his office and introduced her to a junior official from the French Ministry of Defence who was in attendance at the request of the responsible Minister for the occasion of the arrival of this senior US intelligence asset on loan to the French Government.

Despite René's office being quite large, it could best be described as busy, with rows of filing cabinets against one wall, and a desk-top computer with an exceptionally large screen and telephone on a small desk. Spread over what looked like an oversize kitchen-table against another wall there were various files and loose papers. It was René's preferred working method to spread his materials out over a large work surface when he was busy on a major project. He was always more comfortable with the space that gave him to spread papers and associated materials. He would propel himself on a wheeled work chair along the side of the table to whatever section of the papers and materials he wanted to review, between sessions in front of his computer screen where his fingers would frantically work the keyboard, trying to keep pace with his usually rapidly unfolding thoughts.

At one end of the office under a large window overlooking a small courtyard, double-glazed for the Paris winter rather than for security but nevertheless effective as a measure against the risk of acoustic eavesdropping, there were three small leather tub chairs arranged around a coffee table, for the many meetings René would have with advisers and assistants when working on a particular matter. René was fond of running his case discussions over bottomless cups of coffee as he settled back in his favourite leather chair, which could be identified by the increased wear it had suffered as a result and the coffee cup ring marks on its arms.

'Yes, my trip was fine thanks,' Anne responded. Then more formally. 'The United States is pleased to be able to assist. We will do all we reasonably can to help. It's a global problem. France is the current target but it will be someone else next time, so we all need to work together.'

'Thank you Dr Davis,' smiled the junior official from the Ministry of Defence, 'my Minister has asked that I again convey to you the appreciation of France for the assistance your President has agreed to provide.' Anne nodded an acknowledgment.

René and Anne talked about the need for international co-operation in dealing with terrorism, the willingness of Western powers to work together and share intelligence, and again, how willing the United States was to assist and how appreciative the French were for that assistance. Both had been well-briefed, and were well-informed in any event, on the protocols of international intelligence co-operation. René and Anne were sufficiently senior and experienced to understand the things that should be said in front of the Minister's representative. After ten more minutes of talking in this way René signalled the discussion should turn to specifics by indicating he would give Anne an operational briefing. The junior official took his cue and scurried off to make notes of what had been said so he could faithfully report to his Minister next morning.

After the official had gone René and Anne smiled at each other. They knew the previous conversation had involved necessary protocol, and they had both independently and carefully couched their comments. When the French Minister was briefed by his junior official the next morning on US intelligence involvement and the attitude of the US government to this assistance, both René and Anne had wanted to ensure they had done all they could to foster the cooperative intelligence arrangements which had been put in place, so that those arrangements would be unlikely to be derailed, whether by French pride or political gamesmanship. The reality was there was never going to be such a problem on this occasion, given what France had experienced, but as Ministers always like to have a briefing that confirms their decision making was correct it had been appropriate for René and Anne to take some time to reinforce the value of the arrangements and their mutual support for them.

René began his briefing by bringing Anne up to where he had got to in his thinking and planning.

He spoke of the Charlie Hebdo attack, covering it in some detail, explaining why French intelligence knew early on the attack was undertaken by assailants with some professional training.

'The shooting was quite controlled. Victims were taken out using a single shot, or sometimes two. The shots were usually to the head, to ensure a kill. When confronted by an oncoming police car in the street as they were leaving the gunmen didn't panic. They shot carefully at the approaching police car, and nine of the rounds through the windscreen were closely grouped right in front of the driver's position. That's the mark of careful and competent shooters and it was effective. Those people were trained.'

'AQAP took credit for the attack at Charlie Hebdo,' René continued, 'and we have no reason to doubt they truly were the group that planned and arranged the execution of the attack by the Kouachi brothers whom they had recruited.'

Anne knew AQAP, the acronym for al-Qaeda in the Arabian Peninsula. It was an extremely militant Islamist group, principally based in Yemen. It prided itself in reaching beyond its geographical position to attack Western interests throughout the world. The attack on the USS *Cole* while in the port of Aden was an AQAP bombing. That attack killed seventeen United States Navy personnel. The infamous underwear bomber's attempt to bring down Northwest Airlines Flight 253, which failed when the explosive sewn into the bomber's underwear failed to properly detonate, and other attempts to place bombs on civilian aircraft, were also the work of AQAP.

René was confirming what she and her colleagues at Langley had themselves concluded within hours of the Charlie Hebdo attack, that AQAP was responsible.

René described his initial concerns about Charlie Hebdo triggering even more lone wolf attacks.

'Of course we had security issues before Charlie Hebdo. Over a horrendous three day period during the December preceding Charlie Hebdo the depth of this problem was clearly demonstrated. On the twentieth police in Tours were attacked by a knife wielding individual. The next day an attack in Dijon saw an individual deliberately ram his car into a group of pedestrians. Then on the twenty second another car ramming of pedestrians occurred, this time in Nantes. I was worried Charlie Hebdo would encourage more individual attacks of that nature.'

'Witness statements police gathered at the time had each one of those individual attackers shouting "*Allahu Akbar"* as they attacked, so motivation was clear. Calling out "*God is Greatest"* seems to be their bloody licence to do these things,' René continued, letting just a hint of anger show through his normally professional demeanour.

'Since Charlie Hebdo there have been other lone wolf incidents, including the beheading of a worker at Saint-Quentin-Fallaviar last June. These solo incidents are so easy for the attackers to carry out and so hard for us to prevent. But then we had the attacks last November. We were completely blind-sided by those attacks, centred on the Bataclan. We hadn't anticipated an organised group attack by trained gunmen against multiple targets. It was like a military operation.'

There had been no prior warning signals which could have alerted them to an imminent attack he said. The level of communication between persons of interest had not increased and there were no meetings observed, particularly with the normal giveaways of occurring at unusual times or places. The overall level of intercepted electronic chatter had not shown an increase.

'*Merde*, it was all below the radar,' René exclaimed, before calming and resuming his briefing, setting out his priorities.

'I want to ensure France is as safe as we can make it from another terror attack. That is a combination of raising awareness with a request to the public to be alert, and our own security services prioritising what they do. One risk I am very conscious of is the reaction of Daesh to any losses they may suffer on the various battle fronts in which they are engaged as a fighting force, Syria in particular. If they start to lose ground there I think there is a real risk we will see an escalation of attacks in western cities.'

Anne knew he was probably right about that. Daesh would be motivated to undertake "easy" attacks in an endeavour to preserve its standing as a force to be reckoned with by the West if Daesh began suffering losses on the battlefield.

René continued. 'A campaign has been launched as part of our initiatives to persuade people to call in anything they observe which is unusual, or just different. People are being encouraged not to be embarrassed about whether they are right or not. We just want them to call anything in, and if it turns out to be nothing, no problem.'

'This public reporting campaign has been called "*Signalons*", and it has been operating for the last few weeks. "*Signalons*" effectively means "*Report It*". We are ensuring the campaign is widely known and easily used. People can report electronically via smart phones, notebooks, computers et cetera, using a simple three question on-line submission covering what, when, and where. Of course they can also add more detail or call something in verbally if they wish.'

'In addition our intelligence services have reviewed watch lists and are implementing stepped-up surveillance where thought valuable. Increased electronic surveillance has been established, as well as more human intelligence where appropriate. There is an analysis and assessment being undertaken of the value and ability to insert more under-cover operatives into some of the known hot points in our minority communities.'

'We are paying particular attention to points of entry to France. Border authorities have the usual passport alerts, and that list has been expanded so person-of-interest alerts are now also raised by anyone with sufficient tell-tales. We have lowered the threshold at which someone may become a person-of-interest as a result of tell-tales. Tell-tales included are short duration multi-country travel particularly to flagged countries, historic travel patterns, lead-time to making travel booking and mode of travel payment, you understand Anne,' he said knowingly as he trailed off. Anne nodded acknowledgement, but said nothing. She recognised the French were clearly wanting to lift their intelligence game and she understood why.

'Spot-checks are to be increased regarding freight coming into the country. We can't check everything, the volumes are too great, but we are stepping up inspections where we identify factors that indicate increased risk, and the government is arranging for border control to have more staff and funding to do this as well as running some random checks from time to time. We are doing the electronic equivalent with funding flows and inter-bank transfers, to try to intercept financial arrangements which may indicate some terrorism activity.'

'We have put in place a central data system to ensure comprehensive reporting and matching of all matters of interest. I particularly want to avoid a situation where something occurs which we find later might have been investigated had some information buried somewhere in another area been linked. So we have a very large centralised data cache that receives and holds all information collated from across our various data capture points.'

'Importantly, with regard to all the information we collect, we have developed a special algorithm to help us identify and match seemingly random pieces of information. Much more than standard information matching.'

Anne looked closely at René. She saw the fierce determination in his eyes and the jut of his jaw. She could see he was ready to join battle with the terrorists who had so damaged his country. He was clearly totally committed to doing everything within his power to prevent another terrorist attack in France.

'René that all looks fine to me,' said Anne, 'the one additional thing I would note is the sharing and use of intelligence information ex third party agencies. I can help there because I am authorised to share with French intelligence all relevant information the United States has, either itself or via its allies. This is more than the usual intelligence sharing we both undertake at present. This is the sharing of our special information, usually held tightly.'

René was pleased. He knew it would mean access to additional intelligence which could be very valuable given its sensitivity.

Anne continued, 'Other European services which share intelligence with us have confirmed we may share their intelligence with you. I realise you may already have some of it direct from them, but, if we share it all nothing should get missed. Our friends at British security have also approved sharing of their intelligence, which is a plus. They can be a bit private sometimes. I suggest I assess and analyse all intelligence received from these external sources by the United States, and also all relevant material developed by the United States itself from its own resources, and report it to you so we can decide how best to use it.'

'Thank you Anne,' René responded, sounding slightly short, 'that would be good. When I referred to material available in the central data cache I was assuming it would also hold data logged as a result of intelligence provided by our counterparts in allied countries.'

61

Oops, thought Anne, taking on the mode of René's response and tone, he didn't like me suggesting there may be a gap in the detail he gave me.

'Great,' said Anne smiling at René, 'tell me some more about the algorithm.'

'The algorithm we have developed will enable us to better process and analyse data received,' René answered. 'It's a step up from standard computer matching, where one of our government departments compares its data with another department's data to identify persons or activity of interest.'

'The enhanced security protocols we have now will ensure any information received is logged to our surveillance system's central data cache. If an algorithm identifies special characteristics in the material held in that cache it will be raised for attention. It is a capable programme, undertaking the usual self-contained sequence of actions, but it has the ability to produce outcomes similar to the results achieved with well-developed artificial intelligence applications. The results to date in various test situations appear to offer intuitive notion capability. That's a huge step forward and gives us the potential to recognise information which may have sat unnoticed amongst mass data. It doesn't replace intelligence analysis, but it will provide many more indicators than at present. We expect it will enable initiation of enquiry and support analysis.'

Anne was impressed. This was a step-up from algorithm functionality as she knew it.

René went on to say there had been a lot of discussion, and occasionally argument, when the *Signalons* system was set up by the French authorities. In the end those advocating for three simple questions, what, when and where, which could be answered quickly and anonymously by on-line submission won the day as that was considered more likely to be successful in engaging public response.

If a reporting system was simple, quick, and anonymous, it was thought people may be more prepared to report something they thought unusual or suspicious. Relatively quick, and no embarrassment if it turned out to be nothing of any consequence it was said.

Anne recognised there was value in people reporting anything unusual by being able to log the matter relatively quickly and in a simple format. Easy access to an on-line form facilitated that. Three basic questions: what are you reporting; when did it occur; and where did it occur, would make the system workable. She also knew the value of capable algorithms. The United States had spent considerable money and time in enhancing its capability in this area, but the French algorithm René was referring to represented a marked advance in the data processing and autonomous reasoning she was familiar with at home.

Given the French government's desire for the public to report anything unusual or suspicious it had been expected the volume of information would be high, and would probably include a lot of valueless information. That had proven correct René said, and it confirmed again it had been the correct approach to avoid providing a lot of human resource dedicated to receiving information. Public acceptance and government efficiency dictated the preference of direct public input into the system electronically without the need for human intervention, at least until the algorithm had done its work and signalled matters of interest which should be reviewed.

As it had turned out, the public had been responsive. The *Signalons* campaign had produced mega-loads of data every day, with most of the data input directly by the simple on-line submission process.

'Everyone has a mobile phone these days,' René observed, 'which is great, because it enables instant reporting of something seen or suspected. Eighty per cent of submissions are coming in from a mobile device, so people are reporting it as it happens. If it had to wait until that night when home in front of a computer I suspect we would lose some information as the immediacy factor contributes to reporting propensity, well, that's what our experts tell me,' he laughed, as he realised he was sounding a little formal.

Anne knew processing the consolidated data reported from multiple sources around France could well facilitate some meaningful intelligence insight. She knew also that computing power gave intelligence services significantly enhanced capability, but only if the data was properly manipulated by the relevant computer programme and linked to events that could be connected. Too often she had seen in the past one federal organisation with some pieces of data which, if they had been put together with another agency's data, could have provided a picture that would have avoided something remaining undiscovered until too late.

A capable algorithm of the type René was telling her France had developed could turn a huge mass of data into something useful. As Anne knew, every tool was welcome in dealing with terrorist threat, and the French algorithm was a tool well worth having in the fight against terrorism.

Chapter Five

The container on the wharf at Marseille-Fos, the main commercial port in the south of France, was one of thousands owned by the Mediterranean Shipping Company, one of the world's largest container shippers. The container was coloured in the company's rather drab corporate colour, a dull yellow, and carried its well-known stylised "MSC" logo. The container had been on a ship which had arrived at France's main southern port in the early hours of that morning, after a voyage from Chennai, India.

In the Port Inspector's Office at Marseille-Fos, Delmar Dubois opened the screen on his computer which showed containers arriving at the port during the previous twenty four hours.

Delmar Dubois was an ardent participant at the largest mosque in Marseille, not because of any deeply held religious belief, but because of the support he felt he received when at the mosque. A single, prematurely bald portly little man of forty years of age, he had been, at least in his opinion, unfairly treated by life. He knew he could have been one of Marseille's business success stories if only his luck had been better and if only people had been fair to him. But instead, and through no fault of his own, he had found himself unsuccessful in business and alone most of the time outside work, with few friends. Until he had discovered the mosque and how kind and welcoming members of the Muslim faith were.

Delmar was quietly spoken and was not used to being the initiator of conversations. He was more a conversation participant, when he could. He considered himself a good Muslim, but that self-assessment was simply based on the fact he regularly attended the local mosque. Frequency of attendance trumped depth of belief for Delmar. One had to be seen to be a believer, and he made sure he was regularly seen participating at the mosque.

He had found people at the mosque who would be his friend. Always keen to seek out approval from others, when Delmar was at the mosque he found it relatively easy to join in discussions and strongly voice opinions to receptive ears about the many matters he disliked in the West. The sordid lives led by infidels and how coming Islamic rule would curtail such behaviour was one of his favourite topics. He knew that was what his new friends wanted to hear, and he revelled in the agreement and acceptance by others for what he said. It gave him a huge sense of belonging. Something that had been largely absent from his life until he had found the mosque and its members.

Because of that sense of belonging Delmar was always keen to make friends with anyone who offered him acceptance. One morning he had been introduced to a man whom he had not previously seen at the mosque, who told him he was a committed Muslim who had heard about the good things Delmar had to say. Delmar immediately saw another person who was going to be a good friend to him. The man said he was an importer and understood Delmar worked at Marseille-Fos. Delmar confirmed that, and for some days after the initial meeting Delmar and his new importer friend met daily and became close.

When Delmar's new friend asked if Delmar would be able and willing to assist him with a special importation, as a good friend and also for a small sum of money to recognise his time and trouble, Delmar agreed without hesitation. Not only was Delmar happy to take a bribe, he had done it before on a number of occasions, this man was his friend and a fellow Muslim. To Delmar, the cash incentive offered was a sign his new friend was not just taking him for granted in asking him for help.

It turned out that what Delmar was going to facilitate was the importation of a container carrying a load of cigarettes. The importer who had asked him to help by facilitating release of the container without any inspection of its contents, while a friend, was a bit stupid Delmar had thought. He had been unable to prevent Delmar discovering the container carried contraband cigarettes. Delmar was intelligent enough to pick what was going on. The cigarettes would not be declared to Customs and would be imported without payment of any duty. Delmar didn't mind if the French authorities missed out on receiving some cigarette tax, for the benefit of his latest friend, but he was slightly put out that he had to use his clever detective-like skills to find out what he was dealing with, rather than being taken into his new friend's confidence.

On his computer screen, Delmar Dubois of the Marseille-Fos Port Inspector's Office entered some item identifiers into the freight information system, looking for the particular container he had been asked to watch for.

Every container carries a unique number code to confirm its ownership and use when shipped. That code contains a check digit, and no freight information system will accept a container number with a check digit which does not match the outcome of a system checking process when all the container's data is input. After a moment's delay while the system searched in response to Delmar's query, there it was, the container he wanted. The container's codes and registration number matched the information he had been given, and the container's provenance had been confirmed by the check digit. So far so good.

Next, Delmar accessed the border inspection schedule for last night's inbound containers. He needed to see if this container was to be physically inspected as part of the process of its entry to France. He thought it unlikely, as the shipper, point of origin, and declared contents of agricultural machinery parts would probably not indicate any risk requiring the container to be physically inspected. But he was also aware that screening had been stepped up, and additional border control staff were being hired and trained to allow extension of inspection processes, so you never knew when an additional, random, inspection was to occur.

He entered the container's identification number and waited. In just three seconds, although it seemed longer than that to Delmar as he sat and waited in front of the screen hoping no one would come into his office, the Marseille-Fos freight control system told him no container of that number was scheduled for inspection. It was available for release from the port. *Dieu merci* he thought, an easy one thousand euros, just for ensuring a container load of cigarettes entered France without the risk of his new friend having to pay the substantial duty due. He reached for his mobile phone and called the number he had been given.

'Your container has been released and may be picked-up,' he said quickly when his call was answered. Then he disconnected the call and went back to his normal office routine, trying not to think what he might do with the money he had just so easily earned.

Despite considering himself a good Muslim, Delmar Dubois spent some of his time frequenting the seedy clubs near the Marseille waterfront. He knew what he would do with the thousand euros he had received, but he didn't want to admit it to himself, nor could he afford for anyone at the mosque to ever know. In his favourite local brothel they had some young girls, recently "imported" from Morocco. They were expensive because of their age, and he normally wouldn't pay the going rate for that, but he planned to use the money he had just so easily earned to buy a session with one of the girls. He had been told he could do anything he liked with those girls, if he paid, and Delmar Dubois had some strange likes. He felt a growing anticipation, and shut his eyes thinking about the girls and what he would do. He started to breathe a little more heavily than he would normally.

By the end of that day the container Delmar Dubois had been checking as part of his special arrangement had been uplifted from the wharf, and was on a truck parked in a secure transport compound on the outskirts of the City of Marseille. The container, with its forty tea chests filled with the cake left from processing castor oil beans at a plantation in India was ready for delivery, first thing next morning.

When Aashiq entered France at Paris Charles de Gaulle Airport in late April, on his way to Montfavet to oversee preparations for the attack, his passport caused a flag on the border control system. Aashiq knew something was wrong immediately he saw the manner of the young woman in the booth at passport control suddenly change from polite but bored to an alert approach. And that had occurred just as she had run his passport through her scanner and then taken a second look at the screen's response to the passport scan. She had tried not to show anything different in her demeanour, but her second glance at the screen to read something unexpected and her change in composure told Aashiq he had been flagged.

As the border control agent somewhat clumsily thumbed through his new and for that reason largely empty passport, Aashiq realised she was time-filling. Sure enough, within a minute of the agent discreetly pressing her "alert" button after seeing the flag on her screen two plain-clothes policemen approached Aashiq and after identifying themselves politely but firmly invited him to accompany them to a small interview room to answer some questions. As he accompanied the police officers Aashiq wondered what could have gone wrong for him to have been intercepted at the French border.

Unknown to Aashiq, he was experiencing first-hand the implementation of additional vigilance by the French. Border authorities in France were now required to interview anyone raising an alert on presentation of their passport. Matters for which previously no alert would have been set on a passport, or certainly would not have resulted in an interview, now formed part of the wider circumstances to which French border authorities would respond.

Aashiq Ahad's passport had been issued only weeks prior in place of an older passport due to expire. It was a Syrian passport, and showed his recent exit from Syria. Under the new border regime these matters alone would have resulted in some standard questions being asked of this traveller by the young woman in the booth, but what had caused the special flag on Aashiq's passport was his possible support of Islamic fundamentalism. Early in 2015 he had written an article for his mosque's monthly broadsheet where he had, rather carelessly in hindsight, expressed some anti-authority sentiment as part of a piece on Charlie Hebdo. Someone who had seen it was clearly not part of the intended readership and he had been recorded as a person of interest, deserving a flag on his passport.

'Have you previously held a passport?' questioned one of the policemen, looking at the newly issued passport Aashiq had presented on arrival at Charles de Gaulle, as soon as they had sat down in the small harshly lit interview room.

'Yes,' replied Aashiq, looking him directly in the eye. He knew he must give his answers with conviction if they were to be accepted more readily. No downward glances, or shifty sideways looks. Look at him directly, and smile. 'But it was due to expire, and I always like to have at least nine months before expiry when I travel, so I got a new one.'

'Where have you travelled recently before getting your new passport?' A necessary question as the travel history shown on the notation pages of a passport is lost in the case of a newly issued passport, unless an electronic search is made on the old passport, and that couldn't be done to assist this interview as the trace would be too time-consuming.

'I live in Syria. I went to India in early January, Chennai in particular. Nowhere else,' Aashiq said, knowing that if they wanted to check they would eventually discover that trip, so no point in not saying he had been in India, although as he mentioned Chennai he immediately regretted it. His internal movements in India would probably have remained unknown, so he need not have added that extra detail.

'Why did you go to India?'

'A business trip,' he replied.

'What do you do in Syria?' Another question, this from the second policeman. A sudden change, to unsettle.

'I live there most of the year,' Aashiq responded, 'and I am involved in the export of cotton.' He wasn't part of the family business anymore, but he knew enough about the industry if asked specific questions.

'Address of your business please? ' the first policeman followed up. Aashiq gave him the address, knowing that checking his participation was almost impossible given the state of most of Syria. Anyway, even if a check was possible it would take a while to confirm he was no longer involved in the business. Appear confident and deliver answers in a positive way. That was the way to deal with these people.

'Where are you going in France and what for?' he was asked.

'Touring around, on holiday.'

I'm getting a little annoyed with this thought Aashiq, but he knew better than to show it. Co-operate, appear calm and polite. Keep smiling. Any other approach to airport border personnel would be counter-productive at the best of times, and certainly not now when he could not afford to be detained for further enquiry. He was in the course of finalising a major operation.

After some more questions, probing his views about "ISIS", the policemen seemed satisfied that despite his mosque article he was not a public risk, and they let him go, warning him they would be checking the detail he had given them. Aashiq knew they probably wouldn't. Too difficult to confirm and there was insufficient reason to make any enquiry from what they had heard. As well, the confusion in Syria would help discourage them from pursuing any enquiry.

The policemen went off to complete their report which would be logged to the new centralised security data cache established since the Bataclan attacks, together with a series of images of Aashiq Ahad's face, captured as he had answered questions in the interview room. Facial recognition was now an important feature of security, as many members of the public were becoming increasingly aware. It had become relatively common for passport applications to be rejected, for a range of what appeared to be random reasons. Where the accompanying photograph of an applicant had "insufficient face to background space ratios," or simply showed the "applicant smiling" a rejection usually followed. Facial recognition software struggles with a smile.

Aashiq headed downstairs to the Paris Charles de Gaulle Airport rail station to catch the high speed train, the *Train á Grande Vitesse,* commonly referred to by its initials "TGV", to Avignon. He felt somewhat relieved now his brush with authority was behind him. But at the same time he was dismissive of the efforts of the French border control agencies. The policemen would never know they had had in their hands an important Daesh operative who was currently organising a fresh terror attack on France. Their questioning had been inadequate. Aashiq felt superior.

As he moved through the airport he noticed the increased security presence at the airport, understandable and expected following the events of a few months ago he thought.

Three young soldiers, probably not much older than twenty, all hefting grey sub-machine guns, rode down on an escalator towards Aashiq as he sat having a coffee adjacent to the train platforms, at the bottom of the escalator. Thirty minutes until his train departed from the TGV platform.

As the soldiers were borne down towards him by the escalator he found himself thinking about the security now operating in places such as Paris Charles de Gaulle Airport. The increased security presence was largely a political response. Let the public see armed military personnel in public places and they would feel something was being done. But how good would the security be if there was an event? Probably better than nothing he accepted, but it wasn't optimum.

He could see the young soldiers were inexperienced and not well briefed. If that was not the case, Aashiq thought, why would they stand clustered together, travelling down on an escalator from which they could not get off until reaching the bottom? A gunman waiting near the bottom of the escalator, probably using one of a number of the columns in the area as cover, could easily pick them off as they slowly came towards him on the escalator. They would have no-where to hide because the escalator confined them and they would just be carried inexorably down as any shooting started, delivered mercilessly towards the gunman.

One at a time on the escalator to ensure cover from the others, surely boys, he thought. He definitely felt superior.

Hussein Nasser was an angry man, and his anger was directed at the West, the United States of America in particular.

Some years earlier, when he was a busy and engaged high school science teacher at a secondary school in northern Iraq, he had considered himself happy. He had enjoyed his teaching, and in his spare time he had participated fully in the activities of his local mosque. At that time in his life he had felt quite satisfied.

Hussein was a member of Iraq's Sunni Islamic denomination and while Sunnis were the minority they had held all the power in Iraq. Their strong-man Sunni leader, Saddam Hussein, had ensured Shiites were excluded from any government function, and he had encouraged his Sunni followers to attack Shiite citizens and their holy sites.

Then the United States of America had led a coalition force in the invasion of Iraq and displaced Saddam Hussein. In the aftermath of that war there had been confusion, as is so often the case following major conflict, and a power vacuum. Sectarian violence had erupted between Shiite and Sunni groups. It had got so bad that in 2007 the United States had felt obliged to try to bring the violence under some sort of control and increased its military presence in Iraq, the so-called "surge" of troops described by western media.

That increase had some success, with the violence reducing, but many in Iraq were still subjected to isolated and unprovoked sectarian attacks.

So far as Hussein Nasser was concerned the increased sectarian violence, which he considered began after Saddam Hussein was toppled and the Shiites decided they could assert themselves within Iraq, was entirely the fault of the United States of America. He had had a good position and life as a Sunni before the Americans came, but now as a result of physical damage caused by the war and through what he considered the Americans' negligence in failing to establish adequate governance for Iraq after the fighting, he had found himself on the receiving end of some very unpleasant activities by Shiites enjoying their new-found freedom.

While he had had no conscience about repressing Shiites when part of the Sunni power bloc, and had happily played his part in Shiite oppression, he felt utterly betrayed by events driven by the United States and its coalition partners which had left him suffering. Now he was angry, and he wanted to hit back at those he blamed for the position in which he found himself.

There was also a practical reason for his position. He became unemployed as a consequence of his school having been destroyed in military action during the war. That too was the fault of the Americans in his mind.

Hussein now had a role which would again give him not only a sense of purpose but the opportunity to strike back at the West. Hussein's Imam had approached him one evening some months ago after sunset prayers, and requested Hussein join him in his private room for a conversation. Mystified by the request, and slightly apprehensive, he had followed the Imam into a small windowless room lined with shelves of Islamic texts and had sat down on some large cushions where indicated by the Imam.

The Imam had then brought in to the room a tall young Syrian man, who began talking to Hussein about the continuing conflict in Iraq which had originally started in 2003 when foreign forces had invaded the country. The man told him it had been unjust for the foreigners encouraged and led by the United States of America to invade Iraq under the guise of wanting to ensure Saddam Hussein did not use the weapons of mass destruction they claimed he possessed. There were of course no such weapons and it was just an excuse for the Americans to secure petroleum supply he had said.

The Syrian had worked himself up into a real anger as he continued to speak in his marked English accent. Hussein had heard similar rhetoric before when the Imam preached in the mosque in front of the faithful. But he had never seen the Imam deliver with the rage this man was showing. Same message as he had heard many times from the Imam, but this was being delivered by the Syrian with much more vehemence. The Imam recognised this too, and knew it was because this was the main chance they had to persuade Hussein to do something special for Islam. The final push after months of grooming of Hussein, the angry man who had lost his career and way of life in the United States led conflicts, so the Syrian was giving it his best.

'First they made up lies about weapons, then they attacked and destroyed much of our country, and once they had succeeded in destroying great parts of our cities and towns they destroyed our society. We thought the worst was over when many of these foreign devils left after doing that damage to us, but then they came again, saying they must fight more.'

'It is the US Satan who caused you loss and pain and I can help you fight back for the wrongs you have suffered and our country has suffered,' the Syrian had said more quietly, through thin lips as he fixed his eyes on Hussein's. Hussein had felt uncomfortable under the man's gaze, but even before he was asked, and he had guessed what was coming, Hussein knew he would cooperate and do whatever he could to hurt the West for their attacks on Iraq and its people, and for what it had done to him and his family.

Now, some months after that approach, Hussein was in France living in a small apartment, a *pension,* in Avignon ready to do his part for Islam.

Hussein Nasser was enjoying the south of France immensely. The pace of life in Avignon was relaxed and measured, at the other end of the scale from what he had known in Iraq. The climate was pleasant with day-time temperatures of around twenty five degrees centigrade most days, although when the *Mistral*, a strong cold north-westerly wind blew, it could be a lot less. Every day he would catch the local bus to the nearby town of Montfavet where he was working on a project for the Syrian, a man he now knew was called Aashiq Ahad.

Montfavet was a particularly quiet place, especially near the Caumont Airport where he was working in a warehouse, but Hussein enjoyed the atmosphere of the place. The airport did not appear to be very busy. It was small and seemed to be served in the main by a range of turbo-prop regional airliners. A sleepy little town, Montfavet was just a short ride on a bus from old Avignon, with its historic walled part of the city and the magnificent Popes' Palace.

Hussein was enjoying exploring Avignon when not at work in the warehouse at Montfavet. As well as the many fascinating and grand historic buildings in Avignon, Hussein had discovered the perennial tourist favourite, the special bridge on the Rhone the subject of the well-known nursery rhyme "*Sur le Pont d'Avignon*". The rhyme misnamed the bridge Hussein now knew. The bridge is actually *Pont St. Bénézet,* but long ago it had become known as *Pont d'Avignon,* and that's the name children all over the world continued to use when they sang about the famous bridge.

The project Hussein was working on took all his science skills, and he was enjoying the challenge immensely. Because he was very busy in the warehouse, he would often take a break to refresh, and walk around the local area, relaxing in the quietness of the small town of Montfavet. Then revitalised by his walk and the fresh air he would return to the warehouse and continue his work with renewed enthusiasm and vigour.

While Hussein thought of his work as just another scientific task to be undertaken, he was well aware it was a key part of an attack planned on France, one of the guilty western countries supporting the United States in a war with Islam. He did not dwell on the specifics of what his work would result in, and the effects people would suffer because of his work. He didn't like thinking about things at that level. Better to take a broad view, without specifics.

So far as he was concerned he was simply helping punish the West for their attacks on him and his country. Not for him that innocent people caught in the attack would become sick with fever, a cough, and then breathing difficulties and, after days of intense suffering, succumb to an uncomfortable death

Hussein had been preparing three small aluminium hoppers to be attached to the four-rotor commercial drones acquired from a dealer in Marseille. He had also been busy readying some equipment that would enable him to process and extract a toxin from the castor bean oil cake received at the warehouse some time ago, and stored since then, packed in a series of tea chests.

The extraction of the toxin, ricin, from the oil cake would be difficult he knew, but he had researched it, understood what was necessary, and had ensured the tools and equipment needed were available to him at the warehouse. Very soon he would have ricin available in the form of a light dust which would be put into the aluminium hoppers attached to the drones.

Chapter 6

Aashiq had been in Avignon for nearly six weeks since his brush with authority at Paris Charles de Gaulle. He was undertaking final preparations for the attack and knew he must test both the operation of the GPS navigation and the ricin dust delivery system to be used by the drones. Of course, he would not rehearse the dust delivery using ricin. Unnecessarily risky. Aashiq planned to use some talcum powder which had a similar consistency and weight to ricin dust according to his scientist Hussein.

Aashiq and Hussein, the former high school science teacher who would contribute to anything causing the West to suffer as some sort of payback because his homeland had been invaded and his life disrupted, drove into the countryside from the village of Montfavet. They had been busy finalising all that was necessary to ensure the drones could operate as planned and today was test day.

They drove west along highway D900, past the interchange serving the road connecting the towns of Cavaillon to the south with Carpentras to the north, until they reached an open area of pastures and small trees in a wide valley below the village of Gordes. Leaving D900 at the small village of Coustellét, with its narrow streets and stone cottages, they continued until they encountered a farm track leading off the road. Turning on to the track, they then followed it for at least a kilometre to ensure they were some way away from the public road they had just left, which carried a lot of tourist traffic, mostly on its way to see the so-called perched village that sat high above. They did not want to be able to be easily seen from the road.

When they stopped Aashiq removed the drone from the back of the van they were using and gave it a quick pre-flight check. Not too much to it really. Just check the rotor blades are secure and each of the four rotor heads turn freely, and ensure everything else on the drone is adequately attached and secure. Aashiq poured the talcum powder into the hopper and securely attached the hopper to the drone's underside using the specially designed clips Hussein had developed and fixed to the drone's body for just that purpose.

Programming the on-board GPS unit took only a short time. The GPS was set to have the drone fly a race-track like pattern, fifty feet above ground level, at thirty kilometres an hour. The drone would fly one minute legs along each side of the race-track pattern, and would make a left turn of one hundred and eighty degrees at the end of each of those one minute legs.

Those turns at the end of each leg were programmed to be completed at the rate of three degrees per second. At that rate the drone would take one minute to reverse its direction after beginning a turn.

The timer controlling the solenoid which would open the apertures in the hopper when signalled was set for two minutes. That meant the hopper would be opened when the drone had completed its first one hundred and eighty degree turn and was beginning the return leg of the pattern.

Power off time was set at four minutes after launch. That would ensure the drone landed in close proximity to the position from which it was launched, after completing a full circuit of the programmed race-track pattern.

Reviewing his settings on the GPS, Aashiq confirmed he had set up the drone to fly away from him in a straight line for one minute, which would be sufficient time for it to travel some five hundred metres at its thirty kilometres per hour speed setting. Then, following the completion of its one hundred and eighty degree left turn at the end of that first one minute leg, it would have reversed its direction and be about to fly back towards him.

As the drone commenced the return leg of the programmed pattern two minutes would have passed, so the hopper would be opened by the solenoid. Then gravity, assisted by the flow of air into the hopper, would take the talcum powder out of the drone and the area being overflown should receive a dusting of powder. At the end of that leg another one hundred and eighty degree turn would bring the drone back close to where it had been launched from some four minutes prior, and at that time it would land automatically.

With the drone properly set-up for its circuit, Aashiq quickly visually assessed the route he had programmed it to follow, checking there were no trees or obstructions within its flight path. A collision with a tree at this stage of his preparations would not be good. Satisfied all was well he launched the drone.

As the electric motors spun up the quadruple rotors the drone lifted off the ground and climbed vertically, as programmed, to fifty feet above ground level. Its on-board GPS guidance then steered it down the first side of the pattern. After a minute Aashiq saw the drone enter a gentle turn to the left. After a further minute it had effectively reversed its direction. It straightened and flew a track parallel to its outbound track, back towards the area from which its flight had begun. At the same time a stream of white came from the bottom of the hopper as the solenoid did its work, opening the hopper apertures and allowing the talcum powder to escape. The powder hung in the air and then drifted down in great sheets before settling on the ground.

As the drone reached the end of its return leg it again entered a gentle left hand turn. The talcum powder was now exhausted so the white dust trail in the air had ceased. At the conclusion of this next turn the drone's power was automatically reduced by another command programmed into the on board computer and the drone descended and landed safely, about fifty metres from where Aashiq had launched it.

Aashiq was delighted. The drone had worked as it should with the payload it carried, its internal control programme had steered it as required, and the solenoids had opened the hopper apertures to release the powder at the correct position based on the time calculations he had made.

'Perfect,' he said to Hussein, who was very happy the hopper and its timer he had installed on the drone had worked as required. Hussein had expected the steering of the drone around the pattern by the GPS programme would be fine, but the solenoid and effectiveness of the system of apertures had been less assured and he had been concerned whether or not the dispersal system would allow the dust to be spread as required. It was essential the dust should be subjected to positive pressure to ensure it left the hopper in a reasonable flow. The hole he had made in the front of the hopper facing the relative airflow as the drone flew along had ensured that result. Hussein was happy his positive pressure theory had worked.

On the way back to Montfavet, Aashiq said little. He was deep in thought about what was necessary to get the three drones ready to deliver the ricin to the main town square in Avignon. Hussein had to complete the preparation of the concentrated ricin powder. Aashiq had to programme each drone's on board computer control with a route to and over the town square, and calculate solenoid control times to ensure the hoppers opened as the drones entered the square and were above the crowds.

What neither Aashiq nor Hussein knew was their drone's practice flight had been seen. A local farmer's twelve year old son had been working on a tree-house he was building on the family farm. He had heard the sound of the drone's rotors, and looking down into the valley he had seen two men flying their drone. He had also seen what he thought was white smoke coming from the drone through part of its flight. Fascinated, he had been about to run down to the men to see what was wrong with their drone, but they had landed the drone, picked it up, and driven away before he reached them.

Disappointed he had not been able to see the drone close up, he realised it was time he headed home. Papa wanted some firewood brought in before dinner, so he needed to move, otherwise Papa would be angry. But, he knew he had something to tell Papa. Papa would be very interested in hearing about the drone he had seen being flown by two men who had come on to their farm.

When a long established castor oil bean processor based in Delhi submitted its required oil cake disposal returns, the volumes were substantially down on prior year, notwithstanding general harvest levels were known to have been similar year on year. That caused an enquiry by the Indian governmental authority charged with monitoring such disposal. Why were the volumes of oil produced and cake disposed of by the Delhi processor so much less than the previous year the bureaucrats wanted to know?

The reason the amounts were well down on previous years, it turned out, was that much of the castor oil bean crop from the Chennai region the Delhi processor would have normally crushed had not been received this year. Apparently a new processor had offered crushing capacity in that region and had taken some business away from the Delhi processor. That was the reason there was a marked drop in the amount of oil produced and cake disposed of this season.

Still smarting from losing business to the new facility established at the Prasad family plantation, the established processor in Delhi had been quick to suggest a check of the new operator's disposal records may be warranted. The Indian bureaucracy swung into action, always keen and virtually unstoppable whenever it identified an issue involving official records. Inconsistencies must be reconciled, changes must be understood, and questions will always be asked to ensure bureaucracy is properly satisfied. The returns filed for the Prasad family plantation would be checked to ensure its processing volumes reflected amounts lost from the Dehli processor's returns this season.

Now, Inspector Kan Rajeed, a senior investigator for India's Directorate for Agricultural Trade and Practices, was puzzled. He had retrieved and examined the castor oil bean cake disposal records filed for the processing undertaken at the Prasad family plantation. The reason for his puzzlement was that the amount of castor oil cake said to have been disposed of by this new crushing operation did not match the amount of oil cake expected, given the castor oil volumes shown to have been produced by the new processor. Neither could he reconcile Prasad's oil cake disposal volumes with the amount by which the oil cake disposal volumes of the Delhi processor had reduced. There would be a simple explanation he was sure.

To resolve the apparent discrepancies Inspector Rajeed decided to follow up with more enquiries, this time of the new processor operating near Vandavasi. It was a long way from Delhi, where Inspector Rajeed was based, to Vandavasi, which was south west of Chennai. Probably just a clerical error he thought. I will settle it by telephoning the manager of the Prasad operation. It wasn't worth a special trip, but he did want to be satisfied about the accuracy of records.

As he talked to Akash Prasad on the telephone, Inspector Rajeed became more concerned. He thought Prasad was being deliberately vague and evasive, and Prasad certainly could not explain why his expected volume of oil cake disposed of was less than anticipated given the amount of processing taken by Prasad from the Delhi processors. Neither could he explain why the volume of oil produced by his crushing operation did not match the expected cake volume left after processing was complete. Inspector Rajeed accepted different processing techniques and equipment could account for some of the discrepancy, but this was a significant shortfall.

For his part, Akash was rattled. He thought no-one really cared about exact detail of oil cake disposal. And what really worried him was the payment he had received for the cake. Not declared for tax purposes and certainly not to be shared with the wider family of investors in the plantation. It had to stay his secret if that was to continue, to say nothing of a prosecution by the tax authorities for failing to declare some income. Now the Inspector was telling Akash he may have to come to Delhi to be interviewed if the discrepancy could not be resolved. No, no, no, this is getting out of control. Akash's mind raced.

'I donated some cake to a pharmaceutical company for medical research,' he blurted out in an attempt to bring Inspector Rajeed's enquiry to a close, with a simple explanation as to the reason the amount of oil cake disposed of to an official site appeared incorrect against processing and oil volumes.

Why on earth was such a fuss being made Akash worried, these returns have always been treated with relative informality, with no close scrutiny previously, at least so far as he was aware. But whatever happened, he wasn't admitting he received payment for the oil cake. A prosecution for false tax returns was what concerned Akash most. In a get-tough campaign there had been talk by the authorities of imprisonment in appropriate cases. He didn't think fifteen thousand US dollars would get him into that league, but he wasn't even going to risk it. Thus, come clean about "giving" it to a Swiss company, and don't even mention a payment he had decided. That explained the shortfall and avoided a tax prosecution. At worst a small fine for incorrect cake disposal returns. No-one would care about some of the cake going to a pharmaceutical company instead of to a dump he thought.

Inspector Kan Rajeed was silent for a moment as he considered what Akash Prasad had just told him. Should he just leave it at that, and perhaps prosecute Akash for filing a false return or for not using an official disposal site. The fines were small, was there any real point? Then, as he thought about it some more, he realised he had to make further enquiry. The reason disposal was controlled, or at least had to be reported, was that castor bean oil cake contained a nasty toxin and the government needed to know there had been safe disposal.

'OK, thank you for that. I will need to know how much oil cake you gave to the pharmaceutical company and which company it was.'

'I don't know the name of the company, only that it was Swiss,' gulped Akash, 'and I gave them one tonne.'

'Well, if you didn't know the name where did you send it?' asked the Inspector.

'I just emailed to an address I had been given saying the cake was ready and a container was sent to the plantation for loading. Later the same trucking contractor who had delivered the container picked it up, and that is all I know really. Oh, the contractor was from Chennai, I know that. I didn't know where the oil cake was going, but I remember the contractor's truck had a name on the cab door, *"Chennai Road Transporters"*. I can look up the email address I used, but my recollection is that it was associated with the trucking contractor anyway.'

'Thank you Mr Prasad, send me that email address please. I will make further enquiries and you can expect to hear from my department in due course. Good-day,' and Inspector Rajeed was gone, leaving Akash Prasad to worry about what may occur when he heard from the Indian Directorate of Agricultural Trade and Practices again.

Within a week, Chennai police, acting on Inspector Rajeed's request to investigate the transfer of a certain container, had interviewed the driver who had delivered the container and then later collected it from the Prasad family plantation. They had also spoken with executives at Chennai Road Transporters. The police enquiry had ascertained the container had been shipped to Marseille, France, on behalf of a French agricultural machinery importer bringing in some harvesting equipment parts. That was all anyone knew about the container and its shipping.

When Chennai police reported this to Inspector Rajeed he decided the fact the contents had been misrepresented, as had the importer, required more investigation and a report to French security. They should know someone had gone to some trouble to obtain and ship castor oil bean cake, a regulated material, at least so far as its disposal was concerned, to France. As for Mr Prasad himself, a further interview was clearly required. Inspector Rajeed wanted to know more about this matter, given that what had been described as agricultural machinery being imported by a well-known industry participant in France in official shipping arrangements had in fact been castor oil cake given to a Swiss company.

Since her arrival at DCRI some months previously, Anne had been becoming accustomed to the way the French service dealt with intelligence reports. She had also been busy preparing analyses of the intelligence she regularly received from Langley, some of it generated by the United States and some of it simply raw undeveloped reports the product of intelligence sharing by allies of the United States.

As well as regularly discussing and liaising with each other, every Monday morning Anne and René would have a formal meeting to review any matters that might have some importance. To date nothing they had received or analysed indicated any matter they could connect to any terror network or activity.

Anne was enjoying Paris when not busy in her office at DCRI. She thought Paris a beautiful city, and she would spend hours wandering around through some of its narrow streets, with their small shops, cafes, and *pensions*, or alongside the Seine, or past Notre Dame on the Ile de la

Cité. She had been also to the Louvre, and gazed on the famous smile.

Not usually a great shopper, although her credit card had been known to take a beating on occasions, particularly when she got into some of the fashionable establishments of downtown New York City, Anne was very taken with Galeries Lafayette, and could spend hours exploring its various levels. She also had her favourite cafes and bars and would often join others from DCRI at those places, as officers of the DCRI she had come to know at work began to accept and include her in their social activities.

Anne had also spent some time exploring outside of Paris. She had been to the marvellous palace and grounds at Versailles, and she had made a sobering trip to Normandy, on a day outing arranged for her by René. She had been to the actual beaches the Allies had used for their landings during World War II, including the beaches code-named Utah and Omaha used by US forces for the D-Day invasion. It was a surreal feeling looking at the sandy beaches and the blue Atlantic surf on a warm afternoon in June 2016, and reflecting on how it would have been on those beaches at dawn on a June day in 1944, as the boys had come ashore. When she walked into the beautifully manicured Allied war cemetery near where the landings had taken place tears pricked her eyes as she looked at row after row of small white crosses, so many of them, set out with great symmetry. Seeing the level of sacrifice made some seventy two years previously to ensure freedom from the Nazis made her present role defending western freedoms against terrorism even more compelling.

Anne had been with René and his fellow skeet shooters to the local range on a number of occasions when they were practising shooting targets hurled into the air by some launching mechanism. She had tried a shot herself, but failing to bind the butt of the shotgun firmly into her shoulder had seen her suffer a painful bruising as the shotgun recoiled on discharge. René had just laughed at her.

When assessing various possible scenarios arising from matters noted in intelligence reports received, she and René would sometimes continue working on into the night, eating a quick dinner together at a local café before heading to their respective homes for the night. Anne was in a small apartment not far from DCRI offices.

Anne recognised she and René were spending a lot of time together, both in and out of the office, and she had noted René had become quick to flirt when he saw what he considered an appropriate opportunity. As a consequence Anne had become mindful of the possibility the flirting could develop into something more, and she was alert for any sign René might want to move their relationship beyond a professional level. It was the last thing she wanted, not that she found René an unattractive personality. She just knew any intimate personal relationship with René would unnecessarily complicate things during an important time.

So one evening, after sharing a pleasant Coq-au-Vin, with its rich sauces suitably infused by the café's chef with copious amounts of *vin rouge*, when René had said he would walk with her to her apartment, her antennae were up. She spent a good part of the short walk to her apartment thinking how she would handle any suggestion from René he come in with her for a night cap, coffee, or some similar code men sometimes used when they had greater aspirations than a drink of some sort. Then, as they had reached her apartment, René had simply leant towards her, kissed each of her cheeks as Frenchmen are want to do, muttered *bonne nuit*, and turned and walked away. I'm being paranoid Anne scolded herself, resolving not to be so suspicious in future, but she did continue to wonder how she might have reacted to a different approach from René.

Anne was in René's office at one of their regular Monday morning conferences, reviewing and discussing various analyses of intelligence reports received over preceding days. At each of the formal Monday meetings Anne and René would discuss what information had been received during the previous week and what analysis had been, or should be, undertaken.

This morning René was having his habitual black coffee, which he liked strong. The smell of coffee in the air was pleasant Anne thought, but nevertheless she had preferred a cup of tea today. She declined the offer of a biscuit. René always had a biscuit, or two, with his coffee and Anne, more than once, had wondered about his sugar intake. Still, there are more pressing issues than René's sugar intake levels she thought, at the same time questioning somewhere in the back of her mind why she was even noting it. A sign of how much time they were spending together she decided.

In accordance with normal intelligence protocols, when meeting to review intelligence received Anne and René would endeavour to construct a hypothesis from the matters of fact identified by the various reports they were reviewing. It was an established process to group together facts based on some commonality, so-called "clusters". Then those clusters were assessed to gauge whether they offered any indicators of possible terrorist activity.

Anne and René would also apply assumptions in an attempt to help them understand what the clusters may be indicating. When any assumption was being applied it had itself to be tested in an endeavour to ensure, so far as possible, the known factual information was being sensibly interpreted. In intelligence work an assumption is never applied unless it has first been tested for reasonableness.

Sometimes multiple assumptions are necessary, applied to known facts in sequence. Steadfastly working through all assumptions, considering every one of them in turn notwithstanding some may look better than others at the outset, ensures thinking is not limited when seeking to interpret what the facts may be indicating.

Anne and René would always carry out a full exercise by applying every assumption considered reasonable, and prioritising each resulting scenario. This approach meant there was a lesser risk of a possible scenario being completely missed because an assumption that may have helped explain some known fact had been dismissed at an early point.

The overall objective of this intelligence methodology is to test whether there is any scenario indicated by facts known and assumptions made.

Sometimes the hypothesis built up in this way by Anne and René was found to be tenuous, sometimes more possible, but in every case when they tested the hypothesis critically there was always something which showed the theory developed was unlikely to be correct. They judged that on the balance of probabilities.

This is how intelligence agencies have operated for years, using pieces of information, factual and reasonably assumed, to see if they can be developed to identify a possible threat scenario.

Anne's experience and knowledge in these processes were invaluable. Often she was able to identify gaps in the logic in the hypotheses formed. Quality intelligence analysis requires quality thinking, and Dr Anne Davis, PhD, senior analyst from the CIA, always delivered on that score.

This particular Monday morning René had some intelligence which immediately got Anne's attention.

'This report from Indian intelligence regarding some castor bean oil cake shipped to France from Chennai in March. Apparently what started off as a simple administrative enquiry into oil cake disposal records has turned into something more, with the discovery the cake was shipped covertly to France,' René said. 'A trucking operator has confirmed he transported a container from a castor oil bean plantation to the port at Chennai for loading in early March. The Indian shipping agent concerned has confirmed the container was recorded as carrying agricultural equipment and was bound for Marseille. The container looks to have actually been carrying oil cake according to our Indian sources.'

René continued. 'So, because we have indicators of covert activity with a dangerous substance we need to have the authorities at Marseille-Fos check what containers they received from Chennai during the relevant period, late March. If the container came to Marseille-Fos, as appears to be the case, they will be able to identify the container in question. I will get some checks made.'

Within forty eight hours the port authorities at Marseille-Fos, in association with local police, had some answers. They reported the arrival of a container ship from India at the end of March which had carried forty nine containers originating in Chennai. The container thought to be carrying the oil cake was one of the forty nine. The container had been released the day after it arrived. Further enquiry had found the agricultural equipment contractor shown on the shipping documents as the end recipient knew nothing about it, and had confirmed they had not received any shipment from India at the end of March.

'There must be a trail René?' Anne said after René outlined these developments to her. 'A container can't just arrive, be uplifted, and disappear, surely?'

'Well, yes and no,' René said, not very helpfully thought Anne. 'Whoever was waiting for the container, they had to know when it had arrived and when it would be available for collection. They needed to get hold of it before any contact was made with the company shown as the recipient, otherwise questions would have been asked. So that means active enquiry for one container in thousands arriving every week, and that can only be done by checking the computerised records of containers arriving. Such an enquiry would leave a trail. Marseille-Fos ran an audit of its inbound freight control systems to see if there had been any enquiries about the container.'

'That audit turned up an unexpected log-in and enquiry as to whether a particular container had arrived and whether it was on an inspection schedule. It was the container in question. The enquirer, an employee called Dubois, has been interviewed and has admitted to making the enquiry on behalf of some person he had met, but who now seems to have disappeared according to local police. We got the mobile phone number Dubois called to advise the container was ready for collection, but as you would expect it was a pre-pay and it hasn't been shown to have had any ongoing use. It's probably in a river somewhere. I have asked about CCTV at the port and that is being reviewed now to see if the vehicle collecting the container can be identified.'

Anne thought about what she had just been told by René. 'Okay,' she said, 'we have these facts. Castor bean cake has been shipped covertly from Chennai to France. It was shipped to Marseille-Fos with a false recipient and content disclosure. Someone, not required as part of their usual role at the port, undertook a computer search to ascertain arrival. That same individual also checked the freight system to see whether there was to be a border inspection of the container, and reported to some unknown third party on the end of an untraceable mobile the container was released and could be picked up.'

'Now,' she continued, 'I take from those facts someone has gone to a lot of trouble to acquire and import castor bean oil cake without anyone in authority in France being aware of it, and to hide where it was going once it left port of entry. Procured in India, Chennai really, false story about end receiver and contents, cut-outs to try to prevent tracing.'

René and Anne looked at each other in silence. They both knew what the clandestine importation of castor bean oil cake meant. Someone in the south of France now had the raw material to produce ricin, a highly toxic poison, and probably intended to use it illegally given the circumstances of its shipping.

The hypothesis that followed, as two highly skilled intelligence officers analysed what they knew and developed some assumptions to assist analysis of the facts, led to a conclusion about the possible use of ricin in a terror attack. The issue now for René and Anne, if their hypothesis was correct, was how would that ricin be used, and where?

Chapter 7

René was looking happy as he told Anne CCTV footage of the Marseille-Fos freight collection zone covering the day in question had been obtained and reviewed.

'Luckily the good people at Marseille-Fos keep their CCTV images from security areas for three months so coverage for the date of the container's arrival at the port was available. A review has found the container was picked up by an operator identified as a small one truck business in Marseille. The name of his business was clear on the side of his truck. You and I are flying to Marseille today Anne. The local police have the operator concerned coming in for an interview with us at one thirty this afternoon,' René grinned, clearly pleased with progress.

Anne nodded. This was good progress. They should know by the end of the day where the container had been delivered. Then they would be able to plan an operation to locate the container and the oil cake it carried, and, if their terror attack hypothesis was correct, secure the oil cake, or the ricin if the terrorists were at that stage in their preparations.

Their ricin-based terror attack probability stood, despite a number of reviews and testing Anne and René had undertaken. Unfortunately nothing had unravelled the terror attack scenario developed from the facts known and the assumptions made relating to the oil cake, particularly the circumstances of its arrival in France. They had not been able to identify another more innocent scenario relating to the discovery of the covert importation of the oil cake, the raw material from which ricin could be taken.

Just after midday the Air France flight from Paris carrying René Sharen, head of counter-terrorism in France, and Dr Anne Davis, specialist CIA analyst on secondment, touched down at Marseille Provence Airport. Met by local police they were driven directly to Marseille's principal police station, the Commissariat de Police, an unattractive building situated on La Canebière, one of the principal thoroughfares in Marseille.

The driver who had picked up the container from Marseille-Fos was waiting nervously in an interview room, desperate to get outside and smoke a cigarette, something not allowed in the building itself. He was a small time owner-operator in the trucking business. He was very conscious of the fact that this interview was costing him important time on the road. He was anxious about getting back behind his wheel and completing that afternoon's deliveries as soon as possible, without too much delay here at the police station.

René introduced himself to the truck-driver as a security official, but with no other detail, and Anne was simply described as a person assisting him. No need for the driver to have any more information than necessary. After some preliminary questions confirming who the driver was, where he lived, and how long he had operated his trucking company, René told the driver the cargo in the container he had picked up had important security connotations and it was imperative it was located as soon as possible. The driver knew the container pick-up René was referring to as he had already spent some time with local police identifying that pick-up and all the circumstances he could recall about the order and payment for the job. He had been able to recall all that quite easily, even though it was some time since it had occurred. The reason for his ease of recall was because he had been approached by someone who had come into his yard and paid him the necessary fees in cash at the time of order. The driver had not thought that to be suspicious, but it was different from normal course of business so he had remembered it when asked initially by police about picking up the container. And no, the driver had told police, he didn't have a contact address for his client, just a mobile number. It turned out to be the same number Delmar Dubois of the Marseille-Fos

Port Inspector's Office had been given. It was not traceable.

Yes, the driver said to René in response to René's query, he did understand the importance of the issue and yes he would do his best to answer all the questions. His instruction had simply been to collect the container from Marseille-Fos, hold it overnight, and then deliver it to a truck-stop near the town of Arles, about an hour and fifteen minutes from Marseille early in the morning. There the driver had met another truck as arranged by his client, and the container was transferred to that truck using the on-truck crane. And no, he did not know where the container had gone from there.

René was stunned. He had thought the driver would have been able to give him the container's ultimate destination or at least a trail, but clearly that was not going to happen. René probed some more.

Was there CCTV at the truck-stop? No. Could the driver remember the name of the trucking company taking the transfer of the container? No. Could he remember the name of the other driver? No. Was anyone else there? It was very early, so not at that time of the morning.

Negative answers to all. The consignment note signed by the driver of the other truck acknowledging receipt of the container had nothing useful and a largely illegible signature. Fuck it, thought René as he terminated the interview after trying various other lines of questioning in an endeavour to elicit some useful information about the container's likely whereabouts, but to no avail.

'Sorry Anne,' he said after the driver had left, 'that was a lot less useful than I had expected. 'There is nothing more here for us. Let's fly back to Paris and review all we know in the morning.'

'Sure,' said Anne, feeling fairly deflated herself, 'let's do that.'

Next morning, back in Paris at René's office at DCRI, and acutely conscious of the fact a promising lead had turned out to be nothing, Anne and René began reviewing all the information they had, including the latest intelligence reports. They were keen to see if there was another avenue they could pursue.

They were both becoming increasingly anxious about their inability to pin down any useful information which might enable them to identify the whereabouts of the container. Locating the container and its destination were key. They had nothing more than their basic hypothesis which assumed the possibility of an attack in France involving ricin, a view developed as a consequence of the discovery of the covert shipment of castor oil bean cake. Nothing else. There were no other indicators to help them with how an attack may occur, where, or when.

The data Anne and René continually received for review from the central security data cache now maintained by France comprised raw intelligence, in that there had not been any analysis of the data prior to them receiving it. But it was data that had been processed by the special algorithm looking for linkages, or threads as they were known. As part of the French security initiatives implemented following the Bataclan attacks, the algorithm was continually busy as it worked through all of the data now being accumulated and added to the data cache daily.

A border control report from Paris, logged to the central data cache at the end of April as a matter of course, had now been noted by the algorithm and it had been raised for review. The algorithm had identified the report as worthy of some additional analysis as it had crawled through the data, seeking threads in the vast mass of information in the cache. It would have taken human analysts weeks to review, and even then they may not have identified any data linkages in what was there. This was big data personified.

The border control report related to one Aashiq Ahad, and contained information adduced from his responses to questions during an entry interview at Paris Charles de Gaulle Airport.

The report had not been flagged in its current state when first logged to the data cache as there was nothing remarkable about it requiring it be raised for review. The report had just resided in the cache as part of the overall information held. What had made the difference, and which had now resulted in the Aashiq Ahad border control report being raised by the algorithm for review, was the recent report logged to the central data cache by DCRI regarding the discovery of the covert shipment of castor oil cake from Chennai to Marseille. That had been logged by DCRI when the shipment had been reported to French security by Indian authorities. DCRI had also logged as part of that report the circumstances surrounding the container's release from Marseille-Fos discovered on further investigation at the French end.

The DCRI report regarding the covert shipment of castor oil cake, including information about the involvement of a corrupt border official and an inability to trace the container's movement or persons associated with its uplift, had now been identified by the algorithm as having a common thread with items in the report relating to Aashiq Ahad's interview at Paris Charles de Gaulle.

The border control report on Ahad noted he had been interviewed on entry because he had demonstrated some anti-western sentiment in the recent past. The report also included his mention of a recent visit to India, where he had noted he had visited the city of Chennai.

Initially the algorithm had linked the reports because of the geographic commonality of Chennai, mentioned in both the border interview report and in the report regarding the covert shipment of castor bean oil cake. But geographic commonality by itself was not sufficient to trigger a review flag. The algorithm continued manipulating the data and eventually raised it for review because it recognised additional factors beyond the common reference to Chennai.

The coincidence of the date period Ahad was in Chennai with the date period during which someone had arranged the acquisition and shipping of the castor oil bean cake, the fact that someone with anti-Western sentiments was involved, the reference to the shipment being covert and involving a dangerous substance, and the operation of cut-outs preventing the tracing of the container or of those involved in France with the container's importation, were additional factors the algorithm had the intelligence to recognise. There were matters in each data set which caused the algorithm to report, so that someone might look at the detail to see whether further enquiry was warranted. The algorithm couldn't decide this last issue, but it could certainly act with some intelligence and link and identify matters which should result in questions being asked.

In completing this work, the algorithm was clearly demonstrating how its capability had moved beyond simple mechanical linkage and data matching to notional intuition, providing outcomes similar to those found in the autonomous reasoning of advanced artificial intelligence applications. It had the capability to recognise suspicious circumstances attaching to factual situations, and that is what it had done to link and raise these two reports for review.

'Ah ha,' exclaimed René as he looked at the analysis, 'a thread development.' Anne looked at him expectantly.

René continued, 'We have a suspected Islamic activist entering France at Paris Charles de Gaulle, who in the course of a border entry interview said he had recently been in Chennai. The oil cake was covertly shipped to France from Chennai. The algorithm has connected these sets and raised them for review because of the circumstances of each report, with suspicious elements present.'

'We should follow this up. The person concerned is Aashiq Ahad. I will put an alert out on him to see if we can pick up where he is now. He told border control he was on holiday, touring France.'

Anne agreed. What were the odds that Chennai should come up in two different data sets in the particular circumstances applying? Yes, definitely worth a follow-up, and of course locating and interviewing Aashiq Ahad could answer some questions currently unanswered. He may not be involved in anything, but interviewing him would clarify that fact, and it was the only lead they currently had.

A week had passed since the algorithms had raised the name Aashiq Ahad as part of its linkage involving the oil cake shipment, and Ahad had not been located. Then his Euro-currency card was used at a bank in Avignon. When the bank computers recorded the withdrawal of seven thousand euros in cash from a currency account in the name of Aashiq Ahad the system recognised the name as a result of alerts from French security. Now they knew where to look. Ahad was in Avignon.

Then the algorithm provided some more linkages. In mid-June a farmer near Gordes, in the south of France not far from Avignon, had logged into *Signalons* that his son had seen two men flying a drone in a valley which formed part of his farm. Logging a matter to *Signalons* meant it automatically became part of the centralised data cache. The drone was said to have flown one large circle. It was trailing smoke just before it ended its flight so the farmer thought it may have malfunctioned and crashed, but he was unsure because the men flying it had picked it up when it landed and quickly left.

Flying a drone is not that unusual, but the farmer noted the men had travelled well off the public road to access his valley. The farmer had reported the incident fully, principally because he was angry strangers had entered his property. He hoped that in some way his report might result in police activity which would deter future trespassers. That's why he went to the trouble of outlining what had been seen in a bit more detail than merely what, when and where, filling out the comments box with a sentence about the "smoke", and the rapid departure of the two men when the brief flight of the drone had ended, as though they were well aware they were trespassing on his farm.

Initially that report had sat un-reported by the algorithm amongst all the data in the central data cache because there was nothing noteworthy about the detail it recorded. That would change within days, when another report logged to the central data cache triggered a linkage report by the algorithm.

A shopkeeper in Marseille had mentioned to a policeman friend some details about an unusual sale of three small commercial drones he had made recently. The drones were advanced four-rotor models, fully equipped with in-built GPS guidance and capable of carrying up to five kilogrammes each. The shopkeeper had told his friend about the sale because the purchase of three relatively expensive drones, they cost four thousand five hundred euros each, was completed in cash, and the buyer seemed uncertain as to drone capabilities. At the time the shopkeeper had thought it all very unusual.

Thirteen thousand five hundred euros was a lot of cash to carry, and the buyer, despite being prepared to spend that amount, seemed to know little about drones and was cagey about proposed use during the shopkeeper's friendly conversation with him as the sale was completed. The shopkeeper had felt suspicious about the buyer and remembered the transaction, telling his policeman friend about it some weeks later over a glass of old Cognac following the monthly Chamber of Commerce dinner for small businesses in his area. The policeman had been guest speaker that evening on the subject of "Prevention of Fraud in Business". The policeman asked the shopkeeper if he had logged it under *Signalons*. He hadn't, so the next day the policeman had himself logged the information to the central data cache, following the general instruction now in force to ensure anything different or unusual was logged.

The algorithm, continually working its way through the mega loads of data in the centralised cache linked these two reports and raised them for review. The report from the farmer about the drone flight on his property and the report from the policeman about the purchase of drones had resulted in the algorithm noting a thread. Initiating factors were drone commonality, the localised geographic area involved, and the narrow occurrence period. But then the algorithm had gone on, with its artificial intelligence reasoning capability noting circumstances justifying a review when it also recognised an outside norms purchase, a suspicious buyer, and the observation of a drone flight in unexpected circumstances. The drone commonality, occurrence period, and localised geographic area involved, were the precursors to making a linkage, but insufficient on their own. It was the particular associated circumstances that had led to the thread being raised for review by the algorithm.

'So, what do you think we have René?' asked Anne after seeing this latest information thread, one of a number raised that day for review. Anne thought she knew the answer to her question but had decided to let René lead on this. No sense in risking having him think she was taking over analysis. She would be confirmatory. She knew him well enough now to recognise he wanted to lead and announce what the algorithm may have identified.

This thread was getting their special attention because they had actively been thinking about how their assumed ricin attack might be carried out. Anything that could facilitate delivery of ricin in any attack was of special interest.

'Well Anne, the algorithm has reported a number of separate sets of data linkages for review, so let's go back. The first data set linked the discovery of a shipment of castor oil bean cake, originating in Chennai and arriving in Marseille, with our person of interest, Aashiq Ahad, who acknowledged a recent visit to Chennai. Those threads were raised for review because of the special circumstances surrounding those basic positions. Covert activity, dangerous substance, traceability blocks, and involvement of a suspected fundamentalist.'

'We concluded there were sufficient indicators from those data to raise the possibility of terrorist activity in France involving a ricin attack. We wondered about options for the delivery of ricin should there be an attack. Nothing in any of the reports raised has assisted us to date with regard to mode of delivery, but now I think we have some data which raises an option we should consider.'

'In the second set of data raised for review we have a high-capability drone acquisition in Marseille, which looks unusual because of the number purchased, in cash, and by someone who didn't seem to know much about drones and who didn't want to talk about the role in which the drones were going to be used. Then what appears to be drone testing is observed, also in unusual circumstances. Two strangers entered private property near Gordes, not a great distance from Marseille, flew the drone briefly, and then left in what was reported as "in a hurry". The drone was reported to be emitting smoke just before landing. Separately these two incidents, drone flying on the farm and purchase of drones, mean little, but together and taking into account the surrounding detail of each matter reported, they have been raised as one of a number of matters we should review. I think this data set relating to the drones needs more analysis.'

'So René, what are we to think?' Anne repeated, encouraging René.

'I have a view,' René responded, 'but before I give it I would be interested in what you make of it.'

Polite of you thought Anne, somewhat surprised. Maybe he doesn't want to commit to a theory until he has heard my take she thought, somewhat cynically, which was out of character for Anne. She immediately recognised that herself. Damn, what is it about this guy, but she dismissed her thoughts and moved on.

'Okay, here's my view. We have a series of reports which individually signal nothing of real concern. But when the algorithm identifies threads which are suspicious, using its near AI capabilities, it looks different. We have a possible suspect entering France and turning up in Avignon. He is known to have demonstrated some anti-western sentiments in the past and he has recently been in Chennai. That's where the oil cake came from. That cake is now likely somewhere in the south of France, but we are not sure where, as it has not been traceable because of the deliberate actions of some.'

'Then we have an unusual drone purchase not far away, in Marseille. A non-commercial drone buyer seeking three advanced drones, paying a large amount in cash, and reported as being cagey about his planned use of the drones. I say non-commercial because he didn't seem to know much about drones and wouldn't engage on drone operation in conversation with the shopkeeper. Could be nothing, just a socially inept would-be drone operator, but that doesn't sit easily with his acquisition of three expensive drones. Then, separately, we have a drone flight observed, conducted by two strangers trespassing on private property. It was suggested the drone was trailing smoke, but it wouldn't be smoke. Drones are battery operated. So that raises a concern for me. What was going on?'

Anne continued, 'We hypothesised a ricin-based terror attack as a possibility when we found out about the covert shipment of castor oil bean cake. We could move forward on that and make a preliminary assumption Aashiq Ahad may be involved, because of the Chennai commonality and his suspected sympathies. If ricin is to be used in an attack it has to have a delivery mechanism. So we have to think about any ways the ricin could be delivered.'

'I think it reasonable, for the purpose of constructing a hypothesis as to how ricin might be used in any attack, to say the algorithm has reported matters that allow us to develop a possible scenario involving a drone delivering ricin. We have a suspicious drone purchase, and I am going to make the assumption that what was seen by the farmer's son may have been a test flight.'

'Given we have drone testing activity near Gordes and a party we think may have a possible connection, Aashiq Ahad, in Avignon, I think we can also assume, for the purposes of our hypothesis, any attack will be in the vicinity of Avignon.'

'René I accept there is no direct evidence, but when we use the linkages the algorithm has given us to develop our hypothesis it does point to the possibility of a drone-based ricin attack.'

'If that attack hypothesis is valid, and I think it reasonable on the balance of probabilities given the work of the algorithm in identifying the threads and our analysis, then for the purpose of our exercise we need to consider possible targets in the area. Is there a major public event to occur, let's say somewhere in Provence, in the next month or so which could be the target if we are correct about such an attack?'

René looked thoughtful. And then he knew. There was only one major public event scheduled in Provence in coming months.

'The Arts Festival. The Avignon Arts Festival. If our scenario is accurate they might be going to attack the festival with drones dispersing ricin. It's the only major public event planned for the area in the near term,' René answered.

Anne agreed, but she knew also how easy it was to make a false assumption and associate it with known data to come up with something unjustified, so she insisted she and René spend more time testing the hypothesis there was to be a drone based ricin attack, probably on the Avignon Arts Festival. Her role in this was to develop alternative explanations for facts as known and to again test all associated assumptions to ensure they were reasonable. This would enable them to see whether some other scenario could be supported. In turn, it was René's task to counter Anne's alternative propositions and argue for acceptance of the possible attack scenario they had developed from information known and assumptions made.

By mid-afternoon Anne and René were satisfied, on the balance of probabilities, the test intelligence agencies in the United States normally applied in their scenario assessments, and which Anne had persuaded René to accept, their hypothesis of a ricin attack using drones had been confirmed. Balance of probabilities meant that after considering all known facts and assumptions used, the scenario established was more likely than not to be correct. Anne had tried all types of alternative explanations, but when tested neither she nor René had been able to safely displace the drone terror attack risk identified.

The facts of the matter supported the scenario developed by Anne and René. Oil cake which has no use at all, other than to produce ricin, had been covertly shipped to Marseille-Fos and had then promptly disappeared. There had been significant organisation behind the arrangements for the importation of the oil cake. Specific procurement in India, false shipping documentation, bribed employees at the port of receipt to ensure facilitation of the passage of the relevant container, and cut-out arrangements so the container's delivery route could not be followed nor its recipients located. That had led Anne and René to the view a ricin based terror attack was a possibility to be considered.

Then some further facts reported had to be considered when offered by the algorithm as linkages justifying a review. Somebody had made an unusual purchase in Marseille of high-capability commercial drones, in unusual circumstances. A lot of cash had been involved and there had been a refusal to enter any discussion about proposed use. Different, but not facts which on their own were compelling. But then another report had been linked. A drone flight had been witnessed in circumstances which were not entirely normal. When these two drone reports were linked by a very capable algorithm, the circumstances resulted in a flag being raised for two senior intelligence officers to review matters further.

Anne and René had already identified the possibility of a ricin based terror attack on receiving information about the covert ricin shipment. They had been mulling the form in which such an attack could occur, and where. Then the algorithm had located indicators in the mass of data held and raised them for review, allowing Anne and René to identify a probable attack scenario.

While the target itself was open to more question, a suspected Islamic activist who had been associated with Chennai was now known to be in the vicinity of Avignon. The festival was the only major public event coming up in the area within a reasonable time window.

Both Anne and René knew they could be wrong about the form of the attack and the target, but they agreed there was sufficient to focus on the festival in Avignon given the known facts and the scenario they had developed. This was standard intelligence work, but it had been initiated by clever technology.

Confidential alerts were sent out to police, military, and security services around France, warning of the possibility of drones being used to mount a terror attack, so at least there was some awareness of the particular risk of such a mode of attack. No mention was made of the likely target at this time.

Two clear strands of work had come out of the analysis of intelligence data to date. It was imperative to locate and question Aashiq Ahad as soon as possible. And, planning how to defend against a possible attack on the festival. Cancellation of the festival was another option, but it would not be popular.

'Cancel the Festival,' the Minister queried, 'on what basis?' René was in the office of the Minister in charge of the French security services. He had just briefed the Minister on all data, assumptions made from analysis of that data, and the attack scenario developed and tested.

'As I have said Minister,' René answered, 'it is our considered view that a drone-based poison attack may be planned for the Avignon Festival. We can't be sure of course, but that is the likely scenario that stands on the facts as we know them and the analysis we have undertaken. One sure way of avoiding any risk of an attack on the festival is to cancel.'

After a short pause, the Minister gave his response. 'No,' he said, 'we are not going to have terrorists dictate how we live our lives. That in itself is a victory for them. If you think an attack is a distinct possibility then commit whatever resources you need to identifying those involved and foiling their plans. We have a drone defence system that interferes with control signals to drones developed for just this situation. Put it in place at Avignon. I am not approving cancellation because I have confidence that you and your department have the skills and resources to prevent such an attack, or at least to ensure it does not succeed if attempted.'

René understood the not so carefully concealed political messaging. He would go down if there was a successful attack. Responsibility would attach to failure to locate those involved and to prevent a successful attack. It wouldn't be the Minister's fault, by not supporting cancellation.

René walked slowly back to his office, deep in thought. If he and Anne were correct in their scenario assessment then once again his country was facing a terror attack that would shake France. It made him angry to think there were people somewhere in France who were at this moment devising an attack that would kill innocent members of the public. All in the name of Islam, which he knew was unfair to the majority of Muslims who were as shocked and angered by terror attacks as were most other right-minded people. These crazy terrorists, doing what they do, still believe they are avenging Islam. What crap he thought, angrily.

In René's view, Daesh, which he suspected was once again involved in planning attacks on France, comprised psychotic idiots who enjoyed some perverse excitement in waging war against innocents in an attempt to make some point only they thought justified what they did. René was determined he would locate the terrorist cell he and Anne believed was in France and planning an attack in Avignon. He would destroy that cell and prevent an attack occurring. He had to.

Chapter 8

Square Agricol Perdiguier is an area of immaculately prepared gardens situated just inside the southern walls of the Old City in Avignon. It is easily accessed through Porte de la République, one of the many gates in those walls, and then via Cours Jean Jaurès, which is the avenue immediately beyond that gate.

Just past Square Agricol Perdiguier the avenue becomes Rue de la République, which then runs right up to the main town square of Avignon, Place de l'Horloge. The name of the town square is a reference to a well-known clock situated there. Ironically the clock has become largely obscured by building development over the years, and is now difficult to see from the square.

Avignon's City Hall, like all such places in towns and cities throughout France, is known as *Hôtel de Ville.* It dominates Place de l'Horloge, taking up a good part of the town square's western side. Many of the city officials who work in *Hôtel de Ville* have offices with a pleasant outlook over the usually busy square. Offices with such prime views are keenly sought after by those working in the building, but even at this level generational influences are at play. Offices are allocated on the basis of length of service, so younger staff members, even though they might hold more senior positions with more responsibility, have to accept the ensconced position of older employees. Many of those older employees are basically time-filling, awaiting their retirement day and pension. France is a lovely country, but its work ethos could best be described as relaxed.

Square Agricol Perdiguier was originally the area in which Benedictine monks who lived there in the Middle Ages had established gardens next to their abbey. It was developed to its present form in the early 1990's and is known for its extensive colourful flowerbeds containing a wide range of bright and attractive Mediterranean plants.

Square Agricol Perdiguier is often referred to by locals as "*Le Petit Jardin*", "the small garden".

Large trees planted randomly around the square at some time in the past now provide pockets of shade from the intense summer sun. There are also many large tall clay pots positioned through the Square. The oversize pots mostly contain flowers with vibrant colours, but some hold only simple waxy green succulents, many of which spill over the edge of their pots and hang precariously, swaying gently when the wind blows along the avenue and into *Le Petit Jardin*.

The gardens provide a sense of peace and tranquillity, in marked contrast to the nearby avenues bustling with traffic and people. It is an area that has long been a haven for busy workers and shoppers taking some time out to enjoy the calming atmosphere of the trees, plants, and gardens.

No one knew that this place, a pleasant oasis for locals and visitors alike, was to be used as the area from which a cruel and deadly terrorist attack would be launched.

As he walked around Square Agricol Perdiguier, Aashiq Ahad was pleased with what he saw. He had been looking for an open space from which he could launch the drones for his attack. This place, and its proximity to Place de l'Horloge, where many would gather to eat, drink, and enjoy their day during the Festival d'Avignon was ideal. It was a mere 600 metres from Place de l'Horloge.

Aashiq looked around trying to determine where best to park the van he would be travelling in on the day of the attack. He wanted to park the van, which would be carrying the three drones to be used, in a position where the drones could be taken out of the van and launched relatively quickly, before someone saw the activity and caused a problem. Mind you, thought Aashiq, why should anyone automatically think the drones were to be used for the purpose he planned. They could just be for filming for all an observer knew, or part of a festival display. But

Aashiq knew there was always a risk of third party interference, so a quick launch from a relatively quiet area close to the target zone was what he wanted, and that is what Square Agricol Perdiguier would provide.

Next to the remains of the old cloister of the Benedictine Abbey was a small gravelled area, usually used for parking by the workers who tended the gardens. It sat slightly apart from the main areas of the gardens and would provide an ideal spot to prepare and launch the drones. Aashiq knew that during the opening day of the festival, a big event in Avignon, it was unlikely workers would be in the Square, so the parking area should be free for him to use.

Having satisfied himself as to the best place from which to launch the drones, Aashiq walked out of the Square, turned right, and slowly made his way along the avenue towards Place de l'Horloge. With him was a man he knew only as Youssef, a local petty criminal who had supplied and who would drive the van Aashiq was using. Youssef was not an intelligent man, but he was useful.

As Aashiq walked from Square Agricol Perdiguier to Place de l'Horloge he kept looking up and around, checking for obstructions which could interfere with the flight path of the drones which in just a few days' time would fly low along the avenue to deliver their deadly cargo to those celebrating as part of the festival. Aashiq was satisfied that apart from some trees in Cours Jean Jaurès there was nothing which could obstruct the flight of the drones provided they did not descend below fifty feet above ground level. Anything flying below that height would be at risk, principally from the various power cables and telephone lines festooned from numerous poles along the avenue.

Youssef, walking with him, but a pace or so behind, observed what Aashiq was doing but didn't ask why. In fact he didn't really care. He was being paid to provide his van and driving services. All he knew was the police may be attacked by the people he was working for and he had no problem with that, he hated the police. He had come to France from Egypt some years ago and had been constantly harassed, and on occasions beaten, by police during that time. If the people carrying out an attack they were calling "Haboob" wanted him to be available to help, and to be discreet, then no problem. He was no friend of the police.

As Aashiq moved he held in his pocket a small GPS unit. He had armed it to record points along the route he was walking, beginning at the area in which his van would be parked on the day of the attack, at Square Agricol Perdiguier. He proposed to walk from there to the far end of Place de l'Horloge, recording positions enroute by pressing the button marked "MEM" on the GPS unit in his pocket as he passed each point he wanted marked in the GPS memory. They were the way-points of the GPS track the drones would be programmed to follow.

The first way-point had been logged in the GPS memory as he stood in the workers' carpark area in Square Agricol Perdiuier. The next way-point logged was after he had turned right towards Place de L'Horloge on exiting the Square and had walked along the avenue until he was clear of the trees bordering that avenue. Once past those trees he recorded the position at which he was standing as the next way-point, after ensuring he had a clear view from that point back past the end of the old abbey to the position from which he would launch the drones. That satisfied Aashiq the drones could fly from their launch point in a straight line to the point at which he now stood, avoiding the trees lining the avenue.

Then a further way-point was logged into the GPS memory as he entered Place de l'Horloge. The final way-point would be recorded when Aashiq reached the far end of Place de l'Horloge.

The GPS would remember the way points and guide the drones automatically along the track Aashiq had created during his walk, flying straight lines direct between the way-points created by each press of the MEM button. Aashiq was careful the track he established in the GPS maintained a good margin from the buildings lining the street.

When Aashiq reached the far end of Place de l'Horloge he stopped, and pushed another button on the GPS unit to calculate and then hold the track required to fly between the way-points established in its memory. So far so good. Tracking arrangements complete, although he would have to manually programme into the GPS units in each drone the initial climb to fifty feet on launch.

'Let's get back,' he said to Youssef.

There had been some discussion between Hussein Nasser and Aashiq, while Hussein had been working on making and installing the aluminium hoppers on the drones in the leased warehouse, regarding the possibility of just manually programming the proposed track into the GPS, but Aashiq had not been satisfied about the accuracy of that method. A minor miscalculation could have the drones crashing into a building façade or a tree he had said. He knew that if he walked the track, recording the required way-points on the GPS as he was at each position destined to be a way-point, the GPS would faithfully replicate a track between the way-points he had created as he walked, when the time came. Because the drones would follow exactly the path he had set, that meant no risk of a programming error allowing a drone to collide with a tree or building.

As a consequence of his firmly held view about this Aashiq had steadfastly refused all offers of programming from his scientist, Hussein. While Aashiq may have been right about reduced risk of track inaccuracy by undertaking the required way-point recording walk, there was another risk he had not thought of that arose from his walk.

After Aashiq Ahad had been placed in Avignon as a result of a banking transaction using his currency card being identified, René had put out a special alert. Police had Ahad's facial image available, courtesy of his border control interview at Paris Charles De Gaulle. As a consequence, as well as ensuring police on the streets were keeping an eye out for Aashiq Ahad, public CCTV coverage of areas around Avignon was now being subjected to scanning by DCRI computers using facial recognition technology.

Facial recognition is a major tool for many security agencies, including the French. The software that drives facial recognition systems analyses the relative position, size, and shape of prominent facial landmarks, such as eyes, nose, cheekbones, jaw, and then seeks to match them with similar features shown in base images held in another source. This is the so-called geometric approach to facial recognition.

If facial recognition software is to operate accurately, there must be an accurate "clean" base image. Once a compliant base image of a face has been established to the required standard as part of data held, recognition software can interpolate newly captured images even though those candid images may be affected by real world circumstances. The image of Aashiq Ahad was sufficiently clean to provide the necessary base image.

A public CCTV camera high up on the side of a building on Cours Jean Jaurès was the first camera to provide a hit. Then another camera, in Rue de la République, picked up an image which the software again matched to the image data of Aashiq Ahad. A further camera, at the top of Hôtel de Ville in Place de l'Horloge, was the next to record Aashiq's image, and once again the facial recognition software successfully did its work matching that image.

René was delighted. Target identified and importantly he now knew Aashiq Ahad was still in Avignon. The question for René was what was Ahad doing in Avignon? Watching the CCTV record showing Ahad, René thought he now knew.

'Anne,' René exclaimed, 'look at him, walking slowly through the Old City.'

René had arranged for the full images from the CCTV cameras seeing Ahad to be sent to him once the facial recognition software had identified Ahad. When René had looked at the full data recorded on CCTV he had observed the slow measured walk and the constant scanning undertaken by Ahad as he had walked along the avenue and across Place de l'Horloge.

'That is a reconnaissance exercise if ever I saw one,' René said grimly.

Anne nodded, 'I think we can safely assume Ahad is involved, and we were right to identify the festival as the likely target. We have to find this man and locate his base. If we can't do that then we will only have defensive strategy to meet the attack and that's always last resort. We really need to find him and stop him before he can implement his attack. And look René, he seems to have a buddy.'

The software had not matched Youssef to any available image data, but when the CCTV data from the cameras which had seen and provided matches for Aashiq Ahad was reviewed by René and Anne, Youssef, the Egyptian driver, was clearly identifiable as an accompanying person. Anne had noticed him and was highlighting his presence to René.

'You are right,' René confirmed, 'he has a friend, but we have no match at present unfortunately, so all we can do is take a good image from this data and use it as base material for future comparison. Then if his friend features again we can match at that time. We won't necessarily know who he is as a result, but we will get more information about his movements if he shows up in scanned CCTV data again.'

'Agreed,' said Anne, crisp and efficient as she moved into operational mode. Then she went on. 'We need to physically locate and detain Aashiq Ahad as soon as possible. The festival opens soon. If the festival is going to be attacked, and that is our agreed scenario based on what we had, now reinforced by this,' gesturing at the wall where the CCTV images had been played, 'we have very little time.'

'I know,' responded René. 'We should get the CCTV coverage of the area from where the various metro buses depart near *Porte de la Règublique,* to see if we can see Ahad or his friend using a bus to travel. It is not public CCTV so it will not have been scanned, but we can ask the bus company for its images showing the bus boarding and departure area covering, say, 3pm onwards yesterday. That timing encompasses the period during which the public CCTV recorded Ahad and his friend in the area looking like they might be going to the bus stops near the old walls.'

'Good idea,' Anne said smiling, recognising the professional leadership and initiative René was showing. He could be insightful and proactive in what was a difficult intelligence exercise.

Twenty four hours later René had received the bus company CCTV data for the agreed period. A review had found Aashiq Ahad and his accompanying friend boarding a local bus at 5pm. Digital enhancement had not been sufficient to read the signage at the front of the bus showing its destination, because the angle at which the bus had parked prevented a clear view, but a bus company manager had been able to help. When interviewed he was able to confirm the stand from which the bus departed at 5pm meant the bus was going to the small town of Montfavet, on the outskirts of Avignon.

'Montfavet is a small place Anne. Actually it was once well known as a place for treatment of psychiatric disorders, with quite a large hospital there catering for the affected. Now it's predominantly a dormitory town where a lot of those who work in Avignon live. Cheaper accommodation and close, only a short ride away.'

Anne nodded as René continued. 'I have again alerted police to look out for Aashiq Ahad and his friend. Photos have been widely distributed to officers on the street. I have also tasked some plain clothes officers to hang around the few bars and restaurants in Montfavet, watching for either of these gentlemen.'

'And if they see one of them,' Anne asked, 'what then?'

'Observe only, and follow. We need to find their base.' Good, thought Anne. That's dead right. Any attempt at detention could well leave us with no trail to follow, and just warn others in the group the authorities are aware of an operation.

Montfavet does not appear a wealthy town, but it hosts Avignon's principal airport, Caumont, and it has a range of light industrial and trade activity complementing its dormitory town status. Near the main town square in Montfavet there is a range of small shops, mostly dealing in the basic fundamentals, groceries, bread, and meat. Smart shopping requires a trip to Avignon.

Sometimes, for special occasions, the Montfavet locals will organise a band to play in the open area next to the town's fourteenth century church, with its tiled spire that stands above all the surrounding buildings and provides something of a landmark. The band members are usually enthusiastic locals rather than professionals, but they can nevertheless put on an entertaining evening.

There is a couple of bars near Montfavet's main square, and one of them also has a small restaurant. Basic fare in the restaurant, but reasonable value.

Then of course there are the ubiquitous pâtisseries found in most small French towns. Only open at certain times, sometimes to the frustration of tourists looking for something light to eat at the wrong time, they produce tantalising pastries and breads, and have cheeses that are ripe, smelly, soft, and delicious. As would be expected in France.

It was what appeared to be a local man eating by himself at one of the tables in the bar's restaurant and continually casting his eyes around the room who had attracted the attention of a plain-clothes officer put in place in the bar by one of René's operatives. The dining room was relatively empty, but the bar area was busy and noisy as patrons, who were mostly local workers, drank and told stories to each other about their day, their lives, and their expectations of the local soccer team, due to play an important match the following weekend.

The diner looked very similar to the person who appeared to have been accompanying the principal target identified and now sought by police, Aashiq Ahad, as shown in the photographic image which had been extracted from CCTV data provided to the officer. It was a grainy photo though, and he wasn't sure if it was the same man. I will just watch him for now the officer thought, and try and get a closer look if he comes into the bar after his meal. If he leaves I will follow him the officer decided, thinking it probably was the man reported as accompanying Aashiq Ahad.

Fifteen minutes later the diner got up from the table and headed to the bar at the back of the room. The plain clothes officer also moved towards the bar, to a position where he could more clearly see the suspect. The diner ordered a drink. The officer bought a beer so he could remain at the bar drinking and observing. As he lifted his beer glass and took his first mouthful he looked along the line of the side of the glass towards the suspect. The suspect looked up at that moment and their eyes momentarily locked. Fuck, thought the plain clothes officer and quickly dropped his eyes. Too quickly.

Aashiq Ahad's associate, Youssef, the Egyptian who disliked the police, recognised a cop's look instantly. He had been operating on the fringes of society long enough to be well aware of the signs of "le flic". He was being watched by a cop, and the too quickly averted eyes told him he was definitely the subject of what had been meant to be covert observation. He waited a minute or so to let the moment pass, then put down his half-full glass and moved towards the exit.

The plain clothes officer knew he had been made by the suspect. The eye contact had been bad luck, but it had been enough, and with the suspect suddenly leaving and an unfinished drink the officer knew he had been spotted. No chance of discreet observation now, so better to detain the suspect he thought. He moved quickly after the departing man who was just moving through the outdoor dining area towards the pavement as the officer called for him to stop. Youssef instead vaulted the railing separating the dining area from the pavement and ran. Here we go thought the officer, and set off in pursuit. Youssef turned down a small alley which carried the permanent stench of urine from all those who regularly relieved themselves there on the way home from the bar.

As he chased the officer again called for his suspect to stop, to no avail, but he was closing on him. As he reached Youssef the officer became aware of a drawn knife. Realising he could not outrun his chaser Youssef had turned, with his knife out, and lunged at the cop who he had seen watching him and who was now trying to detain him. The blade entered the upper left arm of the police officer. It didn't hurt, but the officer could feel a wet warmth growing on his arm and he knew he had been badly cut. Youssef stepped back and prepared to stab again, but the officer had drawn his pistol and pointing it at Youssef shouted at him to stand still and drop the knife.

Youssef ignored him and moved forward again. As Youssef closed the distance between them again the officer knew he had no choice, and he shot Youssef twice. The first bullet hit Youssef's left shoulder, doing terrible damage to his shoulder muscle and bone. Youssef grunted in pain but continued towards the officer. The second bullet entered his chest. Youssef made no noise this time. He just silently crumpled to the ground. The pathologist would later say Youssef was going to die within approximately two to three minutes of the second bullet entering his chest, and he would have had only a short time before he became unconscious, as his blood pressure plummeted. The second bullet had sliced through the upper part of his heart, causing catastrophic damage from which there could be no recovery.

As Youssef lay dying, and moments before he lapsed into the unconsciousness that would precede his death, he abused the man who represented all he hated about France and who was the cop who had shot him and ended his life. Through contorted lips he spat his abuse reflecting a life-long hatred of authority and the law.

'Pig, die in Haboob,' Youssef rasped, as he fell unconscious and his life began to end in the urine stinking alley he had run into seeking escape.

The next morning René was angry. 'Fuck it, don't people understand what don't detain means,' he shouted, using his favourite expletive, 'just follow was the instruction.' He had been told about the chase and shooting and he wasn't happy a potential lead now lay dead in the local mortuary.

'To be fair René,' one of his lieutenants, Moriarty, intoned, 'the officer had little choice in the circumstances, so let's not be too harsh.'

While René understood the sentiment being expressed he wasn't going to settle that quickly. René would grumble on for the next fifteen minutes or so before gathering himself and reading the formal report on the incident now on his computer screen. It outlined the series of events leading to the shooting, the situation resulting in the fatal shot being fired, and what had happened in the immediate aftermath as the suspect lay dying.

René forwarded the report to Anne who was working in an adjacent office, asking her to come through when she had read it and they would discuss. He expected that might take fifteen minutes at least, but five minutes later Anne was in his office, excited by something she had seen in the report.

'What is it Anne?' René queried, noting her state.

'I think we now have confirmation there will be a drone attack using ricin,' she said.

'Okay, how do you move from our more probable than not scenario to reach such a definite view?' René responded.

'The person shot has been identified as the man with Ahad captured on the CCTV images. As he was dying the report says he swore at the officer saying he would die in "Haboob". I think "Haboob" may be the name of the operation Ahad is planning.'

'And if it is,' René retorted, 'where does that get us. Most operations have a code name, it doesn't necessarily help.'

Anne looked grim. 'René,' she said, "Haboob" is Arabic for dust storm. I think we can now be reasonably assured that Ahad is planning to deliver ricin by dropping it from an overflying drone. We have the intelligence regarding castor bean cake being shipped from Chennai to Marseille, the suspect container disappearing after arrival at Marseille, unusual drone purchases and flights, and a reconnaissance of streets leading to Place de L'Horloge by a person linked to Chennai who is suspected of supporting Islamic extremism. And now this. In my view we are looking at a ricin dust attack by drones.'

René sat silent. He knew her scenario was likely correct. It fitted everything they knew.

'*Merde*, what is wrong with these bastards,' he shouted angrily, thinking about the horror of drones being used to cover happy crowds at the festival with poisonous dust, like some crop-dusting exercise in the country.

123

Then, suddenly calm and calculated, René lent forward to Anne.

'Thank you Anne. With this final detail we can be reasonably confident we have accurately identified the attack and its form. Now we plan how to combat it and ensure no one is hurt, other than the bad guys. I will hurt them. I will fucking hurt them.'

Anne could see René meant what he said, and while his tone and language had been unexpected she understood his feelings. France had been subjected to a number of terrorist attacks with large numbers of casualties among people who had started their day thinking it was just that, another day. Not the day they would be randomly murdered. Anne had felt the same feelings of anger, as had her fellow students at the time, for the perpetrators of the attacks on the Twin Towers in New York City, back in 2001.

René and Anne worked late into the night the day after the shooting of Ahad's assistant, Youssef, looking at how they might locate Ahad's base of operations and prevent him executing his attack on the festival. But they knew they were running out of time. The festival was due to open in days.

Chapter 9

René told Anne of the arrangements he had made to create a radio frequency block for any drones in the town square, Place de l'Horloge. Because CCTV footage had shown the town square as an area of interest to Ahad, based on the reconnaissance Ahad had been seen undertaking, this was seen as the likely area of attack on the festival.

René was confident the radio frequency jamming capability of the French drone defence system would prevent any drones successfully attacking. No ground-based operator radio signals could reach a drone once the jamming was activated. Without the ability to transmit command signals to the drone an operator could not direct a drone's flight and activity.

'If the drone cannot be directed it cannot fly where it needs to, and neither can it release its dust when required,' René was telling Anne. 'We can block the radio command signals the drone would need to do those things.'

Anne was not so convinced. 'René, what say for some reason we cannot block the signals, for example if we don't have the right frequencies covered?'

'Our jamming equipment covers the full range Anne, and I have had a check made of the frequencies installed in the drones purchased. They are included in the bandwidth we will jam. We will make the drones impotent,' René said, showing his Gallic background a little with that description.

'It blocks the frequencies used by an operator to send control instructions to a drone. It is similar to the mobile phone signal blocking sometimes undertaken to create dead spots for security purposes when important politicians, like your President, are visiting. If control signals cannot be sent to the drone it will not be able to be used in any attack.'

'I think it would be a mistake to rely solely on the jamming system to stop any attack using drones,' Anne

125

said firmly. René raised a questioning eyebrow as he settled back into his old leather chair with yet another cup of black coffee.

'Why are you pushing this view?' he asked. 'We can block the signals if an attack occurs.'

'I know,' Anne said, remembering her briefing back at Langley when the French drone suppressant system had first become known to the CIA, 'it operates in a similar way to the system we use to supress mobile phone signals in an area around a VIP. Stops activation signals to nasty devices.'

'And it will also prevent an operator sending control signals to a drone in flight' René interjected.

Anne replied. 'The drones purchased in this case were said to have GPS capability. What would happen if the drones were pre-programmed to follow a flight parameter set in the GPS memory? No ground-based signal would be required to control their flight and once launched they would go about their business and dead signal zones would be ineffective.'

Anne continued. 'If we attempted to jam the satellite signal frequencies as well to disrupt GPS guidance are we sure the jamming equipment would be effective over a wide area? I understand localised jamming of GPS signals may be possible, but the wide area coverage we need, I am not so sure René. In my view jamming provides no surety of outcome, whether for ground based control signals or terrestrial GPS signals.'

René then spent some ten minutes taking Anne through the briefing he had received from his radio techs, as he called them, who had described their jamming capabilities for all the signals they might want to disrupt, including the signals from GPS satellites.

The techs had confirmed GPS signals from satellites were relatively weak, and sufficient electro-magnetic noise could disrupt those signals. René did concede to Anne the techs had noted some risk around ability to jam a large number of GPS satellites located at different points in the sky, and broadcasting on multiple frequencies to GPS receivers operating over an extended area. René had been lost when the techs had started describing the use of bi-phase shift keying modulation techniques in satellite signal transmissions, which they said made jamming more difficult, particularly when there were multiple satellites involved. But they had confirmed they were of the view the number of satellites in view and the redundancy arising from this modulation technique, while providing increased resistance to successful jamming, was not critical to their likely success in blocking signals. The techs had noted the area a jammer could cover was unclear, but they considered the town square was an area they could effectively shield from all GPS signals "ex terrestrial sources".

After René shared all this with Anne she considered it confirmed her fears, rather than satisfying them. 'The result is not sufficiently certain René,' she warned. 'I think we should again recommend cancellation of the festival.'

'The Minister will not cancel Anne. He says as we have now identified the likely threat we should be able to prevent an attack. He says he will not let the terrorists have a win by causing cancellation of such an important event, and if we cancel this the terrorists will just plan another attack elsewhere, so it could only ever be a postponement of terror attacks, not a win for us. Unfortunately he has a point.'

Anne's turn to get angry. 'For Christ's sake what do we do then, take a risk with the hundreds of people enjoying the festival and its atmosphere, hoping the frequency blocking is sufficient? That's an unacceptable risk in my book.'

René stared at her. Fleetingly angry this woman seconded to him by the CIA would not accept his operational scenarios, he was about to show his annoyance when he realised she may be right. Why hadn't he considered the possibility that jamming would be ineffective, assuming instead there would be no issue with jamming, as his techs had thought? It had always been his training mantra. Presume nothing, test your scenarios, and look for any alternative outcome in case you have become too channelled in your thinking. Always stop and consider what else could or could not happen. God, he had lectured on it enough, and now he was guilty of the same channelled thinking and resulting oversight.

'Ok,' said René, recovering his equilibrium momentarily upset by Anne's position and fairly definite view that had cut across his settled thinking and plan, 'fair point. Let's assume the drones, once launched, can operate unaffected by any frequency blocking. I don't care how they do it, let's just assume they can for present purposes. In that situation I have to agree with you.'

'That's right René, autonomy in their operation, however occurring, is a real risk I think' Anne responded, sensing a softening in René's position.

Then Anne looked directly at René and held his gaze. 'It occurs to me there is something we can do to protect against the autonomy scenario René. In the world in which we operate what I am going to suggest is not a highly sophisticated response, but I see no reason why it would not work.' Then she spent the next thirty minutes outlining her plan and how she thought it could be implemented.

'Oh yes, that's such a practical solution. It's brilliant,' René said at the end of it, and sat back in his chair smiling.

He was increasingly liking this woman. Importantly to René, a man who had never enjoyed the airs and graces of some in the upper echelons of the French intelligence community, Dr Anne Davis was showing herself to be a very practical person, with valuable real-world insight which she was ready to apply.

Standing in front of the equipment newly installed in the Montfavet warehouse, Hussein once again reviewed the process he planned to follow to produce the required toxin, ricin, in the form of a light dust taken from the cake left after the processing of castor oil plants.

The castor oil plants had, he understood, been harvested in late November and through December. Spread out on the ground after harvest the plants had been left to dry in the sun until they had been blackened from that exposure. Then, after workers on the plantation concerned had beaten the plants with sticks to enable the seeds to be removed, winnowed, and screened, the seeds had been collected and crushed, and the castor oil extracted. The residue, the oil cake he was now to deal with, had been waiting for him in the warehouse when he had arrived to take up his work some time ago.

He knew the oil cake residue from the crushing process which had extracted the oil from the castor oil beans would contain about seven per cent ricin. But that didn't mean seven per cent of the oil cake volume he had would be available in the form of ricin. There would be substantial conversion losses as he produced the dust through the special process he had researched and planned to follow. But he would certainly have more than enough ricin dust to fill the hoppers he had had assembled and which were to be attached to each of the three drones.

Hussein's plan was to use a chromatographic technique to extract the ricin from the oil cake. That required him to turn the cake into a slurry, and then filter it with water and hydrochloric acid. Then, once he had isolated the ricin he would sieve it through a very fine mesh and suspend the resulting fine particles in ether to extract any remaining oily substance. After that Hussein planned to stir the mixture, and with fine particles in suspension he would decant the fluid on to a filter.

The resulting sediment would be taken off the filter and air dried, providing a residue comprising highly toxic ricin dust which in due course unsuspecting men, women, and children would inhale in what Hussein considered would be one of the greatest terror attacks in memory.

When ricin dust is inhaled a cough and fever will normally follow a short time later, and death may occur between three and five days after inhalation. Death is usually caused by respiratory failure or in some cases by pulmonary oedema. People would recall the flight of three drones overhead in the town square of the Old City in Avignon, but no-one would realise that what they had thought was display smoke coming out of the drones was in fact something else. It would take autopsies and an official review of events before the terrible truth dawned on France.

While Hussein was aware there may be better ways to attack the West to achieve multiple casualties, using explosives and guns, he thought the drone dust attack was a great plan. He could understand the horror and fear the West would suffer when it became known some drones had laid a poisonous toxin over crowds of people happily going about their day. It was the horror and fear that made this attack so special and valuable for Daesh.

Hussein particularly liked the fact Aashiq had arranged for an addition of colour to the dust in each drone's hopper. One drone would drop blue dust, the second white dust, and the third, red dust. The crowd being overflown and dusted could be forgiven for thinking it part of the opening day's festivities as they observed the colours of France falling from the drones. A wonderful irony, thought Hussein.

Hussein had confirmed to Aashiq how lethal ricin could be, particularly if it was delivered in a closely targeted dose. He had told Aashiq about the devastating effects of ricin on Bulgarian dissident Georgi Markov, who had been killed on a London street by the Bulgarian secret police. Stabbing a ricin-coated pellet placed on the end of an umbrella into Markov's leg had meant he was a doomed man. Markov had died days afterwards. Hussein had noted the wider dispersal method, using the drones to spread toxic dust over the crowd, meant a lethal dose would be inhaled only by some in the crowds standing beneath the drone, not all. Dusting the crowd would not have the same efficiency as a targeted dose of ricin he had said.

Hussein acknowledged there would not be a large body count, but Aashiq wanted this form of attack because it would be seen as horrific. It would cause totally unexpected deaths because people would not realise they were the subject of an attack until too late, and afterwards, when the attack was better understood, France would be rocked, as would its western allies.

Hussein had accepted what Aashiq wanted to achieve. He knew the first symptoms would not show themselves for some hours after the dust had been inhaled. People would not recognise serious illness for some time after that, let alone know, initially anyway, how they had been exposed. Discovery of what it was and how it had occurred would cause a shocked reaction, and that was the principal goal.

In the warehouse in Montfavet, Aashiq was momentarily shaken to hear that Youssef had been shot and killed during a police confrontation. How in God's name did that happen, he asked himself. It was not a major setback he rationalised. Getting another driver was no problem, and it appeared Youssef had been killed in a struggle as an officer sought to detain him, so no risk of any information having been leaked, not that Youssef knew much anyway. Dismissing Youssef's death as unimportant he coldly returned to his discussion with his scientist, Hussein Nasser.

'I have walked the route I want the drones to fly,' Aashiq said, noting as he spoke the scientist did not appear to have wholly recovered from having his suggestion of manually programming the GPS guidance systems in the

131

drones dismissed. So Aashiq took the opportunity to repeat his reasoning.

'Walking the route and letting the GPS record waypoints along the actual track I walk is more certain and accurate than manually programming the GPS as you suggested. Ideally we would just fly the drones on their track by controlling them from a ground position using visual cues from the on-board cameras, but as we have agreed, at least on this point, that is too risky. Not only do I not want to have to control three different drones, the security services would have the ability to block my radio signals to the drone and we would not be able to maintain control in those circumstances. Better to pre-load the route and have each drone operate in a self-contained way, unaffected by any signal blockers. Okay?'

'Okay,' shrugged Hussein grudgingly, 'I accept what you say. Controlling multiple drones via one operator at the same time is not optimum, but I am not sure the French could block drone command signals as you fear, and why should they even think it's necessary, they know nothing of our planned attack let alone how we will implement the attack. And to answer the other question you asked me earlier regarding satellite signals, no, I don't think French security would be capable of blocking satellite signals to prevent the on board GPS units in the drones following the track programmed. While GPS signals sent from satellites are not strong, blocking these signals coming from different positions in space, as they would with multiple satellites in view, is usually only certain if trying to shield a GPS receiver close to the transmitter doing the jamming. It is not easy to shield over a wide area, which is what we will have with our drone flights. So in my view blocking satellite signals is not realistic for French security, even if they knew we were using drones with self-contained GPS track guidance.'

For the next two hours Aashiq went over all the details of the planned attack with Hussein, including the final preparation of the dust and the drones, the trip they would make to the Old City of Avignon in the van provided by the late Youssef, and the arrangements around the actual preparation and launching of the drones. The van they were to use now had signage placed on it indicating it was an Avignon City Parks and Reserves Maintenance vehicle. They would use the van to enter the Old City area at Porte de la République and park it in the caretaker's parking area in Square Agricol Perdiguier.

Once there, the drones would be taken out of the back of the van and launched immediately. As soon as the drones were airborne Aashiq and Hussein would leave. There was no need to stay to see what happened. They knew what would happen.

The drones would faithfully and automatically follow, at their programmed speed and height, the track between the series of way-points imprinted in the memory of the GPS devices in each drone. After one minute the on-board timers would activate the solenoids in the hoppers installed in the drones, and cause them to open. At that point the drones would have covered just over 600 metres from launch point and would be entering Avignon's town square, Place de l'Horloge. Then, as the drones passed over the crowds gathered to enjoy the festival and its carnival-like atmosphere, the dust would begin to fall. Some in the crowd might even cheer and clap as the blue white and red of France began to fall from the drones.

Everything was ready. The installation and testing was complete, including a test flight on a nearby farm which had been necessary to ensure the satisfactory operation of the GPS flight programme, and the operation of the timer and solenoids to ensure the dust would be released at the correct point. Aashiq smiled. He could not see how the execution of his attack could fail. Once French security became aware of the attack, as the drones came into view and began their evil business, it would be too late. Drone flight time from launch until dust release was one minute, and then it would be over. At least for a few hours, until large numbers of the public began presenting with breathing difficulties, rapidly deteriorating in a short time after that, with many dying a very unpleasant death within days.

The search for Aashiq Ahad continued. There was a huge police presence in and around Montfavet. Some of the locals were starting to get a little feisty about the many police stops, identification requirements, and questioning now pervading what was usually a small sleepy village. But the police work, including continued scanning of images on feeds from public CCTV, was to no avail. Aashiq Ahad had not been located.

René and Anne were beginning to accept he would probably not be located in time and the only action left, short of cancelling the festival which the minister refused to do, was to try to stop the attack as it began. At least they were now more confident about where and how the attack would occur. They had been working hard that afternoon, completing their planning and preparation to counter the attack they thought likely.

Anne and René were proceeding on the basis the Festival d' Avignon was indeed the target, with the attack to be carried out using drones to disperse ricin dust over the crowds in Place de l'Horloge. The algorithms had given them the base threads from which they had been able to develop their attack scenario. Coupled with the evidence from the CCTV cameras showing Aashiq Ahad reconnoitring the area and the late Youssef's dying utterance, they considered the evidence sufficiently robust to draw the conclusions they had. They now had to finalise their plans for meeting this identified attack probability.

Frequency jamming was fine, but there was a risk it would not be sufficient, as identified by Anne and now accepted by René. Cancellation of the festival was not acceptable to the Minister, and because they had been unable to locate Aashiq Ahad, intercepting the terrorists and preventing the attack was not currently an option. There was to be considerable reliance on Anne's suggested counter to any drone attack. Hopefully her plan would work. If not, France would suffer badly and the terrorists would again be able to release gloating media pieces about their success and French security's failure. It was an important time for France, and René and Anne were both very aware of that fact.

Chapter 10

The wait was over. The 2016 Festival d'Avignon was about to begin. Months of practise by the many musicians and performers involved had led to this day. Most of the sessions were sold out, and the public were ready to enjoy eighteen days of what many considered to be one of the great arts festivals of France. This year the festival was to run from 6 July through to 24 July.

In Place de l'Horloge, cafes and restaurants had temporarily expanded their footprints, with extended marquees covering the extra tables and bars allowed courtesy of a special dispensation from the Mayor and councillors who were always willing to accommodate the needs of the festival. The brightly coloured canopies temporarily erected around the square under which people sat eating and drinking, and the noise of the hundreds of conversations going on, interspersed with shrieks of delight from the children, and some of the adults, watching the many street performers in the town square, affirmed the popularity of the festival.

Many of the street performers appeared to be of North African origin, and specialised in amazing acrobatics that brought gasps of surprise and appreciation from those watching. Brightly coloured clothing was worn by the acrobatic entertainers, and they were often quick to involve some hapless spectator who had no choice but to become part of the act. Often to their embarrassment, but always to the delight of the crowd, many silently thanking, as they laughed, they had not been picked out and dragged into the act.

In stark contrast to the bright colours and happy activity in the town square was the black combat kit worn by members of the anti-terrorist squad forming part of the security cordon established around the 2016 festival. Members of the squad could be seen standing sombre and alert about three hundred metres down Rue de la

République, carrying automatic weapons. Most of those in the square had come through the cordon as they made their way to the festival venues, and tellingly, none were surprised and most appreciated what they saw. The targeting of France by terrorists, and particularly with Charlie Hebdo and the Bataclan relatively fresh in people's memories, meant the French public were used to such security. Unhappily it was now seen as the norm, and necessary. The public felt a degree of comfort when they saw the security, so no-one objected.

Parked at the southern end of the town square were two trucks. They were identical in type and size, and by the markings they carried were clearly police transport vehicles.

Each truck was a flat deck, with canvas walls installed around the deck extending about one and a half metres above the level of the deck. Because of the height of the top of the canvas walls passers-by could not see into the back of the trucks, nor could they see there was no top cover, with the flat deck exposed and open to the sky behind the canvas walls. And certainly, they could not see what was in the back of each of the trucks, on their flat decks. If they had been able to see they would have been surprised, perhaps apprehensive.

As he and Hussein drove to Avignon from the Montfavet warehouse they had been using for their preparations for the attack, Aashiq became very aware of the sizeable police presence. As they turned into the gate that would allow them into the Old City, Aashiq saw the black-suited anti-terrorist squad members further along the avenue. Momentarily apprehensive, he relaxed a little when he saw the security cordon was further down Rue de la République than he needed to travel. Square Agricol Perdiguier was at least three hundred metres before the security cordon, so he could reach his planned launch point without having to pass through any special security. Aashiq didn't consider the security indicated any particular concern by French authorities about the festival he was to attack. He thought it the standard security now applicable at major public events in France, particularly since the Bataclan.

As the van turned into Square Agricol Perdiguier, and drove to the caretakers' parking area, a policeman sitting astride his pride and joy, a new and powerful BMW patrol motor bike, looked towards them. Aashiq was ready. He was wearing workman's overalls and his van said he was Parks and Reserves maintenance. He waved and grinned at the cop, who nodded back and turned away. When the van pulled into the small parking area used by city maintenance staff, Aashiq saw he had been right. No other vehicle was there. The public wouldn't park in such a reserved area and risk a ticket, or worse still, a tow. And no regular staff were working today given it was festival opening day. It was treated as if a public holiday in Avignon.

Aashiq climbed over the seat into the rear of the van and began to prepare the three drones for flight. First he checked the rotor blades on each drone were secure and that the rotor heads themselves, four on each drone, showed full and free movement when he turned them by hand. Then he ensured the holes in each of the drones' hoppers were covered by a solenoid controlled aperture cover, and that all linkages between the solenoid actuating devices and the covers were secure. Solenoid operation itself had been checked back at the warehouse. The aperture covers would slide aside and allow dispersal of the ricin dust when the timing device carried by each drone activated the solenoid.

Finally, as Hussein again voiced the need for Aashiq to be cautious as he transferred the light dust into the drone hoppers in the confines of the closed van, he put on protective gloves, goggles, and a mask and carefully tipped the ricin dust from each of the three containers he had in the back of the van, one containing blue dust, one white, and the final container, red dust. When he had filled each hopper with its respective colour, Aashiq firmly clipped each hopper to its drone. He was ready to launch.

In the office René had arranged with the Mayor to use, in Hôtel de Ville overlooking Place de l'Horloge, René and Anne sat watching the throngs of people in the square from their second floor vantage point. In the room next to them the radio frequency jamming equipment had been set up and was ready to be activated by a public servant who lived in Lyon, and who appeared to live for the opportunity to discuss radio frequency bandwidth and his abilities in jamming operations. Or so René had thought, as he had hastily extracted himself from the room and the man's conversation after some ten minutes of boring discourse.

'Jesus Anne, I hope we can block signals effectively if there is a drone attack today, and if we can't, well your plan better work.'

'I don't know what else we could have done René,' Anne responded, 'but if drones are sighted then as well as attempting to jam we must also move straight into the response we have planned. I don't want us to sit watching to see if signal blocking works once activated. We have to use all resources together, so while we have spoken of our special response as a secondary plan let's not treat it as an alternative position to be used only if signal blocking doesn't work. Time margins are too tight and we need to have the drones at the entrance to the town square as we activate our special response.'

'We begin jamming transmissions as soon as a drone is seen, but at the same time we activate the alternative response. It will be a lot more public than simply jamming, but there is no way around that. And there should be no jamming until we see drones. If the terrorists can't properly launch a drone from wherever they are situated because of the jamming it gives them an opportunity to do something else when they realise signals to their drone are not available. Let's leave signal failure as a last minute surprise once the drones are committed to flight,' she said.

'I'm confident that any attack will likely come from the southern end of Place de l'Horloge. The combination of city walls, buildings, and lack of a major avenue opening into Place de l'Horloge make any other direction of approach less likely. Using the open route from the south, along Rue de la République, is a practical approach for bringing in a drone without undue risk to its flight path. I don't believe they would want to risk too many obstacles by coming in from another direction, and let's not forget that the CCTV footage of Ahad showed him reconnoitring a route along Rue de la République to Place de l'Horloge. That's further confirmation I think,' René responded.

René and Anne sat in silence. Had they done all they could they were each wondering?

Time will tell thought René as he fingered the two way radio connecting him to the security cordon and to the crew in each of the two trucks with their canvas sidewalls parked at the southern end of the square.

Anne was philosophical. They had received and analysed a lot of information, particularly the data linked by the intelligent algorithm. She was satisfied they had undertaken the threat assessment exercises thoroughly and reached conclusions based on reasonable assumptions made after considering everything available. Hypotheses developed had been thoroughly tested. Textbook analysis and approach. The indications pointing to a drone-based ricin attack had been correctly elevated to a definitive position in her view. They could have done nothing else, but it was frustrating they had been unable to locate the terrorist cell itself and intervene before any attack.

She and René had considered how to protect against the attack they assumed would occur, and that had resulted in two principal responses in addition to the security cordon and heightened police alert status. Hopefully, if there was a drone attack the signal blocking would work, and if it didn't, then their alternative response should work, she was confident. If it didn't work...... and then her thought process trailed off, not wanting to address the prospect of being wrong or failing, with the consequences that might entail for hundreds of the happy people in the square below.

Caught up in their own thoughts, René and Anne waited.

In Square Agricol Perdiguier, just seven hundred metres away from where René and Anne sat, Aashiq Ahad was finalising the preparation of the drones for flight. The timers would open the apertures on the dust hoppers carried by each drone as it entered the town square. The GPS in each drone had identified it was at the start point of its track towards Place de l'Horloge. The batteries were charged, rotor blades secure, and the rotor heads all turned freely. The drones were ready to launch.

Aashiq removed his protective gear, as did Hussein, and then climbed back over the front seat of the van, got out, and walked around to the back of the van and opened its rear doors. He looked around to ensure there was nothing that might interfere with what he wanted to do over the next few minutes. There were lots of people walking along the adjacent avenue which ran towards the town square, but none paid attention to a gardener in his overalls. There was a couple of young boys playing in the trees, but they were similarly uninterested in Aashiq.

Aashiq lifted one of the drones out of the back of the van, placing it on the ground about two metres behind the van. Then the second drone was passed to him by Hussein. Aashiq took it and placed it on the ground about a metre past the first drone. Finally Aashiq took the third drone and placed it on the ground, about metre beyond the second drone he had just placed. The three drones sat there, in a line, with a space of a metre between each drone.

Aashiq had rehearsed the launch many times in the warehouse at Montfavet. The drones were to be started and were to take off in the sequence they sat on the ground. Aashiq started the drone which was further from the back of the van than the others, and it took off and climbed straight up to fifty feet before moving in the direction of the adjacent avenue, its GPS slavishly following the required track embedded in its memory. Five seconds later, the next drone in the line had been started and it followed the same flightpath as the first, also following its imprinted track. And then, after a further five seconds, the third drone followed.

The three drones flew in a line, one after the other, from Square Agricol Perdiguer past the end of the old abbey towards Rue de la République. As they each reached that avenue they entered a slight turn to the right, in sequence, and then flew along Rue de la République towards Place de l'Horloge and the hundreds there enjoying the carnival-like atmosphere of the opening day of the 2016 Festival d'Avignon. The drones flew steadily at a programmed speed of thirty six kilometres per hour, at approximately fifty feet above the ground.

Aashiq didn't stop to watch his drones undertake their task. As soon as the last drone was airborne he got back into the van and he and Hussein quickly drove out of Square Agricol Perdiguer, turning left as they reached the avenue, towards the Porte in the Old City wall. The drones would reach Place de l'Horloge approximately one minute after launch.

The boys who had been playing in the trees were very excited to see the drones launched and fly off towards the town square. They hadn't known there was a drone flying exhibition, so they started to run towards the square to ensure they didn't miss anything.

The commander of the anti-terrorist squad manning the cordon in Rue de la République became aware of the drones approaching at the last moment. He heard them first, and because he had been briefed on the threat he instantly recognised what was causing the growing noise as the drones approached. At first he couldn't see them sweeping relatively low along the avenue as he scanned for the noise source, but then a movement in his peripheral vision caused him to focus and he saw the drones. He was wearing a live boom microphone, which meant it was always open to transmit. 'Three drones, forty to fifty feet, inbound to Horloge via République,' he snapped efficiently.

René, on hearing that transmission, called, 'Three inbound. Go,' into his radio. In the meantime the boring radio man from Lyon had flicked his jamming equipment on in the room next door.

The drones flew into Place de l'Horloge, emerging from Rue de la République in a line, with the first drone about fifty metres in front of the second, and the third a further fifty metres behind the second. The spacing resulting from the five second launch interval between the drones. As well as reflecting the time necessary to allow Aashiq to start and launch each drone separately, the resulting spacing provided a safety margin to avoid any mid-air collision between drones.

The drones were clearly unaffected by the jamming efforts of the man from Lyon. As René watched, the first drone must have been airborne for a minute, as its timer had activated the solenoid to open the hopper apertures. René saw blue dust begin trailing from the first drone, and he knew his worst fears were being realised. Deadly toxic ricin dust being released over those enjoying the festivities in the town square. Some of them would have probably thought, if they were watching the drones as they entered Place de l'Horloge, that it was part of the fun.

Reacting to René's radioed alert, the two men who had been waiting out of sight behind the canvas screens in the back of each of the trucks strategically parked at the southern end of the square stood up, looking over the top of the canvas sides. They immediately saw the drones entering the town square and about to fly past their position, the first drone starting to spew blue dust. Each of

143

them lifted the gun they usually used in their skeet shooting competitions, double barrelled shotguns. Binding the shotgun into their shoulders they slowly swivelled as they tracked a drone, swinging the shotgun through an arc which followed the flightpath of the drone they had been tasked to shoot. Three drones had been purchased, so René and Anne's attack scenario had anticipated multiple drones.

The shooters designated "1" in each of the trucks shot at the first drone. They didn't miss. The drones were bigger and slower than the target discs they usually shot at as part of René's skeet shooting team. The rotors giving the first quadcopter drone its lift and momentum exploded under the hail of shot and some of the pellets penetrated the drone's infrastructure, obliterating its GPS function. The drone fell heavily to the ground.

Number "2" shooter in each truck tracked the second drone, spewing white dust, as it approached a few seconds later. It crashed to the ground after receiving at least one direct blast of shot, with multiple pellets striking it. The third drone, some fifty metres behind was targeted by all shooters. Number 1 in each truck had reloaded and Number 2 in each truck had only fired one shot, so a second shot was already in the second barrel and available. The amount of shot hitting the third drone meant the whole thing virtually disintegrated in mid-air, its red dust trail tracing the drone's arc down to the ground as it fell out of control, no longer a flying machine, just shot-pulverised aluminium and plastic.

Chemical and biological weapon experts, who had been nearby but out of sight of the square, suitably kitted up, appeared and moved forward to secure the crashed drones. Masked medics moved into the part of the crowd that may have been exposed to the initial opening of the dust hoppers on the drones. The drones had been shot down almost immediately, but there may have been some inhalation of dust so those potentially affected were to be taken by ambulance to a treatment centre René had arranged to be set up.

Aashiq Ahad knew nothing of his failure as he headed for the Avignon TGV station to catch the fast train to Marseille and the escape route which would enable him to leave France quickly and discreetly.

Back in the Old City the police were interviewing two boys who had been playing in the trees in Square Agricol Perdiguier and who had seen the drones launched after they had been taken out of what the boys described as a green Parks and Reserves van. The scene commander immediately sent one of his men to uplift the CCTV footage from the cameras which covered Square Agricol Perdiguier, and issued an alert for a green van bearing Parks and Reserves signage.

A review of CCTV images from Square Agricol Perdiguier showed the Parks & Reserves van parking, and after about five minutes a man appearing from the van and going about setting out the drones and launching them, before quickly driving away as soon as launched. Facial recognition algorithms matched Aashiq Ahad as the person launching the drones. Ahad was re-rated from likely suspect to confirmed attacker in the person of interest alerts already in place.

Two hours after the attack on the festival, the Parks & Reserves van was found abandoned on a road close to the Avignon TGV station. CCTV from the station confirmed Ahad had boarded the Avignon to Marseille train. Unfortunately it had arrived in Marseille and Ahad had disappeared before René's counterparts in Marseille reached the station. But the hunt was on, and unknown to Aashiq Ahad French security had identified him as the attacker and had dedicated significant resources to hunting him, knowing he was in or around Marseille.

While he didn't know French security knew who was responsible for the attack, Aashiq did feel the weight of what he had just done in Avignon. Almost paranoid, he started to think every policeman he saw in the street must notice he looked uneasy, and he felt he was attracting undue attention. The sooner he got out of France the better.

Chapter 11

Anne and René reviewed what they had. They didn't have time to congratulate themselves on having identified the attack scenario that had now played out, an intelligence assessment which had proved so horribly accurate. Now the principal task for them was to locate Aashiq Ahad. That was their total focus. He must be located and detained.

'He doesn't know we have identified him and have his picture, but nevertheless my pick is he won't try to hide with any supporters in France. He will try to get out of the country as soon as possible,' René said, 'and he will not want to risk normal intercept points. He will know all formal border crossings will be subject to intensified scrutiny and questioning of those who fit a profile. Given his experience inbound at Charles de Gaulle he won't want to run that risk. So what will he do to get out of France quickly and covertly?' he asked rhetorically.

Anne spoke. 'We know he has travelled to Marseille. The airport there is being watched, along with every other airport in the country in accordance with the usual surveillance protocols you noted René. That's a normal response following an event like this, and Ahad will be well aware of that as well. I agree with you, he will not take any risks at all. He will be mindful of the fact he triggered an alert at Paris Charles de Gaulle. He will be conscious of the fact that would have been because he was a person of interest, so I don't see him going anywhere near areas with controlled environments such as airports or seaports. I understand all main roads, especially close to borders, have been put under watch with extensive random checks of vehicles implemented, so getting out of France, probably into an adjoining territory as a first step at least, is not the straightforward piece it might have been for him prior to today.'

René watched Anne closely as she spoke. He liked the way she had become part of his team and her clear commitment and dedication to task, and, if he was truthful, the fact she had stood up to him over the signal blocking issues. What really appealed to René was her insight. She had been key to some of the decisions made, and given what had happened she had been right. Her suggestion to emulate skeet shooters shooting at their range targets, using shotguns to bring down the drones, had been a brilliant but simple solution to a complex problem. And, he added as an afterthought from somewhere in the back of his mind, she is an attractive woman. The complete modern woman really, René thought, always the sexist. He smiled to himself, very happy she had been made available to help French security, and him in particular.

Anne spoke again. 'Ahad has limited country exit opportunities, but one avenue available to him is he may try to get out of France on a small boat, from an uncontrolled port. It's a possibility we should cover off. We know he has travelled to Marseille from Avignon. I would doubt he plans to get on some ship out of Marseille because entering a seaport environment has its own security challenges for him, and the same with airports, so what else might a fugitive in Marseille try? A small boat is definitely a possibility, and not from the port at Marseille. In my view he is likely, if small boat escape is his plan, to use a boat from one of the many small harbours along the south coast near Marseille.'

In saying this Anne was recalling some CIA pre-work she had seen. The pre-work had noted a small boat, most likely sailing from a minor harbour, was a possible escape route for lone or small group fugitives to get to an alternative close-by territory without using a land route or passing through seaports or airports when trying to exit a country covertly. Pre-work was a valuable tool for the CIA. It involved analysing multiple scenarios and possible outcomes, so a lot of the thinking, at least at a high level, had been done before any actual occurrence when pressure was high and time was short. It made responses to any occurrence both timely and more accurate as much of the thinking had been completed and tested previously.

'To that end I have been on to Langley,' Anne continued, 'and we will shortly have satellite coverage for movements in coastal waters for the seas around Marseille. Langley has arranged with the military to task a number of low orbit reconnaissance satellites to cover a swathe from Perpignan in the south west to Nice in the south east, and extending out from the French coast for about two hundred kilometres, or further if we require.'

René was surprised the US would make such a commitment just on the possibility of a small boat being the escape mechanism for the terrorists. He expressed that surprise to Anne.

'René,' Anne responded, now icy cold and focused, 'if you accept Ahad is looking for a covert country exit, and we know he has travelled to Marseille, and we assume he will seek to avoid normal controlled exit places and modes because of interception risk, doesn't that make private small boat use a possibility we should cover off? What else could he do? He will be thinking he has to get out of France as soon as possible. Possibly he could be planning to hide up somewhere and to leave after some passage of time, but I doubt it. Passage of time won't lead to a reduction of alerts in the short to medium term, and he will know that, and he will be uncomfortable trying to remain hidden within French territory. No, I think he will try to get out of France soonest, like tonight, before French authorities seal the borders more efficiently, as they will over the next twenty four hours.'

René knew Anne was right. He hadn't previously met someone working in intelligence who was as focused as this woman. She could be forthright, but that was a characteristic René had always appreciated in other people, so long as it was well founded forthrightness. One of his

149

pet hates was people who, as he described it, "pussy-footed" around issues that really needed to be addressed and definitively dealt with. No risk of that with Anne.

'Okay Anne, if your government is good enough to help in this way, I will take all you can give me. I thought small boat country exit was a longshot when you first raised it, and maybe it is, but it's something we should consider and it complements all the other arrangements being put in place at present to locate Ahad, so I'm happy we do what we can with this reconnaissance assistance. We will need to sort out how we identify a suspicious small boat movement. The amount of sea traffic in the area is very large.'

'Thanks René. There is a pre-work for reconnaissance filters, which I will take you through shortly.'

During a quick discussion with Langley via her encrypted sat-phone Anne had asked about reconnaissance availability to cover an area off the southern French coast. Because her secondment had been part of the President's offer to assist France, the President had instructed that Dr Davis get all she reasonably required to help in her secondment. The powers at Langley took that to mean if she wanted something such as localised satellite reconnaissance, she got it.

As they drove along a major auto-route, Aashiq settled back into his seat in the Citroen borrowed from a friend of the late Youssef in Marseille. They were headed to the small coastal commune of Bandol, on the coast between Marseilles to its west, and the city of Toulon to its east.

The Bandol area is well known for its wines, particularly the familiar smooth reds made using the Mourvedre grape, which is the major variety in the region. But Aashiq wasn't interested in the area's wines. Bandol also had a small fishing boat base, adjacent to a large marina which was home to a full range of pleasure boats. The fishing boats at the base were all busy working boats, but one of them, *La Belle Marie,* was something more.

La Belle Marie was owned by a man known simply as "the Skipper" who had called his boat after his wife of thirty years. The Skipper was willing to take people wherever they wanted to go on his boat, and what made him different from other boat operators on the southern French coast was that he would do so without asking who his passengers were, why they wanted to travel, or what they carried.

Aashiq had always proceeded on the basis the French authorities would put in place additional border scrutiny following the attack, so departing France on an airline or on a regular ferry would have been too risky. He didn't want to risk border interception. He also knew main roads would be being watched and traffic checks undertaken. Usually deserted so far as the presence of any officialdom was concerned, given the free cross-border movement allowed in parts of Europe, points at which roads entered countries adjoining France were now likely to be the subject of long queues as vehicles were stopped, drivers questioned, and, in some cases, vehicles searched. Instead Aashiq had planned an alternative way to exit France. He had arranged for a fishing boat to take him to Sardinia, and land him in the fishing village of Alghero on the north-west coast of Sardinia. From there he would make his way to Tunisia and then back to Syria.

Aashiq had approached the Skipper some time ago about passage on *La Belle Marie* from Bandol. He had told the Skipper he was a businessman who needed to travel to Sardinia with a substantial amount of securities in the form of bearer bonds. He had said he would be carrying the bonds to avoid formal banking channels and the usual alerts and interrogatories large overseas currency transfers always raised. A sufficiently thick wad of cash for the Skipper, seven thousand euros taken that day from Aashiq's pre-loaded Euro Currency Card, and the boat was his to take wherever he wanted, no questions asked, no records kept, and, importantly for Aashiq, without risking any formal exit processes when leaving French territory, or arrival processes when reaching Italian territory.

The Skipper had not been particularly interested in the reason for Aashiq's requirement to exit France informally, but Aashiq had told him anyway about the illegal currency transfer he was making. He did not want to risk the Skipper deciding he would not carry a terrorist who had attacked France. An illegal currency transfer was an acceptable activity for the Skipper's passenger, but an attack on France was probably not okay.

'Not so fast, you might attract the gendarmes,' Aashiq warned Hussein who was doing the driving. They were on Auto-route 50, and while the motorway speed limit in good conditions, it reduced when it rained and the road surface became wet, was one hundred and thirty kilometres per hour, Aashiq had noticed they were touching one hundred and fifty. Hussein eased off and Aashiq relaxed as he looked out for the exit that would take them to the regional road to Bandol, via the small town of La Ciotat.

Shortly after his speed warning Aashiq saw the sign indicating the La Ciotat exit was coming up. 'There it is, number nine interchange is next,' and obediently Hussein positioned the Citroen to take the approaching exit. Soon they were off the A50, passing the northern outskirts of La Ciotat, a town of about thirty five thousand people with an artificial sand beach, necessary because of the otherwise rocky coast-line and the local mayor's desire to have a town with a nice sandy beach for locals and tourists alike. They had about fifteen kilometres to run to Bandol.

As they approached the fishing boat wharf next to the marina at Bandol, Aashiq looked for the building in which the Skipper had a small office. The Skipper's office hadn't really surprised him the first time they had met to make arrangements to use *La Belle Marie*, with a single filing cabinet, large table, a telephone/fax unit, and a number of straight backed wooden chairs that looked as if they had been filched from a school classroom. No computer Aashiq had noted. After having met the Skipper, he wasn't surprised modern office technology and comfort were not high on the Skipper's priority list. He operated what he considered to be a simple business with his boat, and didn't appear to be concerned about the availability of modern business aids. Perhaps that reflected the dark side of the business the Skipper undertook, which often involved personal furtive contact and secret cash payments being passed, a situation in which computerised records were probably best avoided Aashiq had thought.

'So you want to go to Sardinia this evening?' the Skipper quizzed, eyeing Aashiq suspiciously. While the Skipper had agreed to carry Aashiq he had not expected such a short notice departure. Aashiq wasn't impressed with the Skipper's attitude, particularly as he had agreed to make the trip whenever required and had already taken his relatively substantial payment.

'Yes,' answered Aashiq coldly, 'unless the conditions enroute make it too dangerous I would like to go tonight. As you know I will not be formally exiting France, nor will we formally enter Italy, which I understand is not an issue for you.'

It wasn't. The Skipper had seen it all before. His regular fishing gave him a reasonable income, but it was the special business, such as was being proposed for this evening that gave him the super-profits to support his lifestyle which basically involved expensive women and smart cars. He was married, but Marie had given up on their marriage years ago. They lived together, but it was just a convenience for both of them. She enjoyed their home overlooking the Mediterranean, and the reasonable amount of money her husband regularly gave her. He enjoyed her keeping the home and gardens tidy, and cooking for him when he was not out partying and playing.

153

So they tolerated each other, but the passion that had led to his boat being named *La Belle Marie* was long gone.

'When can we leave?' asked Aashiq.

'I need to check weather and sea conditions as well as arrange fuelling and provisioning of the boat, and I will have to pick up my personal gear from my home. That will all take at least two hours. Then before we leave I am obliged to record sailing intentions with the Harbour Master. I will note a fishing trip is planned off the coast. The usual deep sea fishing grounds are about seven or eight hours south east from here. I suggest we meet back here in two hours.' The Skipper knew also he would have to make contact with his Italian associates to arrange a discreet arrival for his passenger at the small fishing port of Alghero on the north-west coast of Sardinia, which was to be their destination.

Aashiq and Hussein headed in to the small town centre to find some food and get a drink. In a small café they found some sandwiches that had seen better days, but they managed a reasonable cup of coffee. While eating they saw, on the television attached high on one of the café's walls, news reports about some drones being brought down by shotgun fire at the Festival d'Avignon. Then Aashiq saw his picture, the voice-over confirming he was a person of interest to police. They quickly left the café and headed back to the harbour. Aashiq was stunned. How could French security have anticipated and prepared for an attack by poison-dust carrying drones, and of even greater concern, how in God's name had they identified him as the perpetrator?

Two hours waiting was longer than Aashiq had wanted, now it was an eternity, knowing he had been identified and was being hunted. The apparent failure of the attack hurt as well, even though that had always been a possibility. They hurried back to the harbour. The plan was that once they were back at the fishing wharf Aashiq would board *La Belle Marie* and Hussein would take the car on to Nice, where he had some relatives with whom he would stay for a while until things were more settled.

La Belle Marie was a boat of a type recognised by fishermen in the south of France as an efficient and robust vessel, well capable of handling most seas the Mediterranean would normally produce, but it was not large, at just over eleven metres. A wheelhouse with oversize windows dominated the mid-deck. Inside the wheelhouse, at the steering station, a large wooden wheel acted as the helm. It was not the standard wheel for such a boat. The Skipper had acquired it from a nearby yacht builder after he had seen it in the builder's store-room when looking for some other equipment for his boat. He had been taken by the detail with which the helm had been made, with its smoothly machined wooden handgrips and polished dark wood finish.

Immediately behind the steering station with its beautiful timber helm, was a tall and narrow metal table bolted to the floor and mostly used as a chart table. Its harsh grey metallic look was a stark contrast to the detail and finish of the timber wheel installed as the boat's helm. At the rear, hanging over the stern on quick release davits was an inflatable, with a small outboard motor bearing factory labels confirming it was a four-stroke Yamaha producing thirty horse power.

Aashiq was not happy. He would have preferred something bigger than the thirty seven feet he calculated the eleven metres to represent, but this boat had been the only option for his purposes.

Hussein left Aashiq at the fishing wharf and drove off towards Nice, and the relative safety of his cousin's house on the outskirts of that city. His cousin lived in a converted farm-house in the hills near St Paul de Vence, a picturesque walled town on the lower slopes of the mountains above Nice that ran to the north, rising in height and eventually becoming what was known as Haute-Provence, "High" Provence.

155

Aashiq climbed aboard *La Belle Marie* as the Skipper emerged from the wheelhouse. Noting Aashiq's apparent lack of confidence in heading out into the open ocean, the Skipper spent some time telling Aashiq how *La Belle Marie* was specifically designed for off-shore fishing, particularly with its "deep vee" hull profile. This helped the boat ride rough water the Skipper said, although he immediately went on to assure Aashiq that in fact there would be no rough water encountered on the planned trip in any event, as the weather was fine and the sea was calm. Aashiq just shrugged. He wanted to get underway as soon as possible and he had already accepted this boat was all he had available.

'Please stay in here, and keep low as we exit the harbour,' the Skipper instructed Aashiq, pointing to the small area at the rear of the wheelhouse where there was a day-bunk. 'Lie on that as we pass the harbour-master's building, so he won't see you in the wheelhouse if he has a close look at us through his binoculars as we sail past.'

The Skipper knew the Harbour Master, Raoul Penne, was a nosey bugger, who would indeed watch them through his binoculars as they sailed. If he saw someone dressed in day clothes in the wheelhouse, rather than fishing gear, he may ask who it was. Anyway, the Skipper had only declared two "POB", as persons on board were normally shown in sailing intentions, himself and his young deck-hand. The sailing intention had also nominated the voyage as a fishing trip to familiar fishing grounds about one hundred and fifty kilometres south east of Bandol. He didn't want Raoul to have the chance to get on to his radio to raise an inconsistency with him and start asking awkward questions about who was on board besides the Skipper and his usual deck-hand, particularly as it was an open channel which would be heard by anyone in the area with their marine band radio switched on. The Skipper ran a discreet business. Aashiq dutifully lay on the bunk as they left the harbour, not enjoying the unpleasant smell of the stained and lumpy mattress.

The trip to Sardinia was expected to take about seventeen hours the Skipper said. Sailing at 9pm, and after cruising through the night they should reach their destination about 2pm next day. Sea conditions were calm, with little wind, so the Skipper expected to be able to maintain a cruising speed of about sixteen knots.

As a result of the Schengen Agreement, to which both France and Italy are parties along with a number of other European countries, arrivals from France entering Italian territory are not normally subject to formal border entry checks by the Italian authorities. Given the attack on the Festival d'Avignon the last few hours had seen that situation change, but not in a way that would affect Aashiq.

The port at which Aashiq planned to land, the small fishing port at Alghero, was some distance south of the main passenger port serving that part of Sardinia, Porto Torres. The docking of a small French fishing boat in Alghero would attract no attention and in any event what Italian border control there was in the area, from which the French might seek assistance, operated at Porto Torres. Alghero was well away from any random checks of passengers arriving from France which the Italian authorities might have been asked to carry out by their French counterparts.

Once ashore in Sardinia, Aashiq planned to make his way south on a regional bus to the port of Cagliari. He had planned on the basis that when he reached Cagliari he would be able to use established connections Daesh had there to secure passage on a freighter to Tunis, and once in Tunisia the rest of his trip back to Syria would be relatively easy.

Aashiq settled back on the bunk and dozed, knowing it would be a long night because he never slept well at the best of times, let alone on a smelly, lumpy mattress in the back of a wheelhouse in a small boat making an illicit trip across the Mediterranean.

The early morning sun through the wheelhouse windows woke Aashiq. He had slept fitfully, vaguely conscious of noises and movement on the boat as he dozed, and he still felt tired. It was a beautiful cloudless day, the Mediterranean was relatively flat and there was no wind. Forward, to their left as they made their way south, therefore to our south east Aashiq thought, pleased with his basic situational awareness, was a smudge of brown low on the horizon.

'It's the high country of *Corse*,' said the Skipper in response to a query from Aashiq, using the French name for Corsica. 'We will see the Sardinian coast in a few hours.'

Aashiq felt unwashed and unkempt, so he set about boiling a jug of water which he then poured into a large pot he had found and squatted down on the foredeck to wash, as best he could in the circumstances.

Aashiq was looking forward to seeing al Khayr and reporting to him about the attack. After seeing the news reports while waiting for *La Belle Marie* to be made ready to sail the previous evening, he knew the drones had been destroyed by some shotgun blasts, but he was not sure of the extent of the ricin dispersal nor how many people would have been affected before the drones were shot down. If success was the measure of terror created by an attack, he was confident this attack had been successful. The news bulletins, notwithstanding they reported destruction of the drones, had reflected high degrees of angst as the French government, the public, and security authorities tried to cope with the horror of drones covering a crowd with poisonous dust.

While Aashiq was disappointed his drones had been shot down, a new form of terror attack had been able to be launched. An attack that would have done some damage to people in the town square, and importantly, an attack that would have created more fear. The terror he and his cohorts wanted those in the West to suffer.

Chapter 12

The US military has a number of reconnaissance satellites deployed for earth surface observation. They enable detailed observation of selected targets, via close-look image capture in particular. Computer enhanced super-high resolution gives viewers the ability to see relatively small details from a significant height. The satellite shots the US government released of Osama bin Laden's compound in the Pakistani city of Abbottabad, and of people sighted in the compound's enclosed yard, is a relatively recent and well known demonstration of what can be obtained from space observation. But those shots only told part of the story. The capability of the extreme high resolution now available in the latest iterations in surveillance from space technology, and the detail that can be viewed after the computers have done their work on images captured from space, are now much more advanced and remain strictly classified.

If not in high geosynchronous orbit, which allows a satellite to effectively hold its position over one area of the earth's surface, satellites can only provide surveillance of selected areas of the earth's surface as they pass overhead. Sequencing passes by multiple satellites can produce near continuous coverage of a targeted area if no high geosynchronous orbit satellite is available, or if operational requirements mean that a low orbit look is preferable.

Low perigee orbit was what had been required in the watch for any signs of a country exit attempt by the Avignon attackers, so that was what the United States military was providing to meet Anne's request. A series of satellite passes from low perigee orbit satellites. This form of satellite observation was available as the US military had already programmed some of its reconnaissance satellite resources to be at their lowest height passing over the Mediterranean because there was a lot the United States wanted to watch in that area, especially at the eastern end of the Mediterranean as the satellites passed in the vicinity of countries such as Turkey, Syria, Israel, and Iraq. But for now the focus was further to the west, off the south coast of France.

CIA officers constantly undertook pre-work in developing what they referred to as activity options, reflecting a range of activities a terrorist group might undertake in the course of an operation. It helped the CIA anticipate and identify indicators of particular activity associated with a range of scenarios. Long ago CIA officers had worked up and listed likely elements in any attempt at covert country exit by small boat following a terrorist event. They had developed a series of actions to help meet such a situation. Near space observation of affected waters was one such action. As a consequence of the pre-work completed, a small boat escape scenario was the subject of a reaction plan should an attack occur which triggered the relevant parameters. That had been Anne's pre-work recollection and she had requested, and had now received, the surveillance coverage necessary to cover off the possibility of small boat exit from southern France following the Avignon attack.

The satellite reconnaissance Anne had requested and had been granted in this case was subject to her tasking. Reporting at first level was to intelligence officers in a special ops room set up at CIA headquarters in Langley, but Anne and René were being given immediate raw data via a special link René had arranged to be set up in DCRI's Marseille office where they had based themselves. Anne's sat-phone link remained available for any voice communication required, but the surveillance picture was up on a live screen for viewing by Anne and René in the DCRI control room, and gave them first and best raw intelligence. Any analysis could follow if required.

The satellite surveillance had been established within five hours of the attack. Now, the data plotted in Langley as received from the satellites were showing on the electronic screen in front of Anne and René. At this stage there were six targets on their screen. An identity tag was attached to each target, showing any relevant comments about the target.

Not every vessel could be tracked and reported on, there were just too many. The pre-work protocol had established filters that had resulted in observation reports being limited to small vessels observed more than twenty five kilometres from the coast and travelling away from the coastline. There were only four small vessels more than twenty five kilometres out which were being plotted and shown on Anne and René's screen, and they had been photographed earlier. Three were sailing yachts and one was a large private motor cruiser according to their screen tags. Their type and position made it unlikely they were being used by terrorists trying to escape France.

Large vessels such as container ships, ferries, and the occasional cruise liner were not plotted. They were unlikely to be used by the attackers to make an exit bid it had been reasoned as part of the original pre-work on this scenario, as those vessels would have been subjected to checks and controls at time of boarding or loading.

Any small boat appearing to maintain a track towards either Spain or Italy from the French coastline via a close coastal route was also plotted, even though within twenty five kilometres of France's coast, because that cruise parameter could indicate country exit notwithstanding they were not outside twenty five kilometres. There were two such vessels, both on course for Italy. Both were tagged on the screen.

Anne and René hoped the filter protocol adopted was right, accepting that every vessel couldn't be efficiently tracked, but they saw no reason to adjust the pre-work parameters. The active scenario was to look for something moving away from the country of attack towards some alternative territory within proximate range, and if it was a small vessel it was treated as suspicious until proven otherwise. That fact, and the filters to be used to decide what to track, reflected a lot of thinking and discussion at some earlier time when the pre-work was being developed.

Changes to pre-work outcomes would only be made for good reason if something that could not have been anticipated developed in an actual situation which made some of the pre-work logic suspect, or at least likely to benefit from some flexibility in approach. That would be unusual, but possible, as an ability to react to fresh information remained important. There was however always a recognition of the value of the thought, analysis, and discussion that had taken place to establish the parameters of pre-work activity, all at a time when there was less pressure and when those involved had more time to fully consider and plan. Pre-work protected against an over-reactive approach in real time, as well as providing guidance as to actions to be taken.

The vessels identified and tagged where either outside twenty five kilometres from the coast and maintaining a course away from France, or moving towards Italy via a close coastal route. The small boats heading via close coastal route to Italy would be met on arrival. Those heading away from France, out to sea, would continue to be watched in the interim.

As darkness fell no new targets had been logged on the screen. No further vessel, looking suspicious as a result of its size and course, had been observed. The satellites switched to infrared cameras to continue their surveillance in the dark. Just before midnight, a satellite's infrared cameras picked up a small vessel moving away from the French coast on a course towards the south east. There had been a coverage break between the satellites which had affected continuous surveillance, so this target was in the nature of a pop-up. It was already forty four kilometres from the French coast when first observed. By assuming the vessel had maintained a relatively constant course which was backtracked using a reciprocal of that course, those in the ops room in Langley were able to calculate the area of the French coast from which the vessel had probably emerged.

'Run the track back on that one, and it looks like it's come from an area between Marseille and Toulon,' said the young man in charge of track plotting. 'Its current speed and position indicate it left the coast around two and a half hours ago. That's around twenty one hundred hours, French time. That's an unusual departure time given daylight hours. All our other small boat targets had estimated sailing times no later than sixteen hundred hours French time. So we should look closer at this one.'

One of the pre-work parameters had departure time as a factor affecting degree of suspicion. It was thought a small boat sailing out to sea at night should be rated as worthy of special attention because night sailing was not the norm for small boats. This was particularly so when it appeared to have emerged from a part of the coastline close to where a suspect had been known to be. Again, as in all intelligence, nothing definite, but useful indicators in the world of possibility and probability assessments.

Anne was advised about the degree of suspicion the sailing time and origination point had created, by a sat-phone call. A small boat sailing at that hour and heading directly out to sea from an area of interest was definitely worth looking at she thought. May be nothing, but the question should be asked. And it was time to do something more on the ground.

'René, we need to get the police to focus on small ports along the coast between Marseille and Toulon. We have a reciprocal track calculation indicating a small boat moving away from the coast likely sailed from one of those ports. Police need to find the port from which the boat sailed, probably around nine tonight. It's the only one emerging from the French coast in that area tonight and continuing to cruise away from the coast.'

René had been delighted when Anne had told him the CIA had ensured the US military had put low orbit satellite surveillance in place to cover coastal waters to the south of France. France didn't have such capability available and the coverage provided by the US would help should the attackers' escape have been planned to take them out of France by sea. Now a possible result. He spoke to the anti-terrorist commander in Marseille, who had remained on duty with elements of his team to help with the manhunt.

'Have checks made of all small ports and wharves in every coastal town between Marseille and Toulon. We want to know who and what sailed any time after, say, twenty hundred hours this evening, and where they were going. I have looked at the topographical map covering this area, and it looks to me as if you have about ten or so places to check, from the port near Cassis through to Sanary sur-Mer. Get on to it please.'

By six o'clock the next morning all possible ports identified had been checked, the necessary people woken where required and questioned. One such person, a very grumpy Raoul Penne, who was the harbour master at Bandol, upset about being woken "in the middle of the night", had confirmed a fishing boat had sailed about nine the previous evening, off on a fishing trip to the usual grounds about one hundred and fifty kilometres south east of Bandol. And no, apart from the owner of the boat, *La Belle Marie*, he didn't know who else was on board, but expected it would be the deck-hand. Sailing intentions had recorded only two persons on board, he said.

That information wasn't as electrifying as Anne had hoped it might be. Just a fishing boat off to its fishing grounds. A night-time transit to the fishing grounds made sense, as it would be on-station, ready to fish, as dawn broke. An electronic tag was attached to the relevant target showing on the screen, noting it was a fishing boat on a fishing trip to grounds one hundred and fifty kilometres south east of Bandol. The tag was noted as "Plot 7".

Neither René nor Anne had slept during the night, although at different times both had briefly dozed in their chairs in front of the large screen showing all the target plots. Now Anne sat upright very quickly. On the screen all the small boat plots made and being followed were noted. She had been lying back in her chair looking at each plot in sequence, thinking about what was known of each plot and what the target the subject of the plot was doing. No plot was doing anything unexpected or untoward. Then she had seen it. Plot 7 was doing something that didn't fit its tag.

'René, the tagged fishing boat, *La Belle Marie,* Plot 7, said to have sailed from Bandol last night at twenty one hundred hours, bound for fishing grounds one hundred and fifty kilometres south east. It has just cruised past a position that is two hundred kilometres from Bandol.'

'You're right. That doesn't match what it's meant to be doing.'

Anne was already on her sat-phone to Langley.

'I've asked for a special close image recon on Plot 7, fishing boat *La Belle Marie'* she said to René. 'We should have something within the hour.'

The military satellites tasked to meet Anne's request had the latest in super-resolution imaging, and could pick up the detail of very small objects from ninety to one hundred kilometres above the earth's surface, which is the level their low perigee took them to as part of each earth orbit. For precise imaging taken from that height to be useful, advanced computing power was required, with super computers working on individual pixels in the images captured to allow those images to show the necessary level of detail. The degree of enhancement required to allow adequate viewing of detail captured sometimes involved computations measured in quarter hour blocks. The world did not know about this degree of capability, the US military keeping it a closely guarded secret, but a lot could now be seen from near space. Imagery intelligence had come a long way in recent years.

In fact it was fifty three minutes later Anne received a data link message with confirmation of boat name, and close observation images. The first image was taken from a rear quarter position, clearly showing the boat's name, the aft deck and back of the wheelhouse. The second image, taken shortly after the first as the satellite continued its path across the sky, was from the front quarter. It showed the wheelhouse from the other side and the foredeck. On the foredeck was a man sitting bare chested who had been caught by the camera looking out over the sea, a position that enabled the advanced cameras in the low orbit satellite to capture his facial features. The image had been the subject of a lot of computer manipulation on receipt at Langley, and now presented relatively clear of distortion. The classified computer enhancement programmes and techniques the United States had developed had manipulated every single pixel of the thousands held in the relevant image. Anne thought the resulting image useful, but René had his doubts. 'The face isn't that clear to me Anne,' said René, 'but I will arrange for it to go through our facial recognition systems to see if a computer can recognise the image.'

Facial recognition algorithms use and compare features from a subject's face to make a match with a face with similar features held in a database. Analysis of the relative position, size, and shape of features, called "landmarks", such as the eyes, nose, jaw, and cheekbones is undertaken by the programme used. This is the so-called geometric method. On high priority cases, such as this, a second approach is always added, in case the geometric approach does not accurately record a hit. This second approach is known as the photometric approach, and it uses statistical data collected by assigning values to different parts of an image and then comparing those values with a template which removes variances to assist identification.

While they waited for any identification of the person seen on board the boat *La Belle Marie*, René and Anne continued looking through the other live plots to see if any other target had become of interest. None had.

When René took a call on his secure line, Anne knew from his reaction to what he was being told that it was good news. René disconnected his call, and, smiling at Anne, reported that the facial image captured using the new and secret computer manipulation techniques of the United States military had been sufficient to allow the image to be matched by French security.

'The hit was for Aashiq Ahad,' he said gleefully. 'We have him. International security co-operation at its best,' he grinned.

Ahead of them, just protruding above the horizon, the elevated terrain of the Sardinian interior was becoming more visible. The Skipper said they would be in Alghero just after two o'clock, and when they entered the port Aashiq should again stay off the deck and out of sight until they berthed. A car would be at the wharf to take him to the bus terminus, where regular buses ran down to Cagliari, the main port situated at the southern end of Sardinia.

Anne and René sat in silence behind the two pilots as the French military EC175 helicopter which had picked them up at Marseille-Provence Airport cruised towards Sardinia at 6000 feet. With them in the helicopter were four members of the elite anti-terrorist squad which had been put into Avignon as part of the preparations to protect the Festival d 'Avignon when an attack was just a possibility, based on analysis of a number of information strands pulled together by a special algorithm used by French security.

Then a possibility-based intelligence scenario had been developed. It had quickly morphed into a probability, and then a reality, as the threads were linked and developed by two very capable intelligence officers working together, one from DCRI the other from the CIA.

Another EC175 flew with them, slightly behind and five hundred metres out to their starboard side. As well as its two pilots, it carried six members of the anti-terrorist squad.

Powered by their twin Pratt & Whitney Canada PT6C-67E turbine engines, the helicopters were flying at their maximum continuous cruise speed, one hundred and sixty knots. At their present rate they would reach the coastline at the northern end of Sardinia shortly before midday.

René knew they would have to wait to see where *La Belle Marie* was going, but he thought it would probably be somewhere on the Sardinian coast. It wasn't *Corse,* because the last report had the boat virtually paralleling the Corsican coast about eighty kilometres out, so it looked like the north or west coast of Sardinia was the planned destination for *La Belle Marie.* Time would tell he thought.

The French foreign ministry had been busy in the last hour. Would the Italians let the French anti-terrorist squad, in hot pursuit of a suspect, operate in Italian territory, Sardinia to be precise? It was a delicate issue, because the Italians were proud of their own counter-terrorism units, and allowing a foreign service to operate on their soil with firearms to intercept someone shortly to arrive in Sardinia was not something easily approved at short notice. The Italian Prime Minister was required to give the final sign off and thankfully he had been quickly located and had agreed, with the normal caveats about ensuring public safety in all actions and allowing a senior officer from the Italian police force to accompany the French. They were to land at the airport near the Sardinian town of Fertilia to establish liaison with that officer.

René had no problem with these arrangements. They would reach the airport by midday and the estimate based on the target boat's movement on the screen was that the earliest Plot 7 would reach the Sardinian coast would be about 1330 hours if it was bound for the northern coast of the Porto Torres area of Sardinia, or sometime after that if heading elsewhere, probably somewhere on the western coast.

At the single runway airport they were flying to, officially known as Alghero-Riviera del Corallo Airport, but usually referred to as Fertilia Airport by locals, there is a military operational area. At eleven fifty the two EC135 helicopters of the French military touched down in that area. Inspector Angelo Gaboriault, assigned as Italian liaison, was waiting to meet Anne and René.

René led the way as he and Anne left the helicopter. The anti-terrorist squad members, who had been briefed on the target and task enroute, also left the helicopters and once again set about checking and rechecking their weapons and communication equipment.

Inside the main administration building of the military area of the airport, situated beside some neatly laid out paths, lawns and trees, René introduced himself and Anne to Inspector Gaboriault.

'You will be aware of the terror attack at Avignon yesterday afternoon, an attack we were largely able to counter,' René said.

'Yes,' the Inspector replied, 'I am aware of the incident and I congratulate your services in preventing the attack being successful.'

The world media had been full of the attack. Journalists, so often reporting mass deaths by hand of terrorist, had happily reported the success of counter-terrorism forces and in particular the method used to stop the attack. An enjoyable story to write some had thought, but only because of the outcome, attacking drones brought down by a shotgun bearing anti-terrorist squad before the drones could do too much damage. The fact terrorism attacks were still being planned and executed in France was the accompanying dark side.

'Well,' continued René, with a small nod acknowledging the compliment, 'as the foreign ministry will have advised your government, we have identified the principal attacker, Aashiq Ahad. At this moment he is on a fishing boat approaching Sardinia. We are not sure where he will land, but the boat is being tracked and once we have his arrival point we intend to land our helicopters nearby and take him. We want him alive to take back to France to face charges, but we have operational rules that permit use of lethal force if necessary.'

'I understand,' responded Inspector Gaboriault. 'My government would prefer a low key capture and removal, but we accept the outcomes in these matters are never certain. I will accompany you on your mission, as representative of the country in which you are operating, but I am realistic and accept this might unfold quickly in a number of different ways. My request to you is you keep me informed as to your field objectives as the operation begins and is underway. I am unlikely to veto anything you plan to undertake, but you must understand my principal concern is safety of others on Italian soil. If I think public safety is at undue risk I will tell you, and I want you to acknowledge to me now that you will heed what I say should that circumstance arise.'

'Agreed,' said René, hoping that he did not have to even consider breaching that understanding by ignoring some Italian request that may eventuate as the operation progressed. He knew just how dynamic these things could become.

Marie Marceaux had no idea what was happening. She was in her kitchen, a small room facing the east which ensured the warm morning sun she enjoyed while breakfasting. She had just dipped her croissant into her coffee, her favourite method for dealing with her preferred *patisserie,* when she saw a movement through the window above her sink, still full of dishes from the previous

171

evening's solo supper, solo because her husband had a last minute charter. To Sardinia of all places. She was asking herself what that movement was when her kitchen door was suddenly kicked open and she found herself looking directly into the ugly spout of a sub-machine gun, and then two sub-machine guns as a second black clad and helmeted figure entered.

'Hands in the open. Show me your hands,' the first black clad figure shouted at her.

Then, 'Lie on the floor.'

A series of shouted commands, repeated until she complied, totally confused, shocked and frightened. She wet herself.

The Marseille anti-terrorist squad was raiding the home of the Skipper, following the identification of his boat as the vessel carrying the principal suspect in the Avignon attack. Within twenty minutes a shaken Marie Marceaux had answered all of their questions, including the fact her husband had told her he was going to Alghero in Sardinia. In handcuffs, she was taken outside to a waiting van, to be transferred to police headquarters at Marseille for further interrogation. The authorities did not yet know she was an innocent party, uninvolved in any activities undertaken by her husband, so she was in for an unpleasant time for some hours.

The information regarding the likely destination of *La Belle Marie* was passed to René as he spoke with his Italian liaison officer at the airport near Fertilia in Sardinia.

Chapter 13

As *La Belle Marie* neared the Sardinian coast, the land features became more obvious to those aboard. Ahead and to the left was the small island of Asinara. Further down the western coastline was the cape they would soon have to round to reach their destination, the fishing port at Alghero. That cape, criss-crossed with popular walking trails, was Cape Caccia according to the Skipper. As they continued at a steady fourteen knots the Sardinian coastline continuing to grow above the horizon.

Rounding Cape Caccia, Aashiq could see the town of Alghero ahead in the distance, its small port surrounded by stout sea walls with tonnes of large rocks dumped on the seaward side of the walls to combat the waves generated by the strong winds from the west and south to which Alghero was exposed. The town's cathedral sat just beyond the port, dominating the skyline above the various wharves and jetties constituting the harbour facilities, such as they were at a small port like Alghero. No large cranes or gantries here. Those things were reserved for larger ports, but then so was the security apparatus Aashiq was keen to avoid by coming in to a quiet fishing port.

To the north of Alghero, at the end of the bay they were crossing to reach Alghero, Aashiq could see an urban area on the water's edge which he knew would be the town of Fertilia. There was an airport near there he had originally considered using when formulating his plans, but had long ago dismissed. Too much security and associated risk for Aashiq to try to use an escape route involving passage through an international airport which would probably be on an higher alert following the attack, even though this was Italy, not France. No, he was happy with his plan to get a bus from Alghero to travel south for the length of the island, and to hitch a ride on a freighter sailing from Cagliari with the help of a Daesh sympathiser who worked at the port.

As he watched, gulls screeched and screamed as they whirled and dived around *La Belle Marie*, thinking it a working boat which should be producing some morsels for them to seize and fight over. Aashiq also saw the amount of man-made rubbish floating in the sea. He found himself wondering why people were so careless with their rubbish. There seemed no concern by some for the quality of the environment. Aashiq, something of an environmentalist, thought it unacceptable the way people chose to use and dispose of the plastic bags and bottles he was now seeing floating in the sea. Some people give no thought to the consequences of their actions he thought. The irony of his concern for mankind was completely lost on Aashiq.

La Belle Marie continued to push through the water which was now showing the occasional whitecap with some of the swells starting to crest and break as the wind increased a little, but it was still a pleasant sunny and warm day. The Skipper confirmed they would be berthing in about fifty minutes, and reminded Aashiq he should again move into the wheelhouse and stay out of sight as they entered the harbour. More time on the smelly mattress thought Aashiq, but he understood why it was necessary, and moved into the wheelhouse.

While the two EC175 helicopters had been on the ground at Alghero – Riviera del Corallo Airport, René and Anne had obtained an update on the position, course and speed of *La Belle Marie*. It had been tracked approaching Cape Caccia. The destination of *La Belle Marie* was Alghero, according to what the Skipper's very frightened wife had told the anti-terrorist squad members who had swooped into her home earlier that morning.

René calculated it would be about an hour before the boat berthed in Alghero's harbour. René looked at aerial photographs of the area around the harbour given to him by the Captain in charge of the control room. René was looking for a place relatively close to the harbour where the helicopters could land.

'I want to land close, and to be in position before he berths,' René said to Anne as they looked for suitable sites. Anne agreed, nodding her head.

One of the pilots had joined them to give advice on a landing site. 'Here would be okay,' he said, pointing to a large open area immediately over the road from the harbour site. 'It is a large area with an open approach from all directions.'

René and Anne looked closely at the area the pilot had indicated. They could see it was a large area, used for public parking. Tour buses also used it, and in the aerial photograph there were eight buses angle-parked along the town-side boundary of the parking area. Towards the harbour-side of the parking area, separated from the harbour precinct by a dual carriageway road, the area was used solely for the parking of cars. It was a large site, so there should be room for the helicopters to land safely.

'What if the parking area is full, and there is no room to land?' asked Anne.

'Unlikely,' the Italian liaison interjected, 'I know the area well. That parking area always has lots of space where the helicopters could be landed, and if for some reason it is unexpectedly crowded there are open fields you could use just five hundred metres north.'

'Yes, I see them,' said René. 'OK?' to the pilot, who confirmed the open fields would be a "good alternate" if necessary.

Anne called the satellite team in Langley, seeking confirmation of *La Belle Marie's* current course, position, and speed. The boat was reported as appearing to be on course for Alghero, and was now travelling at a reduced speed of 10 knots.

'Thanks,' Anne said to the team sitting around the speaker phone in Langley, 'your help has been much appreciated.' The team leader in Langley, picking up on

Anne's use of the past tense, asked if "eyes were still required" to which Anne responded 'Negative. We are complete on surveillance.'

That suited Langley. They had been on it for a while, and with mission accomplished they were ready to release the satellites for the other tasks to which they had been assigned before the urgent request following the Avignon attack.

'Eyes are off,' Anne said to René, feeling slightly awkward at her terminology which she realised might have been more appropriate in some box office espionage thriller. René just nodded and smiled. Bastard, thought Anne, he's teasing me.

The helicopters were airborne within fifteen minutes, racing along at eight hundred feet about one kilometre inland from the coastline towards Alghero, some nine kilometres to the south.

The Skipper eased back on the throttle of *La Belle Marie,* and slid the wheelhouse door back so he could lean out for a better view than he could get through the marked and salt-encrusted wheelhouse forward windows. He had just received a radio message, coded given it was an open marine frequency used by most of the small boats in the area. His associates in Alghero, who had helped him in the past when he had wanted to bring someone or something illegally in to Italian territory and whom he had contacted about this trip, were warning him of an unexpected reception party at the harbour. They had agreed a warning procedure years ago when first establishing their arrangement, but this was the first time a warning had actually been necessary.

His shore-bound associates had seen the two low flying grey helicopters circling and descending over the town and landing close behind the harbour area. What were helicopters doing landing in the middle of the car-park they wondered? When they saw the black clad figures exiting

176

the helicopters and beginning to move towards the area of the harbour where the fishing wharves were located they knew it was a police operation of some kind. *La Belle Marie*, the French fishing boat they were to assist with an illegal transfer was due at the fishing wharves shortly. They concluded, fairly quickly, *La Belle Marie* was the likely target.

'No berth is currently free' was the coded radio message they then broadcast. The Skipper knew that meant trouble. As he leaned out of the wheelhouse door, binoculars in hand, the Skipper alerted Aashiq to the problem. 'I've just been warned something is going on in the port and we should not berth.'

Aashiq, lying on the mattress at the rear of the wheelhouse was immediately alert.

'What is it?' and then impatiently, 'By God, let me have a look,' reaching out for the binoculars. 'I can't see anything,' he said as he frantically scanned.

The Skipper took back the binoculars. He too could see nothing. He closed the throttle of *La Belle Marie* completely, and as the boat slowed he stepped out on to the deck, resting his elbow on the wheelhouse infrastructure to help hold the binoculars steady against the wallowing of *La Belle Marie,* lying without power in the swells. At first nothing, but then he saw a number of figures dressed in black moving quickly towards the part of the harbour where they would be berthing, the fishermen's wharves in the northern part of the harbour.

'Look again, to the northern corner of the port, that's at the left hand end from here,' the Skipper said grimly.

'God,' said Aashiq again, as he too saw the figures moving towards the area the Skipper had referred to.

'It's some sort of police operation, I guess,' said the Skipper, 'and I fear your currency transfer may be the subject.'

Aashiq had always presumed that while the Skipper was happy to supplement his income by undertaking occasional illegal trips, he would probably not be happy to learn he was in fact helping the Festival d'Avignon attacker escape from France. Quick money from smuggling people or goods, bearer bonds in this case, was one thing, but helping the man who had attacked the women and children of France was another. That was the reason Aashiq had deliberately misled the Skipper when first arranging the trip, suggesting the trip was to facilitate an illegal currency transfer.

'We must turn north towards Fertilia,' Aashiq snapped, 'we can't go into Alghero now.'

The Skipper had a well-developed sense of self preservation, but he couldn't hide the expression on his face which told Aashiq that the Skipper was now wondering whether there was another reason for Aashiq wanting to leave France covertly and slip into Italy un-noticed. He was clearly wondered why a major police operation would be undertaken for a simple currency transfer breach. Illegal, yes, but warranting a squad like this? The Skipper didn't think so.

'No, we go in,' the Skipper said to Aashiq, avoiding holding Aashiq's eyes which flashed with anger as the Skipper brought the boat's power back up and continued *La Belle Marie* on its course towards the harbour entrance at Alghero some four kilometres ahead.

Aashiq knew immediately what was on the Skipper's mind. He would claim he knew nothing other than a man wanted to be taken from France to Sardinia. Border controls did not apply for travellers between France and Italy, so he was not in serious trouble on that score. It was true the Skipper had thought he was carrying someone undertaking an illegal transfer but he wouldn't admit that to the police. He would claim ignorance about Aashiq's reason for travel. He certainly didn't known Aashiq was the person who had tried to murder many of his fellow countrymen with the poison dust attack at Avignon.

Not normally a person of violence, but like many when their back is to the wall and they are confronted with something that must be dealt with, Aashiq moved out of normal character. He was determined he would not be caught. He grabbed a boat hook hanging on the wheelhouse wall and struck the Skipper without any warning. He had no time to debate his requirements with the Skipper.

The Skipper fell to the deck, his hands grasping at his throat where the boat hook had cruelly sliced him open. Blood spurted through his fingers in pulses, matching the timing of each beat of his heart. He didn't continue gasping for breath or struggling to hold his ripped throat for long. He lapsed into unconsciousness after seconds, and then lay quietly until death came minutes later on his deck, now slippery and red with the blood that had pulsated from his throat wound, but which was now almost exhausted.

The young deck-hand standing behind the wheelhouse stood stunned, mouth open, unable to comprehend what he had just seen. As Aashiq approached him with the boat hook in hand, a grim determination on his face, the deck-hand took the only option he thought might allow him to live. He leapt over the side, into the relatively warm waters of the Mediterranean and started swimming slowly towards the shore. While he was a good swimmer, he wasn't sure if he would have the strength and stamina to cover the distance to shore, but it gave him a better chance than facing the mad man with the boat hook.

On the fishing wharf at the port in Alghero the squad was setting up to ensure the area was well covered and they were ready to take Aashiq Ahad into custody once *La Belle Marie* docked. The Italian liaison had insisted there be no live firing where the field of fire was towards the town. Accordingly the squad was positioned so that if there was any shooting it would be away from town towards water. And it had also been agreed the rules of this engagement would require any shooting by the anti-terror squad to be only in response to direct threat to life by Ahad or anyone with him. René understood and accepted that position. He would seek the same if the Italians were wanting to operate in France, although in fact he was not sure he would have approved of such a situation in any event.

The leader of the squad called out. 'The boat is turning.'

René quickly lifted the binoculars he was carrying and saw that indeed, *La Belle Marie* had turned northward and was clearly travelling at an increased speed given the bow waves and spray it was now sending up.

Fuck, what had gone wrong René thought. 'Back to the helicopters,' René instructed, and all began to run towards the helicopters in the carpark. Damn, he must have seen us and decided we were there for him, thought René, ducking and weaving through traffic as he ran across the road between the harbour and the carpark. The helicopters, their pilots alerted by radio, were running through their start sequences preparatory to spooling up their turbines in preparation for a quick departure.

Aashiq wouldn't know for some minutes yet that those who had been waiting for him near the fishing wharves had helicopters available, but he did expect to be pursued by boat. He was also conscious radio alerts to other police units would result in *La Belle Marie* being met at whichever place it now landed. He needed a plan.

Towards the shore, ahead on his right, he could see what appeared to be a resort hotel with some deck chairs and umbrellas set up on the adjacent beach. Not many were occupied at this time of the day, as most people were taking their lunch on the hotel's terrace. Just north of the area with the deck chairs there was an extensive wooded area, about eight hundred metres long and which appeared quite dense. The tree line began about forty metres from the water's edge. He couldn't tell how far back from the beach the wooded area extended, but it must have a depth of some hundreds of metres as a minimum Aashiq thought, given the lack of light beyond the first few metres he could see into the wooded area. That would be a good place to get ashore and get out of sight he thought.

Aashiq took the sheet from the smelly mattress at the rear of the wheelhouse, and tied one end around the leg of the metal table bolted to the floor which the Skipper had used as his chart table. The other end he tied through the vessel's helm itself, the helm that had been the Skipper's pride and joy. Ensuring the sheet was tight between the helm and chart table, he was satisfied the helm would be held in a position that allowed the vessel to maintain a steady course north west along the bay towards Fertilia. He then adjusted the throttle to reduce speed, and noted the speed indicator settle on three knots after his power reduction. It was a slow speed, just enough for the boat to maintain way. But that suited Aashiq. He didn't want too much speed for his next action.

Aashiq picked up his backpack containing his personal gear, including some papers, money, and fresh clothes, from where he had left it next to the bunk. Sliding open the wheelhouse door, stepping over the body of the Skipper and being careful not to slip on the now greasy surface of the wooden deck, coated as it was in the Skipper's blood, he moved to the small inflatable hanging at the stern. He wedged his back-pack under the front seat of the inflatable. He then took a rope from the rear deck, tying one end of it to the eye ring on the front of the inflatable, taking care to ensure the knot was secure. If it came loose it would be a disaster for him.

Measuring out what he estimated to be about two metres of the rope from where it was tied to the front of the inflatable, Aashiq tied the rope at that two metre point to a cleat on the stern rail, similarly taking care with the security of his knot. He coiled the remaining length of the rope onto the front seat of the inflatable. After releasing the safety mechanism which locked each of the hooks

181

holding the inflatable in position, Aashiq pulled the emergency release mechanism controlling the davits. The lines suspending the inflatable from the davits were immediately released, and they ran down, dropping the inflatable onto the surface of the sea immediately behind *La Belle Marie.*

On hitting the water, with the weight of the inflatable no longer bearing down on the large hooks which had been suspending it from each davit, and with the safety mechanism open, the hooks swung free and the inflatable was released. It started to fall behind *La Belle Marie* until the rope securing it had extended about two metres. At that point the knot tying it to the boat cleat stopped it falling further behind, and the inflatable bobbed along in the wake of *La Belle Marie.*

Aashiq returned to the wheelhouse and increased the throttle setting, noting the speed moving towards fifteen knots as he took a fishing knife and returned to the stern of the boat. Now the inflatable was bucking and heaving in the boat's wake as it was towed through the water at an increased speed as *La Belle Marie* motored towards Fertilia. Aashiq clambered up on to the stern rail and carefully measured his jump to the inflatable. He leapt from the stern of *La Belle Marie* down towards the towed inflatable. He fell just short, his stomach landing on top of the inflatable's bow area, winding him slightly, and his legs trailed in the sea.

Aashiq scrambled to find a grip in case he should fall off and be left stranded in the water. His legs were dragged by the force of the water, pulling at him, trying to dislodge him from where he lay across the bow, partly in and partly out of the inflatable. With some effort he was able to get one, and then the other, of his legs up on to the side of the inflatable. Then he managed to roll in. He crawled towards the front, where the rope attaching the inflatable to *La Belle Marie* was tied, and used the fishing knife to cut the tow rope. Immediately he had done that the inflatable fell away behind *La Belle Marie*, and the bucking and heaving ceased as the inflatable slowed until it was just drifting. Aashiq watched, momentarily out of breath from his exertions, as *La Belle Marie* continued to motor away from him.

After priming the inflatable's outboard motor by squeezing the rubber bulb on the fuel line protruding from the small portable fuel tank adjacent to the engine, Aashiq pulled the starter cord. Nothing. He fiddled with the lever marked "choke" and tried again. There was a slight cough from the outboard, but it did not start. Aashiq felt a growing wave of panic. Surely he wouldn't be defeated by a motor that wouldn't start. He squeezed the rubber bulb again and felt if firm and hard, full of all the fuel it would accept. He pulled the starter chord again. Nothing, and then on a second pull the inflatable's Yamaha roared into life, belching the blue smoke that showed it had been over-primed. At least he was now able to move. Sitting in the rear of the inflatable Aashiq wound the throttle fully open and headed for the beach with the wooded area behind it. It would only take him two or three minutes to get to the beach, run across the sand for about forty metres, and reach the relative sanctuary of the treeline.

In the meantime, some hundreds of metres away and getting further away by the moment, *La Belle Marie* and its dead owner steadily cruised towards the top of the bay at about fifteen knots.

Chapter 14

René was stunned. *La Belle Marie* had been, by his estimation, at least four or five kilometres out from the small harbour at Alghero when the helicopters had landed on the car-parking area situated on the town side of the harbour. They had flown inland from the coastline and around behind the town from the airport near Fertilia so they would not be obvious to those on the vessel. Even if the occupants of *La Belle Marie* had seen two helicopters in the distance, why would they assume it was anything to do with them? So why had the boat changed course at last moment? Why had it not come in to the small harbour at Alghero, as the Skipper had originally planned according to his very frightened wife? René shared his thoughts with Anne as they were re-boarding their helicopter.

'It was always possible they may have seen the helicopters René, and decided to be prudent in case the unusual activity they were observing had something to do with them,' Anne responded, 'but I am not sure what else we could have done. We had to be in position before the boat berthed. I agree, at that distance out you would think it was far enough away for the helicopters not to be noticed. Then again, even if the helicopters were seen, why would they be regarded as a threat by those on the boat? But what the hell, they have turned and are clearly not coming into Alghero so we must follow, but carefully. We don't want anyone taking pot shots at us.'

Neither Anne nor René knew the helicopters had not in fact been seen by those on the boat. It was actually the coded radio warning from the Skipper's Italian associates, in response to the squad members moving to deploy around the area of Alghero harbour where the fishing wharves were located, that had alerted those on the boat to an issue.

Once all were back aboard the helicopters they took off, swooping out over the harbour they turned towards

Fertilia, following the direction in which *La Belle Marie* was motoring.

The helicopters climbing to only three hundred feet over the sea. They could see *La Belle Marie* cruising towards Fertilia, about four thousand metres ahead. All were so intent on the pursuit target none of them noticed the dark grey inflatable which had just pulled up on the sandy beach, ahead and to their right, adjacent to a wooded area. Nor did they see the tall slim young man jump off the front of that inflatable and run across the beach into the nearby trees.

On reaching the tree line Aashiq stopped and turned to look back to the bay. He could see *La Belle Marie* continuing to motor towards Fertilia, the tied sheet dutifully holding the boat to its course. He also saw, for the first time, two grey helicopters with French military markings flying past from the direction of Alghero, following the boat.

Aashiq knew then that it was not a police operation by the Italians which had resulted in *La Belle Marie* being warned off as it had been approaching Alghero harbour. This was a French military operation and the black suited figures he had seen through the binoculars were not policemen. Damnation, he thought, they were probably French anti-terrorist squad. How had they located him he wondered? But only momentarily. His priority now was to escape from this area.

He moved on through the trees, and to his surprise found the wooded area not to be as extensive as he had at first thought. After walking through the reasonably dense trees and associated undergrowth for some ninety metres he emerged on to a road. As a car came towards him he put his back-pack on, smiled broadly towards the approaching car, and stuck out his thumb.

Despite untold numbers of warnings from her parents about never picking up hitch-hikers, when the nineteen year old girl driving her parents' relatively new Fiat saw the olive skinned, tall, and smiling man with a back-pack looking for a ride, she stopped. Lowering her window as she pulled up next to him she offered Aashiq a ride. It was only then she noticed his trousers were completely soaked from mid-thigh down, marking the outcome of Aashiq's leap into the inflatable some ten minutes prior. Instantly she realised something was not right and she may have made a mistake stopping. But she was too late, as Aashiq had already pulled open the rear passenger door behind her and slipped in.

Leaning over the back of her seat Aashiq said softly, into her ear, 'thank you for stopping, I will tell you where to go.' Turning towards him, fear and tears in her eyes, she could do nothing but nod her compliance. For his part, Aashiq let her see his right hand which he had raised over the seat back. In his hand he held a small but heavy rock, with sharp edges. 'Don't make me crush your head with this,' he whispered. 'Give me your mobile phone.' Terrified, the driver handed Aashiq her mobile and continued driving along the road as directed.

Within minutes of take off the helicopters were closing rapidly on *La Belle Marie.* They slowed and flew along some distance behind the boat, still at three hundred feet. No one wanted to risk being shot at from the boat by flying closer, and in any event, there was nothing to be achieved by flying right up to the boat. Better to follow it until it reached shore.

A decision was made for one of the helicopters to go ahead and put squad members down at or near the small marina at Fertilia at the end of the bay along which *La Belle Marie* was motoring. The other helicopter would continue to follow the boat, some distance behind it. Those in the helicopter going ahead were tasked with detaining the boat and in particular Aashiq Ahad when the boat came ashore. The second helicopter would land once that had been achieved and there was no further risk of the boat heading off somewhere else.

As *La Belle Marie* approached the top of the bay and was close to the marina entrance at Fertilia, it did not enter the marina as the watchers had thought it might. Instead it continued on and to the surprise of all watching ran straight up on to the beach where it became embedded in the sand in shallow water seventy metres from the eastern side of the marina, near an area used by locals for boat storage and maintenance.

Four of the squad members who had been waiting at the marina observing the approaching boat moved quickly from the sea wall running along that side of the marina, down on to the beach, and then cautiously approached the boat. The remaining squad members stayed on the sea wall, covering those moving up to *La Belle Marie*. It didn't take long.

'One deceased in the vessel. No one else aboard,' René and Anne heard through their headsets in the second helicopter, still at three hundred feet and hovering just off the beach.

'Land,' René instructed the pilot.

Once down on a small grassed area near where *La Belle Marie* had beached, René and Anne climbed out and hurried over to the boat.

'The deceased has been identified by his driver's licence which he was carrying,' said the squad leader as René approached. 'He is the owner and operator of the boat. Address on the licence shows he lived in Bandol.'

'Ok, thanks,' said René wondering where Ahad had got to. We had him on the boat when it was a long way out from the Sardinian coast and the boat has not been observed calling anywhere or meeting another boat during the satellite coverage he thought.

Then the squad leader answered the question in René's head.

'The davits are trailing their lines. They have been released. The boat's tender appears to have gone.'

Fuck, that's what Ahad has done René realised. He's off the boat in its tender. Where did that happen?

'Two of you stay and secure the boat until the local police arrive,' ordered René, knowing his Italian liaison would be there at any time, having driven the short distance from Alghero. 'The rest of you back into the helicopters and look for a small craft that could be the boat's tender. It may be at sea, so watch for wake which might make it easier to spot, or it may already have landed on the shore somewhere, so look for something abandoned on or near the shoreline.'

One of the helicopters was to scour the sea and shore in the bay to the south west of Fertilia, the other, in which René and Anne were travelling, was to scour the sea and shore in the bay to the south east of Fertilia, right back to the town of Alghero.

Within fifteen minutes the helicopter carrying René and Anne had spotted the abandoned grey inflatable on the beach just north of a resort hotel, and opposite a relatively large wooded area that came down towards the water's edge. They landed in the hotel car-parking area and made their way to the abandoned inflatable. It bore markings confirming it was the tender from *La Belle Marie*. There was no sign of Aashiq Ahad and questions of hotel staff and guests elicited nothing more than the fact that a lone man had driven the inflatable on to the beach about thirty minutes ago, and then had got out and moved into the adjacent trees. No one had seen him since. A sweep of the wooded area quickly organised by René revealed no sign of their fugitive terrorist.

It was almost two hours since they had lost Aashiq Ahad, and they were back at the military office at the airport near Fertilia. René was deflated. He looked at Anne.

188

'We had him, and then *phiit,* he's gone,' said René, making a strange sound using his tongue against his pursed lips intended to help him describe a sudden and mysterious disappearance. 'He must have been bloody quick getting off that boat and getting to shore, because we were airborne and in pursuit within eight or nine minutes maximum, after seeing his boat turn.'

'I agree René, it's disappointing he has escaped when we were so close, but at least we know he is in this area somewhere and the police have an extensive search underway around where he came ashore.'

'The Italians want to take over now,' René responded. 'Operating our squad on Italian soil when we were in in hot pursuit of someone fleeing France was okay, but now they say this has become a local manhunt and they don't want the squad to continue as prime operators. You and I have been invited to stay and participate in liaison roles.'

'Paris has confirmed the squad should stand-down. Because of sensitivity to the squad being on Italian soil in an operational capacity the Italian government now actually wants them out of the country. Talk about changing your mind,' René exclaimed rolling his eyes at Anne to emphasise how dumb he thought that decision was. 'I am going to position the squad in Bonifacio, which is the closest French town to Sardinia. They will be only twenty minutes flight time away from Alghero if they are to re-engage in this operation. We are permitted to keep one helicopter here in a transport role, which we should do.'

Anne nodded. She knew Bonifacio from a holiday on the island of Corsica many years ago. A small town at the southern end of that island. It had a port providing facilities for ferries and private craft, and, she recalled, there was a lot of orange-tiled roofs on the buildings atop the rocky promontory on which the town was situated, with steep cliff faces on the seaward side. The cliffs were made up of limestone, giving them a chalk-white appearance. The softness of the limestone also allowed the sea to erode

189

and sculpt the cliffs during storms, and there were some spectacular shapes to be seen on the areas exposed to the open sea. At least the squad would be close if they got to use them again on Italian soil.

'The Italians are going to raise the level of alert at all of Sardinia's exit points, airports and ports, and will also set up random check points on main roads. They have been given images of Ahad and they will raise public awareness by publishing his photo in both print and electronic media. There will be no comment about any connection with Avignon, just that he is a suspect in a serious crime matter. The Italians are setting up a control room for this operation here at the military offices on the airport. I'm happy the ops base is here at the airport because that's convenient should we need to call the squad back at any time.'

'And as well as basing ops at the airport, the Italians have set up facilities to help manage the manhunt and information received. Contact numbers and personnel are in place for all the services that may be involved, from police and customs, to port and airport security. Radio links are also in place to bring in police reports as they are available. A hot line is ready for calls from the public. Computers, linked to the police data-base, are set to ensure a flow of real-time information as soon as loaded by any police unit, so I'm happy as I can be,' René concluded.

Listening to René, Anne knew all René had described the Italians as doing was in response to comments and questions she had seen René carefully interpose as he had spoken with Italian commanders. He knew what he wanted, but he also knew he should, so far as possible, let the Italians feel they were deciding tactics and methods. Sure enough, the Italians had picked up on the comments made by René. They had set up arrangements reflecting matters he had carefully mentioned in his conversations with them, whether a comment they would no doubt be putting certain things in place, or, something he had asked them about, such as how quickly any relevant police reports coming in would be made available to the ops room. That latter matter ensured the real-time reporting pipe-line was set up.

Anne liked the insight into human, or at least Italian, psyche being demonstrated by René. René had achieved not only participation for himself and Anne in the manhunt and helicopter availability, but also all the facilities he had considered would be valuable as part of the operation.

'Sounds good to me René,' she said. 'Now we need to sit down and put ourselves in Ahad's head. What will he do? He probably already knows he has been identified, and he definitely knows he is being hunted. Sardinia is a relatively thinly populated island with only a few places from which he might plan to leave, and he knows we will be watching exit points closely now we know he's here. It's not going to be easy for him, and once the public become aware of the manhunt and his picture is out there he will find it difficult to move around openly without someone spotting him.'

Aashiq's original intention, when he had been working through the planning of his exit from France some months previously, had been to catch one of the many buses operated by *Azienda Regionale Sarda Trasporti,* commonly referred to as "ARST", once he got to Sardinia. There were regular buses from Alghero to Cagliari, the port he wanted to get to. The route he had intended to take was via the town of Sassari. While not direct, there were more buses to choose from on that route and it was busier. He had planned on the basis that he could melt into the crowds more easily by travelling on a busier route and he would be less memorable among many who bought their tickets on the day and travelled on that route. The alternative was the less busy scenic coastal route with a smaller company where he may be more easily remembered. But that planning was all before the earlier events of the day.

191

He had been forced to kill the Skipper, because the Skipper would not agree to run, and had simply wanted to sail in and take his chances, pleading ignorance of his passenger's illegal currency transfer activity. Of course, the Skipper had not known currency transfer was just a cover story. If he had known Aashiq's true position, the terrorist responsible for the drone dust attack on the Festival d'Avignon, he would have understood Aashiq was never going to continue into the harbour at Alghero once the reception committee was spotted. But now the Skipper was dead, and as unfortunate and unpleasant as that had been for Aashiq, it had been necessary. Now, as he sat in the back of a small blue Fiat, being driven by a quietly weeping young woman, he had to re-plan.

This car will do for now Aashiq thought, but I need to have left it before there is a risk of the car and its driver being reported as missing. He knew searchers would probably be able to locate the car quite easily if a general alert went out, as the road network in Sardinia is not extensive. Neither is it busy. And if the car is reported soon, then having gone missing in the area where he had nearly been intercepted by what he now knew was a French anti-terrorist squad, it would be an assumption that he may well be involved with the disappearance of the car and its driver. So locating the missing car and its driver would get a lot of resource from local police.

Okay, he rationalised, let's assume once the car and its driver are reported as missing those looking for me decide there is a risk I am involved and prioritise a search response involving road patrols and public assistance requests. I should give myself no more than three hours before I quit this car. After that time has elapsed the car will become a liability he decided.

That part of his plan settled in his mind, Aashiq now had to find a good place to dispose of the car. Somewhere it would not be easily seen and somewhere near access to public transport to Caglairi. He still had to get to that port town after abandoning the car.

And the driver he thought to himself? He knew the answer to that difficult question. He could not risk her escaping, or managing to signal to someone she was being effectively held against her will. He would do what had to be done soon, once he identified a suitable spot off the road. Then he would drive the car to another place where he could abandon it, close to where he could get the bus he needed.

Looking ahead as they drove south on highway SS131 Aashiq could see they were approaching an area of higher terrain, and, sure enough, soon they were driving through an area of mountains, although they were not particularly high. Maybe three to four thousand feet he thought. He could see there would likely be ample wilderness areas here which would give him the opportunity to dispose of his driver and then continue on driving himself to some suitable place where he could abandon the blue Fiat.

I have to do it, he said to himself, when he found himself again questioning whether he could kill the young girl driving the car.

Chapter 15

Chloe Moreau was a pleasant and intelligent young woman of nineteen. Home in Alghero for the holidays, she had spent most of the last year studying at university in Nice. This summer she had managed to get a vacation job at a motor home and caravan park on the outskirts of Fertilia, just a twenty five minute drive from where she was living during the university break, at her parents' home in Alghero.

The park was on a small isthmus sitting between the Mediterranean Sea on its southern side and a river-fed estuary to its north. Parking-up and establishing a camp among the trees planted throughout the park was a favourite for those in the caravans and motor homes who flocked to the park every summer.

The University of Nice Sophia Antipolis, to give the university she attended its full name, had an excellent academic reputation and Chloe had been delighted to have been accepted to study there. She was based at the Trotabas campus, and had quickly become enveloped in university life in Nice and her study for her chosen vocation, law.

After completing her first year studies, her vacation job at the park would help replenish her savings as she moved into second year study. She was grateful to her parents, both of whom were not particularly well-off school teachers. They had not only found her a hard-to-get vacation job, by calling in a favour from the owner of the park who was an old friend of theirs, but they had also supported her in taking up a legal career. They had helped, so far as they could in their relatively straitened circumstances, with some material assistance. Like the two thousand five hundred euros they had given Chloe to cover some of her expenses when she had got low on funds two thirds of the way through the academic year. That was a lot of money for them, but they had provided it without hesitation at the first indication Chloe was going to struggle financially to get through the remainder of her year.

Chloe had been on her way to work her afternoon/evening duty at the park when she had stopped to pick up the hitch-hiker who had grinned at her as he thumbed a ride. She had thought he looked nice, and she hadn't noticed his wet trousers until too late. Now he was sitting behind her, forcing her to drive past the park where she was meant to be beginning work for the day, through the outskirts of the town of Fertilia, before turning north and heading in to the country. And, this man she had offered a ride was now sitting close behind her with a rock in his hand which he had said he would smash into the back of her head if she did not do as she was told. She was a very frightened young woman, but she was also intelligent and brave. Her mind was racing as she tried to calm herself and think through her situation, and what she may be able to do to stay unharmed.

Aashiq was also busy thinking about what he would do. The arrival of security forces at Alghero had been unexpected and his escape plan had been seriously disrupted by their intervention. He had managed to evade them so far, but he knew a manhunt would be underway. And this girl driving the car, she had to be removed from the equation. He could not leave her to talk to those seeking him. While he hated personal confrontation and violence, which he found quite different to the distant engagement that came from launching a general attack against the public via his drones, he knew he would have to kill her. He had already had to attack and kill the Skipper, and he had now decided, despite his abhorrence of being directly involved in violence, that he could do it again with this girl, because he had no other choice.

Instructing Chloe to follow the main highway, Aashiq continued reviewing his options. He recognised his slight sense of panic. He must be calm. It was affecting his ability to rationalise clearly all factors affecting his plan to get to the southern Sardinian port of Cagliari undetected.

Once there he would contact a person whose detail he had been given. That person in turn would introduce Aashiq to a crew member on a freight boat which regularly sailed between the ports of Calgliari and Tunis. It wasn't a smart boat, but it did valuable work moving small freight between Sardinia and Tunisia. It was the archetypical tramp steamer. Some months ago approaches had been made to Daesh supporters in the area to ensure a person could be carried on one of the freighter's trips from Cagliari to Tunis without anyone in authority, including the captain of the vessel, being aware.

He knew he needed to get himself to a town where he could abandon the car and catch a bus to Cagliari. Aashiq thought the town of Oristano would be suitable. Aashiq did not want to drive the car all the way to Cagliari because it would alert authorities to his presence in Cagliari when it was found, and he was also keen to quit the car as soon as possible, knowing it would be a key factor in the hunt for him.

Yes, he thought to himself, I will find a place to stop where I can deal with this girl, then I will take the car to Oristano, park it in a large public carpark and make my way to the bus station to buy a ride from there to Cagliari. He knew police would trawl through public carparks at some point in their search for the blue Fiat, once that search got underway. But as one of many cars in a parking area it could be expected to take longer to locate there than if it was left abandoned in the countryside outside the town, or even if it was left parked in a street in the town where a passing cop could see it or a local resident report it. Better to be in a large public carpark in town, and that also removed the risk should he abandon the car outside town, of someone remembering a tall olive-skinned young man walking in a particular direction along the highway.

Chloe had been thinking too. Her mother had left her mobile phone charging in the car and had forgotten to take it out before Chloe borrowed the car to go to work. Chloe had been running late and had decided, somewhat selfishly she had acknowledged to herself at the time, not to make herself even later by going back to the house to give her mother her mobile. She had simply put it in the car's dashboard storage compartment. Now it may be useful. Her own mobile had been taken from her by her unwelcome passenger, but he was unaware of the mobile phone sitting in the car's storage compartment.

As they were passing through the area of high terrain he had earlier seen ahead of them, Aashiq noticed what appeared to be a disused quarry.

'Turn in there,' he ordered, pointing to a gravelled road that disappeared between some medium height oak trees towards a cliff standing above and behind the trees. The cliff face showed signs of having been cut away by some sort of quarrying operation in the past. Probably for the collection of the shale-like material commonly used in the area for surfacing paths and drives after it had been crushed.

As the blue Fiat turned off the road into the area he had indicated, Aashiq saw that indeed it was a disused quarry. To the left after they had entered the area there was extensive low scrubby bush cover, and more oak trees. To the right was the cliff bearing scrape and cut markings left after machinery had gone along its face, peeling off layers of shale. A corrugated iron shed, with no windows and what was once a stout timber door, was the only building. The timber door was showing signs of rot, so it was obviously many years since this quarry had been operational. Ahead, over an area of rough gravel and small rocks there was an open area leading to a steep slope down to a fast-flowing stream, some two hundred feet below.

'Drive to the end and stop,' Aashiq said to Chloe. As the car approached the edge Chloe slowed and stopped as required. Aashiq was nervous. He didn't want to kill her but he had no choice. He hated what he had to do. But necessity was his salvation. He had to do it, so expediency displaced morality. There are some situations, he rationalised, where morality doesn't dictate, and this was one of them.

He was already not feeling so anxious about what he was about to do. With the owner of the boat it had been an instinctive reaction and was over before he had really thought. The deck-hand jumping overboard to avoid him had been welcome, because that had saved Aashiq having to attack and kill him as well. But now this girl. It was like an execution process playing out, and he didn't like it. But it was necessary, so it was okay he kept telling himself.

'Give me the keys,' he said. Chloe passed the car keys to Aashiq.

'Wait in your seat until I tell you to get out,' Aashiq ordered as he got out of the rear door. He knew he desperately needed to pee. Perhaps it was because he was scared, or was he just delaying the inevitable? Who knows, he thought, and then suddenly, with some unexpected bravado, who cares? He moved about ten paces to the rear of the car and began relieving himself.

In the car Chloe realised they had probably stopped well off the road for more than this guy to have a piss. If he got her out of the car she would know what to expect.

She had decided on her plan of action. She would run, nothing to lose in that, and better than just waiting for her unwelcome passenger to attack her. But she wanted to do more, particularly if she was unable to successfully avoid what she knew was probably coming. Could she do something to disrupt this guy? Then it came to her.

Chloe quickly took her mother's mobile out of the storage compartment next to the steering wheel, turned it on, and muted its ring tones and notifications. Then she unzipped a small pocket at the bottom of the back-pack her passenger had been carrying, which was on the floor within her reach behind the front seats. She slipped her mother's mobile into the pocket, and re-zipped it. She wasn't sure, but she thought her mother's mobile would now quietly signal its presence to nearby cell-phone towers.

She had just replaced the back-pack and settled back into her seat when Aashiq loomed up at her door.

'Get out.'

Chloe got out of the car slowly, watchful and fearful.

'Walk to the edge,' said Aashiq, nodding in the direction of the steep drop-off at the end of the gravel track they had followed into the area. As she walked slowly towards the edge Aashiq stepped in behind her, making an awkward attempt to conceal the heavy rock in his hand by holding it behind his back. Chloe knew what was coming.

As they reached the edge above the drop-off Aashiq rapidly brought his arm up and swung the heavy rock squarely at the back of Chloe's head. At the same time Chloe did what she had planned. She jumped over the edge, plummeting some thirty feet before impacting the sloping ground among some low growing and spikey bushes, and then tumbling on down the steep slope towards the stream at the bottom. Because she had jumped Aashiq's rock had caught her only a glancing blow to the back of her head, opening an ugly gash which bled profusely, but avoiding the serious damage intended by the blow. Her tumble stopped near the edge of the stream, and she lay there, barely conscious, uncertain whether her attacker would climb down to finish her.

Aashiq swore. He knew he had hit her, but he was not sure whether the blow had been sufficient to be fatal. He looked down, and could see the girl was not moving. It would take longer than he wanted to climb down to her to make sure she was dead he thought. He watched for a short time. No movement.

Through half-closed eyes Chloe could just make out her attacker. He was looking over the edge to see whether she remained a danger to him. She lay absolutely still, despite an extreme urge to adjust one leg which was painfully caught between some rocks, and a buttock that was on a spiny bush, a needle-like spike puncturing her left buttock.

Aashiq moved back to the car, started it, and drove back towards the road. But then, after about fifty metres, he stopped, turned off the motor, and quietly walked back to the edge of the steep drop-off after having sat in the car for a further two or three minutes. He wanted the girl to think he had left. If she thought he had gone and she was not incapacitated she would probably have begun moving he thought, and if that was the case he would just have to spend the time and effort climbing down to her and finishing the job.

Approaching the edge of the drop off stealthily, Aashiq stepped up to the edge and peered quickly down towards the stream. Chloe was in the same position and showing no sign of movement. Satisfied, Aashiq went back to the car and drove away, headed for the town of Oristano.

Chloe had seen the movement as Aashiq had suddenly reappeared and looked down at where she lay. She realised he had come back after trying to lull her into a false sense of security that he had left. She was happy she had resolved, despite her discomfort, to make no attempt to move until she was sure her attacker had gone. She had decided to count to four hundred in her head. She had calculated that would equate to about six or seven minutes which she thought likely to be sufficient to ensure her attacker had left. She counted because she could not risk looking at her watch to check the passage of time, as her movement might be observed. Her decision had saved her life. Chloe had been at three hundred and twenty seven when Aashiq had suddenly reappeared. Now, I have to move she thought. No-one will find me lying here.

Pulling back on to the main road, Aashiq drove towards Oristano, carefully, not wanting to either attract attention or risk an accident. After a short time he saw signs indicating the motorway exit for Oristano was coming up. He took the first exit he came to indicating Oristano, which took him on to state highway 292. After following that road for a few kilometres he reached a major intersection from which provincial highway 56 would take him directly into the main part of the town of Oristano, according to the traffic direction sign there.

Approaching the built up area of the town Aashiq saw a major supermarket complex ahead on his left. "Porta Nuova Centro Commerciale Oristano" the sign said at the entrance to the complex. Swinging in to the large car parking area that always comes with such a shopping complex, Aashiq found a parking place for the car. His trouser legs had almost dried in the heat of the Sardinian summer, so he no longer had to worry about looking suspicious because of his wet trousers. After locking the car he walked to the supermarket at the end of the carpark, and went right through the complex, exiting on the far side of the building. The blue Fiat he had left in the car park was just one of hundreds of vehicles parked in the area.

Aashiq continued walking towards the town centre, and eventually reached the town's bus station near Piazza Mannu, an unattractive piazza surrounded by some new commercial buildings that would never win an architecture award. But parts of the town were pleasant enough. As he had walked past the Santa Maria Assunta Cathedral on his way to the bus station Aashiq had thought it a striking building, with its rounded stone walls and turrets atop the cathedral's two high points. The turrets had reminded him of a Muslim edifice rather than a Christian building. Maybe that's why I like it he had thought.

At the ARST bus station he purchased a return ticket Oristano – Cagliari – Oristano. Aashiq had no intention of returning but if someone attempted to follow his trail and investigate his movements he hoped they would be thrown off, for a while at least, by the fact any enquiry would be unlikely to focus on return ticket buyers. If he was identified as the person buying a return ticket, the possibility Aashiq Ahad was coming back to Oristano would also confuse, for a while.

There was a bus departing in 15 minutes. When it pulled in he joined the other passengers getting aboard, avoiding eye contact with fellow passengers, and took a seat near the back where he felt less conspicuous and from where he could watch those in front of him. Settling back into his seat he again went over his plans and what he would need to do on arrival in Cagliari.

'We have a missing vehicle' said the Italian liaison officer to René and Anne. 'A young woman, a student, did not turn up to work at a vacation park near Fertilia as expected, and an enquiry to her home by her employer resulted in the discovery that she had left for work at least an hour previously. We have an alert out for her and the vehicle she was driving, a late model blue Fiat.'

René and Anne nodded, both wondering if this could be connected to their hunt for Ahad.

'Could be connected,' René said, 'so please let us know as soon as there is something to report.'

An hour later there was something more to report. A motorist driving from Nuoro to Oristano had come across a young woman lying beside the main highway in a bad state. She was semi-conscious, had a large head wound, and was badly cut, scrapped and bruised from what may have been a fall. She was in an ambulance, being taken to Oristano hospital after having received some preliminary treatment when the ambulance had first arrived on site. She had been identified as Chloe Moreau, the student missing from work who had been driving her mother's blue Fiat. She had told ambulance staff about being taken and attacked by a man who had been hitch-hiking just north of Alghero. She had commented that her hitch-hiker had been in clothes which were partially wet. René had no doubt it was their man.

Within fifteen minutes of receiving that information René and Anne were in their helicopter being flown to Oristano. Once there the Italian police transported them from their landing site just on the edge of town, with multiple lights flashing and sirens wailing, to the hospital. Chloe was ready, willing, and able to talk.

The Italian policeman in charge agreed to René asking some questions of Chloe. René took it slowly, while Anne sat quietly across the room listening. Chloe was asked to describe her attacker and step through what had happened, detail by detail. She described picking up the hitch-hiker who had attacked her. He was quite tall, thin, and olive-skinned she said. She told them of the stop at the disused quarry, the jump that had saved her life, and her subsequent slow climb up the bank and scramble across the quarry to the main road.

'I put my mother's mobile phone in his back-pack,' Chloe said. 'I turned it on, but put it into mute mode so it would make no sound alerting him to its presence,' she said. 'I thought maybe it could be tracked and show where we were? The battery has plenty of life because mum had been charging it in her car. It was showing one hundred percent charge when I originally disconnected the charger and put it in the car's compartment on the way to work.'

'You brilliant girl,' René grinned, so happy to hear he may have a way to locate Ahad he did not recognise the slight air of patronisation in the way he had expressed his pleasure with what Chloe had done. Chloe just nodded, and lowered her head. She was tired, sore, and feeling a little lost.

Anne intervened. 'We will ensure you get home as soon as the doctors say you are fine. Your parents are on the way and will be here soon.'

René and Anne both knew this was a great opportunity to locate and intercept Ahad. Ahad would have disposed of the mobile he took from Chloe, but he didn't know he was carrying a second mobile, secreted in his back-pack by Chloe while he urinated.

Mobile phones are traceable when they are connected to a network. But even if not connected their sim cards constantly send out signals looking for a network connection. A request was sent to the network operator supporting Chloe's mother's mobile, asking for an urgent check to be made on its network to see which cell towers were receiving signals from the mobile. Unfortunately, while historic traces were found, showing cell towers which had carried a connection for the mobile in recent days, by the time that day's connections were located Ahad had already boarded his freighter in the port of Cagliari, and had sailed out of the area serviced by the network.

All the reports could show when they finally became available late that night was that Ahad had headed south from the disused quarry, and entered the town of Oristano, and had then moved to the city of Cagliari. Sure enough, Italian police found the blue Fiat parked in a large supermarket parking lot in Oristano.

Cell towers along the route Aashiq Ahad had followed had connected with the mobile he was unknowingly carrying. The cell tower records showed his route south, from the disused quarry where he had attempted to kill Chloe, to Cagliari, and from there it appeared he may have been on board a vessel. The last signal recorded from the mobile was at a cell tower on the southern tip of the Sardinian coast near the small town of Domus de Maria. This last signal, before connection was lost, was as the mobile travelled out of cell tower range on a vessel sailing away from Sardinia.

At René's request the Italian police got him sailing schedules from the port at Cagliari. From those, René, using the sailing time and likely period taken to move beyond the range necessary for network connection, was able to identify the vessel probably carrying Chloe's mother's mobile. As a cross check René had one of his lieutenants calculate the likely course and speed of the vessel as it left Cagliari and sailed south, past numerous towns with their cell towers, until finally passing, and then leaving coverage at the last tower at Domus de Maria. The probable course and speed calculated for the vessel matched the time line shown by the records from each cell tower as the vessel moved south. René was confident he knew which vessel carried his man and where he was going. Now he would arrange a welcoming party at Tunis.

Chapter 16

René sat very still, simply speechless, looking at Anne. What she had just said had taken him completely by surprise, and momentarily he didn't know what to say. He was stunned by the proposition she had made, but as it sank in he realised it was something any good intelligence officer would have to consider.

Anne gazed back at René, intently. She knew she had to take him with her on this idea, and it would not be easy.

While René had been liaising with Tunisian authorities to arrange for the detention of Aashiq Ahad as he left the vessel currently sailing to Tunis, and due to berth late morning, Anne had been on her sat-phone briefing Langley. She had brought them up to speed on the activity of the attacker, Aashiq Ahad, since the time he had avoided interception at the harbour at Alghero. She had also told them about a girl called Chloe Moreau hiding her mother's mobile phone in Ahad's back-pack. Then she had raised with Langley her idea to let Ahad run, with the hope he would lead them to additional targets of high value wanted by the United States.

'The target doesn't know it, but he is effectively carrying an electronic tag. We can locate him using that tag,' she had said. 'He will report to his masters when he returns to Syria and that might give us an opportunity to take out a large section of the Daesh leadership in one strike.'

Dave Luscombe and Bob Newhill, both hunched forward over the conference speaker on the table between them, looked at each other. Bob raised his eyebrows questioningly. Dave responded with a slow, almost imperceptible, bobbing of his head, while he thought this through. Dave's body language is definitely affirmative Bob noted, he's going to agree.

Dave asked, 'Anne, thinking about risks. What if the battery runs out and we lose him that way, or what if he simply discovers the phone and disposes of it, or he doesn't keep his back-pack with him?'

'The girl said the mobile had been left in the car to charge, and was fully charged at the time she put it into the back-pack. So, battery life should mean the mobile is capable of bleating for at least ten days,' replied Anne, referring to the regular network location signals mobile phones send out as they seek a compatible network with which they can exchange information via their sim card to make a full connection to the network if accepted.

'As to discovery of the phone, I accept that's a risk. But two things here, our girl was sensible enough to mute the mobile, so no ring tone or notification will alert the target. Also, she put it into a small pocket among a number of pockets at the bottom of the back-pack, all of which she said appeared empty, so the target has no need to go looking for anything in or near the pocket into which the mobile has been placed. As to the back-pack itself, he is likely to keep it as he travels I think. It was all the baggage he had according to Chloe, the driver of the car he commandeered. It's not perfect I know, but I think it's worth the risk.'

Dave's nodding became more pronounced as he listened. He agreed there was risk of losing the ability to electronically locate Aashiq Ahad, but, like Anne, he did not think it an unacceptable risk. If Ahad took them to elements of the Daesh leadership, that was a prize well worth the risk. In any event, he thought, we have identified Ahad, have his images, and will soon have his DNA from the fishing boat after excluding the two crew members from samples taken. We will find him again if necessary, even if it takes a while.

'Bob, where are you on this?' Dave quizzed.

No hesitation from Bob Newhill. 'Let him run. The risks are well worth what it could lead to.'

'Ok, we agree Anne, but it's too big for us to sign off on without running it past the Assistant Director. We will come back to you in thirty.'

True to his word, within thirty minutes Dave was able to tell Anne he had received the Assistant Director's agreement, although persuading the Assistant Director hadn't been easy. He had been very worried about potential political fallout if Ahad was lost, and it came out that the United States had pressed France to allow the approach now being proposed, letting the Avignon attacker run rather than intercepting and arresting. But eventually he had agreed to put his political sensitivities to one side and accept the intelligence value of what was being proposed. Now, so far as the CIA was concerned, Aashiq Ahad should be allowed to run, and be followed. And while it wasn't expressed, that encompassed killing him at an appropriate time, preferably when he was with other senior Daesh leaders who would die with him.

It was now for Anne to convince René that the terrorist who had tried to attack the Avignon Festival should not be detained as he got off the vessel which had taken him to Tunis, but should be left to travel, probably back to Syria.

'Christ Anne,' René exclaimed, 'if this man gets away I will pay dearly. The security services in France are already in the media cross-hairs for past failures and if the Avignon attacker escapes it will be serious for the services. And for France of course,' he added as an after-thought. 'I can't even start to imagine the media and political outcry if having located the attacker we are found to have let him run and then lost him. I'm far from convinced on this Anne.'

Anne talked to René about the high value targets Ahad could lead them to and how striking the leadership of Daesh would be so much more beneficial for the West's counter-terrorism operations compared to simply arresting Ahad, a single player. Anne took him through the risks involved in doing what was proposed, in the same way as she had taken Bob Newhill and Dave Luscombe through them. She also made it clear to René, but in a subtle way, French co-operation on this was expected given the involvement of the United States to date and the fact it was assistance from the United States that had allowed French security to locate Aashiq Ahad in the first place.

As a Frenchman René hated the concept being proposed. He wanted no risks, and early retribution for the attack on France. He was slightly piqued as well at the reminder in Anne's messaging that the United States was effectively leading this operation and he owed them for giving him the ability to locate Ahad on *La Belle Marie*. He put his irritation to one side though, as he knew it should not be allowed to affect his views on what was being proposed. As a seasoned intelligence officer he recognised there was value in what Anne was proposing.

René finally, somewhat grudgingly, agreed with the proposal outlined by Anne to let the terrorist, Aashiq Ahad, run. He had also decided not to escalate the decision making on the French side. There was a risk he could lose control of the outcome if he did that. He would make the call, and if it came to bite him, so be it. He knew his decision could be career ending for him if it went badly, but this woman from the CIA impressed him and gave him the confidence necessary to make the decision not to arrest and detain Ahad at this time.

'Ok Anne, I agree. We let him run. I just hope like hell this is the right decision.'

When the vessel carrying Aashiq Ahad berthed, he made no effort to disembark for some hours after port clearances had been received by the vessel and unloading had begun. Aashiq had decided he would no longer use his passport. He had seen on the television news, when waiting in Bandol for *La Belle Marie* to be readied for departure, the French had somehow found out who he was and had identified him as a suspect in the attack on the festival in

Avignon. Tunisian authorities may have been alerted by the French to watch for him and in that case using his passport would be fatal. Too much risk to continue with his passport.

Instead Aashiq had decided he would use the special *laissez-passer* travel authority issued to him under a false name when the fighting around his home town of Latakia had been at its most intense. Taking advantage of the war zone confusion at the time he had used false worker's papers to obtain the special temporary travel permit represented by the *laissez-passer* authority. *Laissez-passer* is French for "let pass", and the holder of such a special authority can be permitted to travel without a full passport, but only on a temporary basis. It is not a permanent travel authority. Aashiq could use it now only for the purpose of returning to Syria, but by then it would have served its purpose, helping a fugitive to escape.

With his temporary travel documentation at the ready, Aashiq travelled out of the port area in the front cab of a truck taking cargo off the wharf. No one in the port's gate house asked him for any identification, thinking he was part of the truck operator's team. Dropped off in town he made his way by taxi to Tunis airport.

Tunis airport, or Tunis-Carthage airport as it is officially known, was busy as Aashiq's taxi approached the passenger drop-off area. Moving into the terminal Aashiq went to the ticketing counter for EgyptAir where he purchased a one-way economy ticket from Tunis to Cairo with a short connection on to Damascus. He had no checked luggage, just his back-pack which he could take as carry-on. Once in Damascus he planned to purchase a ticket to Latakia. He was looking forward to getting home.

The EgyptAir ticketing agent didn't seem to care about Aashiq's lack of a passport, nodding her approval at the presentation of his temporary travel authority. People in that part of the world understood country disruption and were used to seeing various types of travel authority, and what Aashiq had shown her at the counter looked fine so far as she was concerned.

Having an hour to fill in before departure, Aashiq went to the area of the terminal where computers were available for checked-in passengers to use on a no-charge basis for up to fifteen minutes. He had to show his boarding pass and was then logged on to one of the many computers by a bored looking young man who paid him no attention at all, other than to input Aashiq's new name, he was now Adad Azrack according to his boarding pass and temporary travel authority, and his flight detail. After fifteen minutes the screen would black out the young man explained, and a fee would have to be paid if Aashiq wished to continue at that time.

Aashiq only needed a few minutes to do what he needed. He entered the name of an email service in the internet search box, and then clicked to connect with the site when it appeared on the screen as one of his search results. Once in the site of the email service he entered an email address and its password. The screen showed the inbox for the email address, but there was no mail showing in that inbox. Aashiq clicked on the email's menu, for drafts. In drafts he found a message. It wasn't addressed to Aashiq, in fact the draft wasn't addressed to anyone, but Aashiq knew it was for him. The draft message spoke of a proposed gathering of friends to celebrate the birthday of a certain relative. The birthday celebration was to be at the house of that relative the next day, at five o'clock in the late afternoon.

The relative did not exist. The relative's name was actually the code designating the proposed meeting place. It was to be at a house in the country just outside the small Iraqi town of Anah, some ninety five kilometres from the Syrian border. Likewise there was no birthday and it was not proposed to have the celebration at five in the afternoon. The reference to a birthday was confirmation it was to be a meeting of Daesh's strategic council, a group comprising those who approved any specific attack proposals formulated by Al Khayr and his lieutenants. The meeting was not going to be at five in the afternoon. It would be at nine in the morning. The protocol for setting times of meetings was that they would be held out in any notification as due to occur eight hours later than really planned. The rationale for all of this subterfuge was to ensure any unauthorised observer of the meeting arrangements would be unsure of purpose and place, and misled as to time.

It was an inconvenience for Aashiq, who had wanted to fly to Latakia once he arrived in Damascus, but he knew he should attend this meeting and report on Avignon. He would have to get himself to Anah, and it was too far to drive comfortably from Damascus in the time available. It was over six hundred kilometres and through some risky areas given the political instability throughout parts of Syria and the different warring factions. He decided he would get an onward flight from Damascus to Dayr az-Zawr, a town in the north east of Syria which was only about one hundred and ninety kilometres from Anah. Just over two hours driving, or maybe three if the roads were still in a damaged state. That would be fine he thought.

Aashiq's flights were largely uneventful, apart from some unexpected moderate turbulence on descent to Cairo airport. That had caused screams and frightened prayers to Allah as many of the inexperienced Muslim fliers aboard reinforced their request for the protection they had sought when commencing their journey. *"Fi Aman Allah"* was recited over and over by those in the cabin afraid of the turbulence.

Once in Damascus, after only an hour in transit at Cairo, Aashiq purchased a ticket on a regional air service to Dayr az-Zawr. On arrival in Dayr az-Zawr he took a taxi to the Badi Cham Hotel Deir ez-Zor, checking in to a room with a view of the Euphrates River. The hotel used the alternative name for the city of Dayr az-Zawr in its title, Deir ez-Zor.

The city was originally known as a quiet backwater in Syria, but with the development of oil resources nearby it had experienced considerable growth in the past and had become a favoured site for the regional offices of various oil companies, at least before the military disruption which was to follow. It was also an area known as the centre of a fertile farming area, with cereals and cotton crops growing well due to the climate, but only where the land was irrigated. The famous Awassi breed of sheep comes from this area. It is a hardy breed, which is just as well given the sometimes harsh conditions found in the desert-like areas too far from the Euphrates to benefit from irrigation.

Aashiq knew he had to be careful. While the city was convenient for his planned trip into Iraq, there had been a siege of the city resulting in widespread food shortages and there was still considerable military activity in the area. The siege was largely over, but it was never clear where the boundaries between various forces were, so unexpected confrontations could occur when driving outside the city in the surrounding countryside. But Aashiq felt confident. Should he encounter Daesh elements he would be able to identify himself as a friend of the Caliphate. If it was the Syrian army he encountered, well he was just a cotton trader from Latakia going to a meeting to arrange some exports. There were risks, no doubt, but Aashiq liked the anonymity that came with the confusion in a part of the country subject to frequent change in the dominant influence of the military and continuing upsets in political control.

Aashiq had decided against getting a rental vehicle. In the current situation they were not readily available, particularly to travel outside the city towards Iraq. Instead, he spent some time in a local coffee house talking to the men he found there to see if someone was available to take him to Anah in a private vehicle for, by Syrian standards anyway, a sizeable fee. Eventually he located a man who would take him and arrangements were made for an early pick-up from his hotel. Aashiq needed to be in Anah by nine am. The driver would pick him up at six in the morning. That would allow for any delay at the border crossing between Syria and Iraq, or a slower trip caused by the state of the roads.

Returning to his hotel Aashiq lay on his bed thinking about what had happened to him over recent days. The attack on the Avignon Festival had been executed, but he was concerned his drones had been taken down by shotgun blasts. He hadn't anticipated such a rudimentary response. French security must have known of the risk of a drone attack, otherwise why were they ready with shot guns? How did they become aware of the risk? He could not understand where their intelligence had come from. What concerned him most was the fact he had been identified by French security. How could that have happened he questioned? He knew his days of operating discreetly, under cover for Daesh, were over. He would never be able to safely return to the West.

He knew also he would have some considerable explaining to do when he met the members of the Governing Council and al Khayr in Anah. He had convinced al Khayr to support the use of drones carrying the toxin because of the publicity it would bring Daesh. They had known the number of deaths may not have been high, but what a story, drones flying over crowds covering them with a deadly substance. That was the true rationale of a terror attack, to create terror. The drone attacks would have been successful in doing that.

While Aashiq took some satisfaction from knowing there would be some fear in the West because of the way the attack had been launched, he accepted there had been reputational loss to Daesh in this, as a result of the shooting down of his drones. Aashiq had seen the media reports since the attack. The media was full of how Daesh had been outwitted and failed. The West was being rated as way ahead with its intelligence work and response. God, it was just some shot guns he though angrily, but at the same time he knew that was a flawed position for him to take. The real question was how did French security know to have shotguns at the Festival d'Avignon?

Aashiq knew he would have to be careful at the meeting in Anah. He was well aware there were some on the Council who would like to see him gone. His media successes for Daesh, and his encouragement of the implementation of social media pressure and reach would not be enough to protect him because some damned infidel had found out about his attack and brought it to a spectacular end, an end the media were enjoying reporting.

Daesh had failed on this one and had been left looking incompetent. The Council wouldn't tolerate such a loss of face, particularly as they had been pushed to accept the mode of attack that had so spectacularly and publicly failed. They had just wanted explosives, and not by drone. Bombs in rubbish bins, or in a car or truck, would not have failed they would no doubt say. Aashiq found himself wondering if al Khayr would support him through the meeting, or seek to distance himself from any connection with the failed attack and its disastrous reputational outcomes. Aashiq would try to get ten minutes with him prior to the meeting to see how matters sat in this regard. It was important, Aashiq thought, that the new guard he and al Khayr represented in Daesh was not side-lined by old men in robes.

Chapter 17

Aashiq and his driver had been on the road from Dayr az-Zawr for over an hour, and had just passed through the Syrian town of Abu Kamal. Not far ahead was the al-Qa'im border crossing into Iraq. Their rate of progress was not as fast as Aashiq would have liked, and despite his exhortations to the driver to travel at a greater speed, they continued to move along at a steady sixty to seventy kilometres an hour. Sometimes even slower when the road became uncomfortably rough in parts, marking the scene of anything from fluvial erosion from the downpours that accompanied the infrequent storms which occurred in the area, to man-made explosions, which occurred much more often.

There was little doubt the Syrian transport network had suffered significantly from underfunding and war damage. It would be a long time before the transport infrastructure would again operate efficiently, and that meant any economic recovery after the fighting finally ceased would be slow. The citizens of Syria, as hard-pressed as they were right now with the war, had little to look forward to for many years.

There had not been many in the streets as they had passed through Abu Kamal shortly after seven in the morning, although some traders had been busy setting up food stalls as part of a market day event. Not that much produce was on offer given the strictures of the war enveloping different parts of Syria, including the areas around Abu Kamal.

Just before Abu Kamal there had been a number of Bedouin tents pitched among low scrub-like bushes, the brown sackcloth appearance of the tents contributing to the arid look of the countryside. There had been a few children outside the tents playing, all of whom stopped to watch the passing vehicle. In contrast, the camels tethered near the tents beyond where the children played continued their doleful chew on their cud, and completely ignored all activity around them, including a passing vehicle carrying two men on a journey to Anah, across the border in Iraq.

As they approached the border crossing Aashiq saw the Black Standard of Islamic State fluttering on a pole next to a small hut where figures dressed in camouflage tops and trousers were standing, ready to check any vehicle and its passengers wishing to cross the border. The black uniforms normally associated with Islamic State had been dispensed with for the more practical, from a tactical perspective, fighter's camouflage clothing. Aashiq was pleased. Crossing should be easier with Daesh in control. If it had been units of the Syrian or Iraqi Army at the border check point he would not have felt quite so confident, because they could be unpredictable. And if unpredictable, dangerous.

Automatic weapons were levelled at the car in which Aashiq and his driver were travelling as they approached the border crossing. Everyone was an enemy until shown otherwise.

'Drive very slowly,' Aashiq ordered his driver, 'and start to slow to a stop when I tell you.'

Aashiq knew enough about the mentality of Islamic State fighters to ensure he did what was necessary to ensure the chance of being shot was lessened. He knew in this war such an incident could never be completely ruled out, but cautious and slow, appearing to offer no threat, should mean they were relatively safe.

Telling his driver to stop when they were approximately thirty metres from the fighters, who were still pointing their weapons at the car, Aashiq slowly opened his door, and lent out stretching both arms out in front of him, putting them in the air in the manner of surrender to show he carried nothing and that he was submissive. Stepping from the car he stood still. He knew if he moved forward without invitation he risked being shot as there may be a concern he carried explosives on his body. He called out a request to speak to the senior person at the border crossing.

A young man who looked to be in his late twenties stepped forward, but stopped at least fifteen metres short of where Aashiq stood. If there was a bomb fifteen metres may not be enough, but it would help if it was not too powerful. More importantly leaving a fifteen metre space gave his fighters a clear field of fire to shoot the stranger should that be required.

'What is your business?' the young man asked, presenting as an older and more experienced soldier than his apparent years would indicate. This war ages and gives experience very quickly. He had a look and tone that said he had seen much more than a young man in his twenties should normally have seen.

'I am Aashiq Ahad. I am a friend of the Caliphate and travel to meet our leaders in Anah.' No need to maintain discretion as to who he was and what he was doing for this audience. The senior fighter would be aware Daesh leaders were gathering nearby for an important meeting. The fact the stranger knew about the meeting indicated to the young border commander that Aashiq was who he said he was. Only a few knew of the meeting.

'You may proceed' he said, adding an Islamic traveller's invocation. 'May Allah lighten your journey and make distance easy.'

'*Shukraan*' replied Aashiq, thanking him. 'And may Allah be with you.'

Weapons were lowered. Sand-filled barrels set up to block the road were rolled away. Aashiq and his driver were free to continue their journey towards Anah. They would be there within the hour. As they drove away from the border crossing point Aashiq reminded his driver of the precautions he should take when he re-crossed the border on his return. Aashiq intended to travel with al Khayr after the meeting, so the driver would be on his own when he came back.

In a pocket in the bottom of Aashiq's back-pack, Chloe's mother's mobile continued to bleat, looking for a network with which it could connect. It had been doing that for some time now. The previous day, as the mobile phone hidden in Aashiq's back-pack had attempted network connection, its signals in Damascus and later in Dayr az-Zawr had been detected in the relevant network systems. The CIA knew this because it had covert pipelines which enabled them to monitor activity on any of those networks.

A watch for this particular mobile had been in place since Chloe had told René about placing it in her kidnapper's back-pack. Those who surreptitiously monitored the Syrian mobile networks for the CIA had confirmed the mobile had been detected attempting to make network connections. But the networks concerned had not accepted a connection from the mobile after exchanging interrogatory signals with the mobile's sim card. It had been rejected as a mobile not approved for connection. No arrangement was in place for a foreign mobile from Sardinia to become a customer on the Syrian networks.

Then the mobile's connection-seeking signals, the bleating, had disappeared completely. That had occurred when the mobile had left cell tower coverage some distance from Dayr az- Zawr, as it crossed the Syrian Desert towards the border crossing point. With no cell tower within range at that time the mobile's signals had not been detected by any network and accordingly went unanswered.

Now, as requested by a prompt from a cellular network which had just started responding to the mobile's signals, Chloe's mother's mobile transmitted detail about its identity, taken from its sim card. That had enabled the mobile to be identified by the network and the network had then accepted the connection request made by the mobile.

The network from which the mobile had received a response and a connection was a very special network. It had to be. There were no cell towers within range of the mobile at present.

In the electronic surveillance equivalent of an internet phishing sequence, the mobile was not actually interacting with a cellular network, but with a military drone. The MQ-9 Reaper drone operated by the Special Activities Division of the CIA, positioned twenty two thousand feet above and thirty five nautical miles north east of Aashiq, contained a sophisticated "dirt box" as it was commonly known by those who worked with it, which mimicked cell-site towers operating in Syria and Iraq. The mobile had reacted as if it had made contact with a cellular network when the dirt box answered the mobile's bleat, and had transmitted its unique verification codes to what appeared to be a network with which it could establish a connection.

As a consequence of the dirt box establishing a connection with the mobile, behaving as if it was a real network, the mobile continued to exchange electronic information with the dirt box. Those controlling the drone at Langley, and reading the signals the dirt box was receiving, were able to identify the communication codes as coming from the mobile being sought. Calculating the mobile's position was relatively simple once the cellular link between it and the dirt box was established and locked in.

Within minutes Anne had been notified of the fact the mobile had been located by its unique signature in a drone-based precision cellular geolocation operation over the Syrian/Iraq border, not far from the town of Abu Kamal.

'We have him near the Syrian/Iraq border René,' Anne said, delighted. 'Ahad, or at least the mobile he is unknowingly carrying, has popped up again. The mobile has been interrogating Syrian networks, but on each occasion, because the network was not able to authenticate a key for the phone, it has been denied access to the network. But now we have it, talking to a drone it thinks is a network.'

'I have told Langley they should get eyes on as soon as possible,' Anne continued, 'just in case we lose electronic surveillance for some reason.' Anne was nervous. To lose Ahad now, because he found the phone, or its battery ran out, or for God knows what reason she thought, would be devastating. But at the same time Anne realised she was experiencing some unnecessary panic. She knew battery life was good for some days yet, and why should Ahad suddenly find the phone now? Settle down Anne she told herself, nearly there.

A short time later advice came through that the drone had established visual contact with a vehicle on a path coinciding with the moving location of the target mobile phone which had linked to its dirt box. The drone operators were satisfied the vehicle they were now observing via their advanced cameras on the drone was the vehicle containing the mobile phone. They had established an ongoing connection with the mobile sufficient to track the phone's position, and that matched the position and track of the vehicle being observed.

As Aashiq's vehicle drove along the narrow track leading to the farm house where the meeting was to be held, he was aware of a number of armed men placed strategically nearby, watching their approach. Good, he thought, the council members must be here already given the number of guards in place. As his car came to a stop in the courtyard adjacent to the large double front doors of the house, the doors were thrown open and al Khayr appeared, smiling and giving Aashiq a small wave of welcome.

Getting out of the car, Aashiq embraced al Khayr.

'It is good to see you again my friend,' al Khayr grinned to Aashiq, 'I am pleased you have come.'

'And it is good to see you again too al Khayr,' Aashiq responded, 'but we must talk before going in to the meeting.'

Aashiq was keen to know where he stood with al Khayr and what to expect during the meeting. Just as he said that another vehicle pulled up in front of the house. Out of the Toyota Hilux stepped the senior Daesh commander for Iraq. Two nearby guards who had been standing near the front entrance recognised him, moved back two or three paces, and nodded deferentially to their commander who went past them without a second look and entered the front door of the house in which the meeting was to take place.

The MQ-9 Reaper drone is a sophisticated surveillance platform and weapon. As well as having the clever electronics of its dirt box, it has advanced cameras for observation. It also carries laser designation equipment and Hellfire missiles. Missiles are guided to impact by the laser lighting up the missile's target.

While the particular Reaper now visually and electronically tracking Aashiq Ahad was based in Iraq it was being controlled by an operator in Langley, using signals which were being transmitted directly to the drone via elements of the United States military satellite constellation. Technology had come a long way since the days in which operators had to be in position reasonably close to the drone's area of operation to be able to send command signals to the drone.

In the control room at Langley the Reaper was instructed to zoom in its camera surveillance equipment and record the images of those getting out of the car and anyone meeting the car. That was done and the facial recognition programmes got to work. Very soon it was confirmed it was Aashiq Ahad who had got out of the car and he had been met by Abu al Khayr, an operations director for Daesh.

The controllers at Langley noted another vehicle, a pick-up truck, had arrived shortly after the car from which Ahad had emerged. No image of the passenger had been obtained because of the hooded robes being worn which shielded facial features from the cameras in the sky above, but what interested the operators of the drone regarding this vehicle was the behaviour of the nearby guards, observed through the powerful camera lens from 22,000 feet.

'That's got to be HVT,' said the observer/weapons officer seated next to the drone's pilot in the Langley control suite when they first saw the pick-up truck arrive at the farmhouse. 'Look at them, backing away and bloody near bowing.' The drone crew were trained to watch for such things. They had already noted and reported multiple guards around the grounds of the house being watched, and that itself had been interpreted as meaning important terrorists were there. Simple folk and women and children aren't guarded in that way they knew.

'Confirmed. High Value Targets likely in the house, and two yet to enter.' An execution was being formulated.

'A quick word before you go in Aashiq,' al Khayr said conspiratorially, 'some on the Council are very unhappy the Avignon attack failed. They think your drones being brought down by shot guns is an embarrassment for the Caliphate and shows our capability as inadequate and too easily defeated. Those who said we should just bomb the festival are saying now we should have listened because the drones were always an unrealistic method of attack, destined to fail.' Then al Kahyr turned and walked into the meeting, with Aashiq following, still unsure if he had al Khayr's support. He knew he would need it.

Aashiq was not surprised by what al Khayr had told him. He understood some on the Council disliked him personally because of his non-traditional style. Any opportunity to criticise would be taken, and the attack's failure was a gift to such people. They had forgotten they approved the plan because it had the potential to be the ultimate terror attack. The delivery of poisonous dust spread over a large crowd by drones would have been a wonderful outcome. The fact the drones had been shot down before completing their work was just an unfortunate result of war, because that was what terror attacks were, acts of war and sometimes matters did not go as planned in war. There would be fresh opportunities as the war continued he thought.

Aashiq would face them and argue all this, but he knew some of the traditionalists on the Council waiting inside to see him would remain unconvinced and may also suggest that Aashiq not be given responsibility to plan and deliver any further attacks, or worse. Aashiq understood the politics, and the advantage some would seek to take from his misfortune.

He followed al Khayr through the large double doors at the front of the house and found he was immediately in a large meeting room. The Council members, some seven of them, were sitting in their robes on various low stools and in some cases, on large cushions. Aashiq could see hostility in the eyes of some. Hopefully the majority will accept this was a well-planned operation which could have succeeded with more luck, and recognise the terror element that had been achieved.

Al Khayr began speaking.

Anne was controlling the operation. Langley had passed all it had to her. She knew Ahad was in the house just outside Anah, she also knew that a senior leader, al Khayr, was in the house. Facial recognition had identified the images captured by the Reaper. The tracking of the mobile phone had confirmed Ahad's presence in any event. But what Anne didn't know was who else was inside the house, although she knew there would probably be other Daesh leaders. Langley had reported numerous guards around the external perimeters of the house and the deference shown by some to arriving persons.

'René, we know Ahad and a Daesh leader, al Khayr are in the house. They have been identified by the Reaper. The mobile's location confirms Ahad's presence, or at least the presence of his back-pack. There are probably others in the house who are involved with Daesh given what Langley has reported it has observed via the drone's surveillance cameras. Hopefully everyone in there is part of Daesh, and not an unconnected civilian, but there is a risk here.'

'So what now Anne. Do we get a special service group in there to capture what could be a large number of high value targets? We know there are at least two, and probably more. Or do take out everyone in the house?'

Anne was worried. Capturing elements of Daesh leadership would most likely yield extremely valuable intelligence, and a raid would lessen the risk to any non-involved persons in the house, but it would take a couple of hours to get some Blackhawk helicopters and special-forces there. And she didn't want any mistakes. She knew the risks of a firefight, and losing men and machines was not attractive. There was also the risk the meeting would be completed and the targets dispersed before she could get forces there. She momentarily wondered about trying to raid and capture, with a back-up to launch missiles if the targets looked as though they were complete and about to disperse before the raid could be carried out, but this Reaper was only carrying two Hellfire missiles and she would prefer to attack a localised group target. Easier to take the targets out clustered inside the house than try to deal with them as they emerged and dispersed. Some would get away.

'On balance I think we should take the house out now while they meet,' she said, outlining her reasoning to René.

She is one tough and capable intelligence officer thought René, as he nodded his agreement. His view was that with just al Khayr and Ahad confirmed as present, a strike was justified. And René thought it likely there were more at the meeting who were of sufficient status to justify a strike.

'Agreed Anne,' René said in a serious tone. He knew there were possibly uninvolved civilians in the house as well, but *c'est la vie* he said to himself, or more correctly, he thought, *c'est le mort,* surprising himself with his black humour.

Anne could confirm anytime and the strike would follow shortly after. Unlike military operations the CIA had protocols allowing Anne, as the senior officer in the field on case, to make the call without seeking authorisations further up the chain.

She picked up her sat-phone and spoke again to Langley.

'Two senior Daesh operatives identified as present, including the Avignon attacker. Likelihood of other Daesh leaders as well. Presence of others unknown. I confirm a strike against the target. Execute please.'

In Langley the drone pilot exchanged looks with his weapons controller. The laser target designator was activated and it was directed to illuminate the large double doors at the front of the house. The pilot held the drone on a steady track towards the house in which the meeting was being held, and the weapons controller activated the missile launch system. Within eight seconds a Hellfire missile had been launched and was arrowing down towards the isolated farm house just outside Anah where a meeting of senior Daesh leaders was underway, a meeting attended by the man who had planned and executed the thwarted attack on the Avignon festival.

Inside the meeting room, just inside the front doors through which he had entered, Aashiq was about to address the council. Al Khayr had finished his introductory remarks and had just asked Aashiq to speak. As Aashiq moved to stand up, he had decided he would be more comfortable addressing the council while he stood and he could also then move about to help him emphasise some of the points he wanted to make, he inadvertently knocked his back-pack off the low stool on which he had balanced it when he had sat down. He was surprised by the sound of a loud clunk as the soft bag carrying only some of his clothes and papers landed on the timber floor. Picking up his back-pack he felt underneath it to see what hard object had caused the sound. He felt something he had not expected.

Unzipping a pocket at the bottom of the back-pack he reached in and found the mobile phone. Holding it in front of him he could not understand how it had got there or whose it was. Then he saw an indicator light on the face of the phone blinking. The mobile was on and it was connected. A look of horror crossed Aashiq's face as the implications of what he had found hit him. He opened his mouth to call a warning and suggest the meeting be abandoned at the same time as he, and the members of the Daesh council he was about to address, disintegrated in the blast of the Hellfire missile as it unerringly followed its laser designator and virtually came through the front door and exploded.

After the flash, heat, and blast, there was silence. Aashiq and the others in the room knew nothing and felt nothing from their deaths. It was instant. Memory is necessary for a human to be aware of light, heat and pain, and there was no time for any memory among those killed to process what had happened.

'Mission complete,' the operator at Langley quietly confirmed to those in the control room with him, who relayed it to Anne, on the end of her sat-phone.

'It's over René, they have all been terminated.'

René nodded. He knew it was never easy making a call to release a missile against targets when there was a possibility of non-involved persons also being killed, but he also knew that what had to be done had now been done. Daesh had lost a leadership tier and the Avignon attacker had paid the appropriate price for what he had attempted. He reached out and touched Anne on her upper arm. A gesture of intimacy and understanding.

'Thank you Anne, without your inputs this may not have been achieved.' Genuine thanks and respect.

And for her part, Anne was grateful for the opportunity to have been involved, and, not for the first time, she realised she had developed a close empathy with René.

Epilogue

Back in Paris, Anne and René were lunching at a small café on the hill of Montmartre. René was having his usual lunch, black coffee and a croissant. Not much, but he never ate anything substantial in the middle of the day. Anne had ordered a club sandwich and Perrier water. They were sitting inside the café, leaving the tables and chairs outside on the footpath to the tourists and the additional cost they would face as a result of wanting to sit out on the pavement.

Anne could hear the mix of accents and languages drifting through the open front doors and windows. The cosmopolitan streets of Paris always gave you that. Some were from the States she noted, identifying the unmistakeable inflections of one of the southern states. She also heard some accents that said to her Australia, or perhaps New Zealand, she always struggled to differentiate between those two.

Looking around her she found it slightly surreal this beautiful city and its people could have been subjected to the terror attacks it had, particularly Charlie Hebdo and the Bataclan. And then of course there had been the attempt on the Avignon Festival just days earlier. It had been satisfying to be able to prevent that attack from succeeding, but Anne knew it was a continuing game. The fact the terrorists had tried, and no doubt would try again, to kill innocent members of the public whose sole crime in the eyes of their attackers was that they were westerners who did not follow Islam, was a concern she lived with all the time. As a consequence Anne found her role wearying.

Dealing with terrorism was a constant battle. Like a never-ending game of chess, with move and counter-move. She knew counter-terrorism outcome was decided by the ability to identify a risk, the ability to make a valid risk assessment, and the ability to make the appropriate judgment calls. The algorithm had been invaluable in the

Avignon attack, providing the threads and linkages which had enabled Anne and René to analyse, identify, and respond to the attack on the festival.

'What's on your mind Anne,' asked René as he sipped his long black. He had noticed her pensive attitude and could see she was somewhere else in her thoughts. He wasn't surprised. It was always a quiet time following completion of an operation of the nature they had just completed a few days ago, an intense counter-terrorism operation, including a post-attack pursuit. That of course came after Anne and René had spent months working together carrying out investigation and analysis as part of Anne's secondment to René's section following the Bataclan attacks. The come-down after such a peak in activity was just one step from a minor bout of depression in René's experience.

Anne smiled. 'Just thinking about the operation and its result, which was a good outcome. The algorithm was invaluable in providing the indicators from which we could develop our scenarios. And the tracking of Ahad worked, thank God. But I find myself wondering where the next attack will come, because there will be more. I don't know how we bring it all to an end.'

René nodded agreement. 'I have enjoyed having you work in my section Anne, and before you go back to the States next week I would really like it if you would come down to the south of France with me. Friends have invited me to stay with them in Nice. They own a hotel overlooking the Promenade des Anglais, with wonderful sea views. Please come with me Anne, it will be great,' René almost pleading.

Anne was surprised René was prepared to let her see how very keen he was that she accompany him to Nice. While she recognised René had been a valuable professional to work with since she had joined DCRI on secondment in January, and they had been through a lot together since that time, he had not engaged well with her in their personal interactions over that period.

Sometimes that had been shown by silly flirting, which Anne had ignored, and sometimes it had been shown by René affecting indifference or being condescending. When he had laughed at her after she had hurt her shoulder because she hadn't held a shotgun properly at the skeet shooting range, Anne has been singularly unimpressed with René's attitude. René definitely had not endeared himself to her in a personal way so far in 2016 she thought. Should she go to Nice anyway she asked herself?

René continued pressing. 'I recommend dinner on the hotel terrace with a very pleasant Burgundy. Then we could walk along the Promenade to watch the wonderful fireworks display put on to celebrate the birth of *La République*. It's Bastille Day on Thursday, an event well worth seeing and celebrating,' René smiling, attempting to be persuasive, and making it clear that he was not indifferent to Anne's response. He wanted her to come, very much.

Anne recognised that René was being genuine and showing his humanity, something he usually carefully cloaked. She was also aware René was a person she had enjoyed being around and working with, despite what she considered to be some flaws in his character. Anne made her decision.

'Yes René, it will be good for both of us to have the opportunity to put what we usually do in our professional lives out of our minds, and just enjoy. I would appreciate some relaxation after what we've been doing, so thank you, I'll come.'

'Fantastic,' exclaimed René, 'I will make the arrangements and we will fly down tomorrow. Anne, I'm really looking forward to showing you that part of France. And you are right, it will be a timely break for both of us, getting away from the nastiness we normally have to deal with.'

231

Anne smiled at René. The trip to Nice was a welcome suggestion, and she found herself looking forward to being able to relax with René, free of the constraints of their professional relationship. Yes, Anne thought, a few days in Nice with René will definitely be a pleasant way to finish my stay in France.

At that moment, Mohamed Lahouaiej-Bouhlel was in Nice. A Tunisian, he had lived in France for some years, but in recent times he had become radicalised by continued exposure to social media messaging orchestrated by Daesh.

Now he wanted to be the next *jihadist* to attack the West, and he was planning to carry out his own terror attack. On Bastille Day Lahouaiej-Bouhlel would drive a large truck into the crowds celebrating and watching the fireworks display on Nice's Promenade des Anglais. That would again remind the West of the power of Islam. *Allahu Akbar.*